GLOBE EDUCATION SHAKESPEARE

D0452707

ROMEO AND JULIET

William Shakespeare

Shakespeare and the Globe

Shakespeare was born in 1564, in Stratford, a small town in the Midlands. We know he was still in Stratford as an eighteen-year old, when he got married. By 1592, he had moved to London, become an actor, and become a playwright. Shakespeare died in Stratford in 1616. He probably retired three or four years earlier, having bought land, and the biggest house in the town.

Shakespeare was successful. He became a shareholder in his acting company, and a shareholder in the Globe – the new theatre they built in 1599. His company was the best in the land, and the new king, James I, made them his company in 1603. They were known as the King's Men. Men, because women were not allowed to act on the stage. Boys or men played all the women's parts. Shakespeare wrote at least 40 plays, of which only 38 survive. Only eighteen of his plays were printed in his lifetime. *Macbeth* was not one of them. It only survives because, after his death, his colleagues published a collection of his plays, known as the *First Folio*.

London Theatres

There were professional companies of actors working in London from the middle of the sixteenth century. They usually performed in inns, and the city council often tried to ban them. The solution was to have their own purpose-built theatre, just outside the area the council controlled. The first, simply called *The Theatre*, opened in 1576.

Shakespeare's Globe today

Sam Wanamaker, an American actor and director, founded the Shakespeare's Globe Trust in 1970. Sam could not understand why there wasn't a proper memorial to the world's greatest playwright in the city where he had lived and worked. He started fundraising to build a new Globe Theatre. Sadly, Sam died before the theatre opened in 1997.

The new Globe is the third. The first burnt down in 1613 during a performance of Shakespeare's Henry VIII. *The King's Men rebuilt it on the same site, and it re-opened in 1614. This second one was closed in 1642, and pulled down in 1647 to build houses.*

The new Globe is 200 yards from the original site, and is based on all the evidence that survives. It has been built using the same materials as the original, and using the same building techniques.

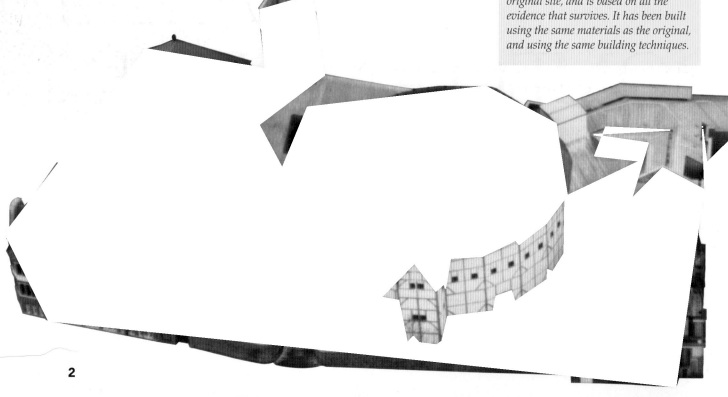

The first Globe Theatre

The Globe Theatre was open-air. If it rained, some of the audience got wet. There was no special lighting; so the plays were performed in the afternoon, in daylight. This meant that, unlike most modern theatres, the actors could see the audience, as well as the audience see the actors (and each other). It may have held as many as 3,000 people, with, perhaps, 1,000 standing in the yard. They paid one old penny (there were 240 in £1). The rest sat in the three galleries, so they were under cover if it rained. They paid more, at least two pence, and as much as six pence for the best seats. The audience was a mixture of social classes, with the poorer people standing.

The stage was large, and extended into the middle of the yard, so there were people on three sides. We think it had three entrances in the back wall – a door on either side, and a larger one in the middle. There was a roof so the actors, and their expensive costumes, would always be in the dry. The underside of this roof, called *the heavens*, was painted with the signs of the zodiac. There was also an upper stage, which was sometimes used in plays, sometimes used by the musicians, and also had the most expensive seats in the theatre. All the rest of the audience could see people who sat in the upper stage area. If you sat there, people could see who you were, that you could afford to sit there, and your expensive clothes.

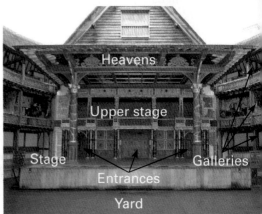

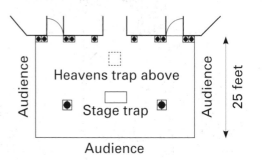

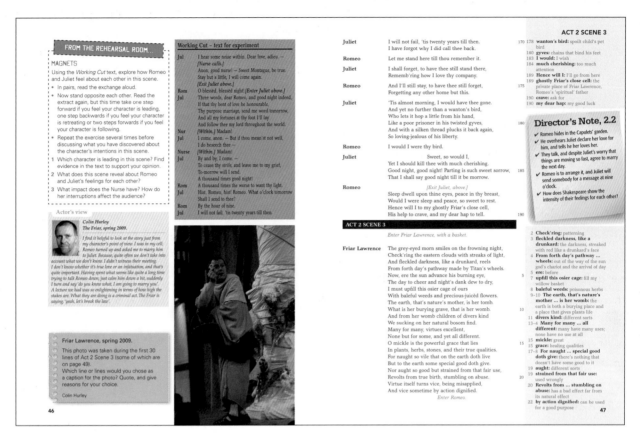

The **play text** is the place to start. What characters say is in black, and stage directions are in blue. Line numbers, on the right, help you refer to an exact place.

> Good night, good night! Parting is such sweet sorrow,   185
> That I shall say good night till it be morrow.
>
> **Romeo**   *[Exit Juliet, above.]*
> Sleep dwell upon thine eyes, peace in thy breast,

Some stage directions, like the second one above, have square brackets. This means they are not in the original text, but have been added to help you when you read. They tell you what you would see on the stage.

> 178 **wanton's bird:** spoilt child's pet bird

The **glossary** is right next to the text. To help you find the word or phrase you want, each entry has the line number in blue, then the word or phrase in black, and finally the explanation in blue again. To keep it clear, sometimes, as in this case, some words from the original have been missed out, and replaced with three dots.

Actor's view boxes are exactly what they say. Actors who have played the part at the Globe tell you what they thought about their character and some of the choices they made.

Green boxes go with the photos. They tell you what you are looking at, and give you a question to think about. Unless the question says otherwise, the answer will be in the play text on the opposite page. The names of the actors are in smaller print.

From the rehearsal room gives you the exercises actors use during rehearsals to help them understand the play. They come with questions that help you reflect on what you can learn from the exercise.

Working Cuts sometimes go with the *From the rehearsal room* activities. They cut lines from the scene so you can do the activity in the time you have available.

Shakespeare's World boxes give you important context for the play. For example, what most people at the time believed about witches is different from what most people believe today. If you understand the difference, it helps you to understand how the characters react to the Witches in the play.

Finally, **Director's Notes** boxes come at the end of every scene. They give you a quick summary of the most important things in the scene, and a focus to think about.

The Characters in the play

This book uses photographs from three productions of *Romeo and Juliet* at Shakespeare's Globe. The actors and creative teams of each production are an important part of the book.

	2004 *Director: Tim Carroll*	spring 2009 *Director: Bill Buckhurst*	summer 2009 *Director: Dominic Dromgoole*
Prince Escalus, ruler of Verona	Joel Trill	Nicholas Khan	Andrew Vincent
Mercutio, related to the Prince	James Garnon	Shane Zaza	Philip Cumbus
Paris, also related to the Prince	Callum Coates	Nicholas Khan	Tom Stuart
The Capulets			
Capulet, head of the house	Bill Stewart	Vincent Brimble	Ian Redford
Lady Capulet, his wife	Melanie Jessop	Golda Rosheuvel	Miranda Foster
Juliet, their daughter	Kananu Kirimi	Lorraine Burroughs	Ellie Kendrick
Tybalt, her cousin	Simon Müller	Marshall Griffin	Ukweli Roach
Nurse, to Juliet	Bette Bourne	Jane Bertish	Penny Layden
Peter, a servant of the Capulets	John Paul Connolly	Nicholas Khan	Fergal McElherron
Cousin, to Capulet			
Petruchio, follower of Tybalt			
Sampson, a servant of the Capulets		Lorraine Burroughs	James Lailey
Gregory, a servant of the Capulets	Callum Coates	James Alexandrou	Fergal McElherron
The Montagues			
Montague, head of the house	Terry McGinty	Colin Hurley	Michael O'Hagan
Lady Montague, his wife	Julia Marsen	Jane Bertish	Holly Atkins
Romeo, their son	Tom Burke	James Alexandrou	Adetomiwa Edun
Benvolio, Romeo's friend	Rhys Meredith	Ben Aldridge	Jack Farthing
Balthasar, Romeo's servant	Tas Emiabata		Fergal McElherron
Abraham, servant of the Montagues		Shane Zaza	Graham Vick
Friar Lawrence	John McEnery	Colin Hurley	Rawiri Paratene
Friar John	Rhys Meredith	Marshall Griffin	James Lailey
An Apothecary, in Manuta	Terry McGinty	Shane Zaza	Graham Vick
Servants			
Officers of the Watch		Ben Aldridge	
Citizens			
Designer	Jenny Tiramani	Ben Stones	Simon Daw
Composer	Claire van Kampen	Olly Fox	Nigel Hess
Choreographer	Siân Williams	Siân Williams	Siân Williams
Fight Director	Rodney Cottier & Jonathan Waller	Alison de Burgh	Malcolm Ranson
Musical Director	William Lyons & Keith McGowan	Stephen Bently-Klein	William Lyons

THE PROLOGUE

Enter Chorus.

Chorus   Two households, both alike in dignity,
(In fair Verona, where we lay our scene),
From ancient grudge break to new mutiny,
Where civil blood makes civil hands unclean.
From forth the fatal loins of these two foes   5
A pair of star-crossed lovers take their life,
Whose misadventured piteous overthrows
Doth with their death bury their parents' strife.
The fearful passage of their death-marked love,
And the continuance of their parents' rage   10
(Which but their children's end, nought could remove),
Is now the two hours' traffic of our stage.
The which if you with patient ears attend,
What here shall miss, our toil shall strive to mend.

Exit.

ACT 1 SCENE 1

Enter Sampson and Gregory, of the house of Capulet, armed with swords and bucklers.

Sampson   Gregory, on my word we'll not carry coals.

Gregory   No, for then we should be colliers.

Sampson   I mean, if we be in choler, we'll draw.

Gregory   Ay, while you live, draw your neck out o' the collar.

Sampson   I strike quickly, being moved.   5

Gregory   But thou art not quickly moved to strike.

Sampson   A dog of the house of Montague moves me.

Gregory   To move is to stir; and to be valiant is to stand.
Therefore, if thou art moved, thou runn'st away.

Sampson   A dog of that house shall move me to stand. I will take   10
the wall of any man or maid of Montague's.

Gregory   That shows thee a weak slave, for the weakest goes to
the wall.

Sampson   'Tis true, and therefore women being the weaker
vessels are ever thrust to the wall. Therefore I will push   15
Montague's men from the wall, and thrust his maids to
the wall.

Gregory   The quarrel is between our masters and us, their men.

Sampson   'Tis all one. I will show myself a tyrant. When I have
fought with the men, I will be civil with the maids, I   20
will cut off their heads.

Gregory   The heads of the maids?

---

1 **dignity:** social status
3 **ancient grudge:** old quarrels
3 **break to new mutiny:** begin new quarrel
4 **Where civil blood ... hands unclean:** fighting and spilling blood even though they are not soldiers at war
5 **From forth the fatal loins ... two foes:** from these two warring households
6 **star-crossed:** doomed by fate
7 **misadventured piteous overthows:** tragic, steps to ruin
11 **but:** except
11 **nought:** nothing
12 **traffic of our stage:** subject of our play
14 **What here shall miss ... to mend:** We'll work hard to tell you the full story

SD **bucklers:** small, round shields

1 **carry coals:** be insulted
2 **colliers:** coal sellers
3 **be in choler:** are angry
3 **draw:** draw our swords
4 **collar:** hangman's rope (wordplay uses collier/choler/collar which sound similar)
5 **being moved:** if I'm made angry

8 **stir:** run away
8 **stand:** stay and fight

10-1 **take the wall:** walk by the wall (the best part of the street) furthest from the centre of the street where the gutter was
12 **slave:** used to show contempt (he thinks Sampson is boasting)
12-3 **the weakest goes to the wall:** from a proverb meaning the weakest must give in
14-5 **weaker vessels:** naturally weaker than men

19 **'Tis all one:** it makes no difference

6

THE PROLOGUE

In seven groups, each group is given a different couplet from the Prologue.

- Identify the key words and images in your couplet.
- Create a freeze frame to illustrate the essence of your couplet.
- Now, speak the whole line, emphasising the key words you identified.
- In sequence, the whole class creates the Prologue by performing their couplets in the right order. Watch and listen.

1 Which words and phrases create vivid images in your mind?

2 What does the Prologue tell us about what will happen in the play?

3 Some directors chose to cut the Prologue, and perform the play without it.

   a) Explain the advantages and disadvantages of cutting the Prologue.

   b) If you were the director, would you cut the Prologue? Give reasons for your answer.

Sampson	Ay, the heads of the maids, or their maidenheads, take it in what sense thou wilt.
Gregory	They must take it in sense, that feel it.
Sampson	Me they shall feel while I am able to stand, and 'tis known I am a pretty piece of flesh.
Gregory	Tis well thou art not fish. If thou hadst, thou hadst been poor John. — Draw thy tool, here comes two of the house of the Montagues.

Enter Abraham and Balthasar, serving men of the Montagues.

Sampson	My naked weapon is out. Quarrel, I will back thee.
Gregory	How? Turn thy back and run?
Sampson	Fear me not.
Gregory	No, marry, I fear thee.
Sampson	Let us take the law of our sides. Let them begin.
Gregory	I will frown as I pass by, and let them take it as they list.
Sampson	Nay, as they dare. I will bite my thumb at them; which is a disgrace to them, if they bear it.
Abraham	Do you bite your thumb at us, sir?
Sampson	I do bite my thumb, sir.
Abraham	Do you bite your tongue at us, sir?
Sampson	*[Aside to Gregory.]* Is the law of our side, if I say 'ay'?
Gregory	*[Aside to Sampson.]* No.
Sampson	No, sir, I do not bite my thumb at you, sir. But I bite my thumb, sir.

25

30

35

40

45

23 **maidenheads:** virginities

25 **They must take ... feel it:** it isn't me that has to take it, but the maids

27 **a pretty piece of flesh:** a fine figure of a man (this starts a series of sexual double meanings)

29 **poor John:** salted and dried cheap fish mostly eaten by the poor

29 **tool:** sword

31 **My naked weapon is out:** my sword is out of my scabbard

31 **Quarrel:** start a fight

33 **Fear me not:** Don't worry that I'll run

35 **take the law of our sides:** seem to be keeping the law

36 **as they list:** however they want

37 **bite my thumb:** an insulting gesture at the time

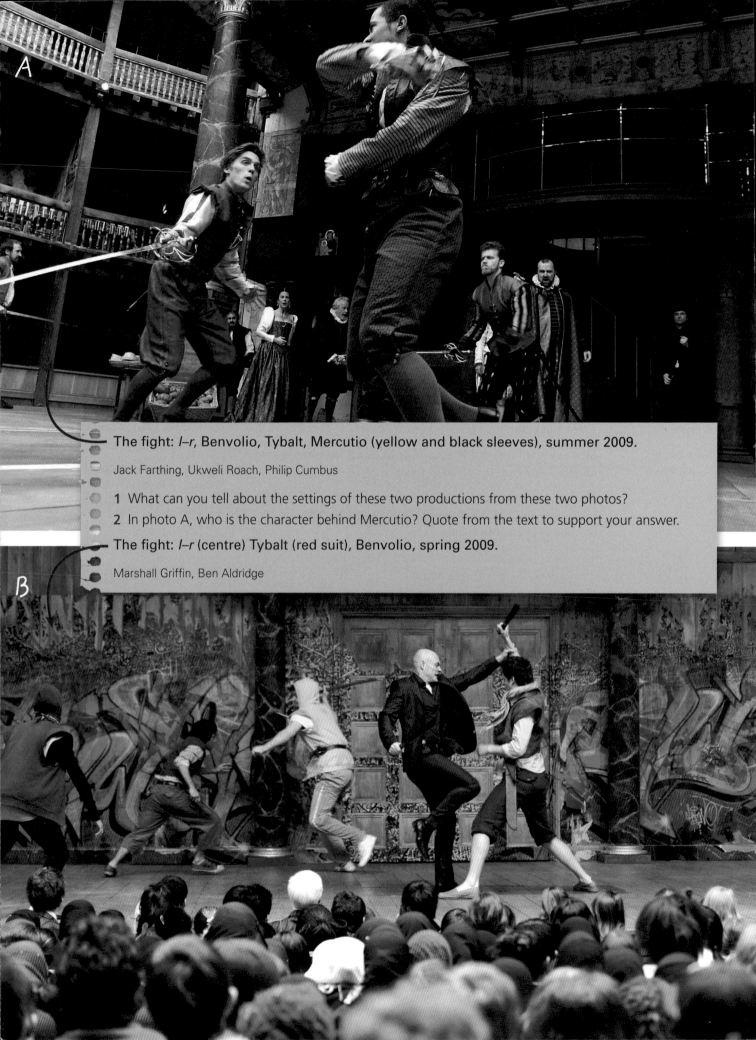

The fight: *l–r*, Benvolio, Tybalt, Mercutio (yellow and black sleeves), summer 2009.

Jack Farthing, Ukweli Roach, Philip Cumbus

1 What can you tell about the settings of these two productions from these two photos?
2 In photo A, who is the character behind Mercutio? Quote from the text to support your answer.

The fight: *l–r* (centre) Tybalt (red suit), Benvolio, spring 2009.

Marshall Griffin, Ben Aldridge

Gregory	Do you quarrel, sir?		
Abraham	Quarrel, sir? No, sir.		
Sampson	If you do, sir, I am for you. I serve as good a man as you.		48 **I am for you:** I'll fight you
Abraham	No better?	50	
Sampson	Well, sir —		
Gregory	Say "better": here comes one of my master's kinsmen.		
Sampson	Yes, better, sir.		
Abraham	You lie.		
Sampson	Draw if you be men. Gregory, remember thy washing blow.	55	55 **washing:** slashing

They fight.

Benvolio	Part, fools! Put up your swords, you know not what you do.		58 **Put up:** put away

Enter Tybalt.

Tybalt	What, art thou drawn among these heartless hinds? Turn thee, Benvolio, look upon thy death.	60	59 **heartless hinds:** cowardly servants (double meaning of female deer without a male for protection)
Benvolio	I do but keep the peace, put up thy sword, Or manage it to part these men with me.		61 **I do but keep the peace:** I'm just trying to stop this fighting 62 **manage it:** use it
Tybalt	What, drawn, and talk of peace? I hate the word, As I hate hell, all Montagues, and thee. Have at thee, coward! *They fight.*	65	

Enter several Montagues and Capulets who join in the fight, also an officer and three of four citizens with clubs or partisans.

Officer	Clubs, bills, and partisans! Strike! Beat them down! Down with the Capulets! Down with the Montagues!		66 **bills, and partisans:** types of spear

Enter Capulet in his gown, and Lady Capulet.

Capulet	What noise is this? Give me my long sword, ho!		68 **long sword:** old-fashioned heavy sword
Lady Capulet	A crutch, a crutch! Why call you for a sword?		69 **A crutch, a crutch!:** she's suggesting it's too heavy for an old man like him to lift, he might as well lean on it, like a crutch
Capulet	My sword, I say! Old Montague is come, And flourishes his blade in spite of me.	70	71 **in spite of me:** scornfully, to provoke me

Enter Montague and Lady Montague.

Montague	Thou villain Capulet. — Hold me not, let me go.		
Lady Montague	Thou shalt not stir one foot to seek a foe.		75 **Profaners of this neighbour-stainèd steel:** who have shown contempt for my orders and God by fighting and wounding fellow citizens

Enter Prince Escalus, with his Attendants.

Prince	Rebellious subjects, enemies to peace, Profaners of this neighbour-stainèd steel, — Will they not hear? What, ho! you men, you beasts, That quench the fire of your pernicious rage With purple fountains issuing from your veins. On pain of torture, from those bloody hands	75	77 **quench:** put out 77 **pernicious:** harmful, destructive 79 **On pain of torture:** unless you want to be tortured as a punishment

The fight, 2004. This shows action from the text on page 9.

1 Compare the setting of this production with the two photos from 2009 on page 8.

2 Which characters might the two actors in black at the centre of the stage be playing? Quote from the text to support your answer.

3 Which character might the woman on the right of the photo be playing? Quote from the text to support your answer.

FROM THE REHEARSAL ROOM...

ANCIENT GRUDGE

Act 1 Scene 1 starts with a fight breaking out between the Montagues and the Capulets. The Prince breaks it up (lines 74–96).

• Working in pairs, read the Prince's speech. Each person reads up to a punctuation mark, and then the next person takes over and reads to the following punctuation mark.

• Now read the speech again: click your fingers on the second syllable of every line and clap your hands on the last word of every line.

1 What do these activities tell you about the Prince's state of mind during this speech? Quote from the text to support your answer.

2 This is the first appearance of the Prince. How has Shakespeare presented him? Pick some of these adjectives, and add others of your own. Support your answer with quotes.

strong/weak/caring/angry/safe/dangerous

SHAKESPEARE'S WORLD

The start of the play

In today's theatres, we see the lights go down, and the play starts. In the Elizabethan playhouses, lit by daylight, this could not happen. Instead, a trumpeter would play a fanfare to signal to the crowd that the play was about to start.

The playhouses were grand and noisy places. The audience arrived well before the start of the play, and enjoyed the social atmosphere. It is possible that they did not always pay attention to the trumpeter's call. Perhaps this is why Shakespeare developed a habit of vivid beginnings to his plays. In *Macbeth*, the Witches enter to the sight and sound of thunder and lightning. Here, in *Romeo and Juliet*, the audience's attention is caught, almost immediately, with a dramatic swordfight involving most of the cast. Shakespeare needed the crowd's attention for the subtler, quieter moments of the play, and so he wrote a scene that grabs it straight away.

Throw your mistempered weapons to the ground,   80
And hear the sentence of your movèd Prince.
Three civil brawls, bred of an airy word,
By thee, old Capulet, and Montague,
Have thrice disturbed the quiet of our streets,
And made Verona's ancient citizens   85
Cast by their grave beseeming ornaments,
To wield old partisans, in hands as old,
Cankered with peace, to part your cankered hate.
If ever you disturb our streets again,
Your lives shall pay the forfeit of the peace.   90
For this time all the rest depart away.
You, Capulet, shall go along with me,
And Montague, come you this afternoon,
To know our further pleasure in this case,
To old Free-town, our common judgement-place.   95
Once more, on pain of death, all men depart.

Exit all but Montague, Lady Montague, and Benvolio.

Montague   Who set this ancient quarrel new abroach?
Speak, nephew, were you by when it began?

Benvolio   Here were the servants of your adversary,
And yours, close fighting ere I did approach.   100
I drew to part them. In the instant came
The fiery Tybalt, with his sword prepared,
Which, as he breathed defiance to my ears,
He swung about his head and cut the winds,
Who nothing hurt withal, hissed him in scorn.   105
While we were interchanging thrusts and blows,
Came more and more, and fought on part and part,
Till the Prince came, who parted either part.

Lady Montague   O, where is Romeo, saw you him to-day?
Right glad I am he was not at this fray.   110

Benvolio   Madam, an hour before the worshipped sun
Peered forth the golden window of the east,
A troubled mind drove me to walk abroad,
Where, underneath the grove of sycamore
That westward rooteth from the city side,   115
So early walking did I see your son.
Towards him I made, but he was ware of me
And stole into the covert of the wood.
I, measuring his affections by my own,
Which then most sought where most might not be
   found,   120
Being one too many by my weary self,
That most are busied when they're most alone,
Pursued my humour not pursuing his,
And gladly shunned who gladly fled from me.

Montague   Many a morning hath he there been seen,   125
With tears augmenting the fresh morning's dew,
Adding to clouds more clouds with his deep sighs.

---

80 **mistempered:** used with a double meaning of 'badly made' (for swords) and 'angry' for the people using them
81 **sentence:** punishment
81 **movèd:** angry
82 **civil brawls:** outbreaks of fighting between citizens
82 **bred of an airy word:** over some trivial remark
86-7 **Cast by their grave ... wield old partisans:** give up the sensible pursuits of old age and take up their old weapons to fight
88 **Cankered with peace:** rusty through disuse in times of peace
88 **cankered hate:** festering hate
90 **Your lives shall pay the forfeit of the peace:** you'll be executed
94 **our further pleasure:** what else I decide to do
97 **set this ancient quarrel new abroach:** started this old quarrel up again
98 **by:** nearby
99 **adversary:** enemy
100 **ere:** before
105 **Who nothing hurt withal:** which, unharmed
107 **Came more and more:** more and more people arrived
107 **on part and part:** on one side or the other
108 **either part:** them both
110 **Right glad I am he was not at this fray:** I'm very glad he wasn't part of this fight
115 **rooteth:** grow
117 **made:** went
117 **he was ware of me:** he noticed me
118 **covert:** shelter
120 **most sought where most might not be found:** wanted most to be by myself
121-2 **Being one too many ... they're most alone:** even my own company was too much for me, my mind was so busy
123-4 **Pursued my humour ... fled from me:** did what I wanted most and avoided him as he avoided me
126 **augmenting:** adding to

11

FIRST IMPRESSIONS OF ROMEO

Act 1 Scene 1 ends with the appearance of Romeo.

- Working in small groups, take one of the sections below, and decide who will read each part. Some of you will be 'listeners'.
- The sections are lines 97–139, 140–177, 177–202, and 203–232.
- As you read through the extract, the 'listeners' should repeat any word or phrase which tells us something about Romeo.

1 Write down or highlight all the words or phrases that you repeated.

- Share your answers with the other groups who worked on other sections of the text.

2 Collect all the words from the entire group and organise them into lists to illustrate what Romeo's parents say about him, what Romeo's friend says about him, and what Romeo says about himself, in the order they are said.

3 What do the lists tell us about Romeo's personality and character? Support your opinion with quotes from the text.

4 How does Romeo feel in this scene?

5 What are the audience's first impressions of Romeo?

Romeo. *Left* 2004; *right* spring 2009.

1 The spring 2009 production was in modern dress. Does this change the first impression Romeo makes? Explain your answer.

2 What parts of the first scene might work particularly well in modern dress? Explain your answer.

Tom Burke, James Alexandrou

	But all so soon as the all-cheering sun
	Should in the furthest east begin to draw
	The shady curtains from Aurora's bed,
	Away from light steals home my heavy son,
	And private in his chamber pens himself,
	Shuts up his windows, locks fair daylight out
	And makes himself an artificial night.
	Black and portentous must this humour prove,
	Unless good counsel may the cause remove.
Benvolio	My noble uncle, do you know the cause?
Montague	I neither know it, nor can learn of him.
Benvolio	Have you importuned him by any means?
Montague	Both by myself and many other friends.
	But he, his own affections' counsellor,
	Is to himself, (I will not say how true)
	But to himself so secret and so close,
	So far from sounding and discovery,
	As is the bud bit with an envious worm,
	Ere he can spread his sweet leaves to the air,
	Or dedicate his beauty to the same.
	Could we but learn from whence his sorrows grow.
	We would as willingly give cure as know.

Enter Romeo.

Benvolio	See, where he comes. So please you step aside,
	I'll know his grievance, or be much denied.
Montague	I would thou wert so happy by thy stay,
	To hear true shrift. Come madam, let's away.

Exit Montague and Lady Montague.

Benvolio	Good morrow, cousin.
Romeo	Is the day so young?
Benvolio	But new struck nine.
Romeo	Ay me, sad hours seem long.
	Was that my father that went hence so fast?
Benvolio	It was. What sadness lengthens Romeo's hours?
Romeo	Not having that, which having, makes them short.
Benvolio	In love?
Romeo	Out —
Benvolio	Of love?
Romeo	Out of her favour, where I am in love.
Benvolio	Alas that love, so gentle in his view,
	Should be so tyrannous and rough in proof!
Romeo	Alas, that love, whose view is muffled still,
	Should without eyes see pathways to his will. —
	Where shall we dine? — O me! What fray was here?

130 **Aurora:** goddess of the dawn (both Benvolio and Montague give very flowery description of dawn)
131 **heavy:** sad
132 **pens himself:** shuts himself up
135 **Black:** gloomy
135 **portentous:** suggesting future misfortune
135 **humour:** mood (also refers to the 'Four Humours' medical theory used at the time where too much of one 'humour' in the body was said to cause illness. Too much black bile caused depression)
136 **counsel:** advice
139 **importuned:** pressed him to tell you
139 **by any means:** in any way
141 **his own affections' counsellor:** is the only person he'll share his feelings with
142 **true:** trustworthy
144 **sounding:** being easy to question
145 **envious worm:** the canker worm that eats through flower buds
148 **from whence his sorrows grow:** what is making him so unhappy
149 **We would as willingly give cure as know:** we want to help as much as we want to know the problem
150 **So please you:** please
151 **his grievance, or be much denied:** what's upsetting him, I won't take no for an answer
152-3 **I would thou wert so happy ... true shrift:** I hope you can get him to tell you the truth (shrift means confessing to a priest)
154 **morrow:** morning
154 **cousin:** used to close relatives and friends
156 **hence:** away from here
162 **Out of her favour:** no longer loved
163 **so gentle in his view:** so attractive as an idea
164 **be so tyrannous and rough in proof:** treat us so badly when we experience it
165 **whose view is muffled still:** refers to the fact that Cupid, the god of love, was said to be blind or blindfolded
166 **see pathways to his will:** still be able to make what he wants happen

13

Actor's view

James Alexandrou
Romeo, spring 2009

Rosaline is the lady he comes on talking about and he's in a woeful mood about and is very melancholy about and absolutely in love with Rosaline when he first comes on, or thinks he is anyway. But yes, he absolutely loves her until he sees Juliet.
I had this theory going into this, Romeo's what, 14, 15, that sort of age and hormonal and, as I did at that age, falls in love all the time with whichever girl caught your eye. With Rosaline, I think she was probably beautifully curvy and gorgeous and sexy and Romeo just fell in love with that.

Romeo and Benvolio, summer 2009.

1 What impression does this give of the relationship between the two young men?

2 The photo was taken while Romeo was speaking. Which of his speeches do you think it best fits? Quote from the text to explain your answer.

Adetomiwa Edun, Jack Farthing

SHAKESPEARE'S WORLD

Elizabethan view of romantic love

In this scene, Benvolio and Romeo discuss how love can make a man act like a madman. Elizabethans had complicated ideas about romantic love. People were encouraged to love their husband or wife. However, loving someone too much was seen as an illness. Elizabethan doctors saw unrequited love or desire as a disease, a type of melancholy sometimes called lovesickness. It was caught through the eye. Symptoms of lovesickness were: fever, mood swings and even shrinking of the heart. Medical writings treated lovesickness as a common disease. Doctors tried various cures. They changed the patient's diet, and gave them herbal medicines. They sometimes sent patients to church, to confess to a priest. They believed that, if lovesickness was left untreated, it could lead to madness.

The lovesick man was a popular character in early modern literature. Shakespeare makes the connection between love and madness again in *Hamlet*, when Polonius believes Hamlet to be mad because of his love for Ophelia.

Yet tell me not, for I have heard it all.
Here's much to do with hate, but more with love.
Why, then, O brawling love, O loving hate,   170
O any thing, of nothing first created.
O heavy lightness, serious vanity,
Misshapen chaos of well-seeming forms,
Feather of lead, bright smoke, cold fire, sick health,
Still-waking sleep, that is not what it is.
This love feel I, that feel no love in this.
Dost thou not laugh?

Benvolio   No, coz, I rather weep.

Romeo   Good heart, at what?

Benvolio   At thy good heart's oppression.

Romeo   Why such is love's transgression.
Griefs of mine own lie heavy in my breast,
Which thou wilt propagate, to have it pressed
With more of thine. This love that thou hast shown
Doth add more grief to too much of mine own.
Love is a smoke made with the fume of sighs,
Being purged, a fire sparkling in lovers' eyes,
Being vex'd a sea nourish'd with loving tears.
What is it else? A madness most discreet,
A choking gall and a preserving sweet.
Farewell, my coz.

Benvolio   Soft! I will go along.
And if you leave me so, you do me wrong.

Romeo   Tut, I have lost myself, I am not here,
This is not Romeo, he's some other where.

Benvolio   Tell me in sadness, who is that you love?

Romeo   What, shall I groan and tell thee?

Benvolio   Groan? Why, no. But sadly tell me who.

Romeo   Bid a sick man in sadness make his will.
A word ill urged to one that is so ill.
In sadness, cousin, I do love a woman.

Benvolio   I aimed so near when I supposed you loved.

Romeo   A right good mark-man, and she's fair I love.

Benvolio   A right fair mark, fair coz, is soonest hit.

Romeo   Well, in that hit you miss, she'll not be hit
With Cupid's arrow. She hath Dian's wit.
And, in strong proof of chastity well armed,
From love's weak childish bow she lives uncharmed.
She will not stay the siege of loving terms,
Nor bide th' encounter of assailing eyes,
Nor ope her lap to saint-seducing gold.
O she is rich in beauty, only poor   210
That when she dies, with beauty dies her store.

171 **of nothing first created:** made out of nothing in the first place
172 **O heavy lightness ... :** the start of a sequence of pairings of opposites
173 **well-seeming forms:** attractive looking shapes
175 **Still-waking:** not sleeping
176 **This love feel I ... no love in this:** I love, but am not loved in return
177 **coz:** cousin
177 **rather weep:** weep instead
179 **oppression:** heaviness, misery
180 **love's transgression:** the way love steps outside its proper limits
182 **pressed:** burdened
186 **purged:** cleaned, purified
188 **discreet:** cautious, prudent
189 **choking gall:** a bitter liquid that chokes you
189 **preserving sweet:** a sweet, healing liquid
190 **Soft!:** wait!
194 **in sadness:** in all seriousness
200 **I aimed so near ... you loved:** I'd worked that out when I guessed you were in love
201 **A right good mark-man:** an excellent guess
202 **A right fair mark:** an easy target
204 **Dian's wit:** the skills of Diana, the goddess of chastity
205 **proof:** armour
206 **From love's weak childish bow she lives uncharmed:** she's unaffected by Cupid's arrows
207–8 **stay the siege of loving terms ... assailing eyes:** listen to a lover's words or even let him gaze adoringly
209 **Nor ope her lap to saint-seducing gold:** you can't buy her love, either
211 **her store:** the virginity she's been saving

15

Benvolio	Then she hath sworn that she will still live chaste?
Romeo	She hath, and in that sparing makes huge waste, For beauty starved with her severity Cuts beauty off from all posterity. She is too fair, too wise, wisely too fair, To merit bliss by making me despair. She hath forsworn to love, and in that vow Do I live dead, that live to tell it now.
Benvolio	Be ruled by me, forget to think of her.
Romeo	O teach me how I should forget to think.
Benvolio	By giving liberty unto thine eyes, Examine other beauties.
Romeo	'Tis the way To call hers, exquisite, in question more. These happy masks that kiss fair ladies' brows, Being black, put us in mind they hide the fair. He that is strucken blind cannot forget The precious treasure of his eyesight lost. Show me a mistress that is passing fair. What doth her beauty serve but as a note, Where I may read who passed that passing fair? Farewell, thou canst not teach me to forget.
Benvolio	I'll pay that doctrine, or else die in debt. *They exit.*

ACT 1 SCENE 2

Enter Capulet, Paris and Peter.

Capulet	But Montague is bound as well as I, In penalty alike, and 'tis not hard I think, For men so old as we to keep the peace.
Paris	Of honourable reckoning are you both, And pity 'tis you lived at odds so long. But now, my lord, what say you to my suit?
Capulet	But saying o'er what I have said before. My child is yet a stranger in the world, She hath not seen the change of fourteen years, Let two more summers wither in their pride, Ere we may think her ripe to be a bride.
Paris	Younger than she are happy mothers made.
Capulet	And too soon marred are those so early made. The earth hath swallowed all my hopes but she, She is the hopeful lady of my earth. But woo her, gentle Paris, get her heart, My will to her consent is but a part. And she agreed, within her scope of choice Lies my consent and fair according voice. This night I hold an old accustomed feast, Whereto I have invited many a guest,

213 **sparing:** saving, hoarding up
215 **Cuts beauty off from all posterity:** will not have children as beautiful as she is
217 **To merit bliss by making me despair:** to earn happiness in heaven through her chastity by making me miserable now
218 **forsworn to:** sworn not to
219 **live dead:** I might as well be dead
223-4 **'Tis the way ... question more:** that will just confirm her beauty
225 **happy:** lucky
231 **Where I may read ... passing fair:** that reminds me my love is more beautiful
233 **I'll pay that doctrine ... in debt:** I will teach you that or die trying

Director's Note, 1.1

✔ Servants of the Montagues and Capulets start a street fight.
✔ The Prince stops the fight, and threatens any more fighting will be punished by death.
✔ Montague is worried about Romeo's behaviour. Benvolio agrees to question him.
✔ Romeo admits he is in love, but the woman he loves is not interested in him.

1 **bound:** ordered to keep the peace
2 **In penalty alike:** with the same punishment for failing
4 **reckoning:** reputation
6 **suit:** request
7 **But:** nothing more than
8 **yet a stranger in the world:** very young
11 **Ere:** before
12 **Younger than she are happy mothers made:** younger girls are married with children
13 **too soon marred .... early made:** they are spoiled by it
14 **The earth hath swallowed ... but she:** all my other children are dead
15 **the hopeful lady of my earth:** she's my only child and will inherit my wealth
17 **My will to her consent is but a part:** she has to agree as well
18-9 **And she agreed ... according voice:** and I'll accept any suitable person she chooses
20 **old accustomed:** traditional
21 **Whereto:** to which

SHAKESPEARE'S WORLD

◇◇◇◇◇◇◇◇◇◇◇

Peter and Will Kemp

In two of the versions of *Romeo and Juliet* printed during Shakespeare's lifetime, the name 'Peter' is replaced in a stage direction by 'Will Kemp'. Peter, the Capulets' servant, is fictional. Kemp was real – he was the actor who first played the part of Peter. Kemp was a celebrity in Elizabethan London, and one of the star attractions of the Chamberlain's Men, the company Shakespeare was part of. Audiences came to watch him for two things: clowning and dancing.

Peter is the clown of *Romeo and Juliet*. It may seem as though he does not have many lines, especially when he was one of the stars the audiences went to see. But clowns often said more than the author wrote, and the crowd enjoyed the sharp wit of celebrated comedians. So, with Kemp playing the part, he probably said much more, and it would have been new every time. Even if he didn't spend much time on the stage during the play, Kemp certainly dominated it afterwards. Every play, whether it was a comedy, tragedy or history, would finish with a jig – a dance, often with a comic song. Kemp was an undisputed master of this part of the performance and his jigs were every bit as famous, and as popular, as Shakespeare's plays.

Romeo and Peter, summer 2009.

1 This photograph was taken during the text on page 18. Pick a line which you think fits with this photo as the one being spoken when the photo was taken. Give reasons for your answer.

Adetomiwa Edun, Fergal McElherron

Such as I love, and you among the store,
One more, most welcome, makes my number more.
At my poor house look to behold this night
Earth-treading stars that make dark heaven light. 25
Such comfort as do lusty young men feel,
When well-apparelled April on the heel
Of limping winter treads, even such delight
Among fresh fennel buds shall you this night
Inherit at my house. Hear all, all see, 30
And like her most whose merit most shall be.
Which on more view, of many, mine being one,
May stand in number, though in reckoning none.
Come, go with me. *[To Peter, giving him a paper.]*
       Go, sirrah, trudge about
Through fair Verona, find those persons out 35
Whose names are written there, and to them say,
My house and welcome on their pleasure stay.

Exit Capulet and Paris.

Peter   Find them out whose names are written here.
It is written, that the shoemaker should meddle with
his yard, and the tailor with his last, the fisher with 40
his pencil, and the painter with his nets. But I am
sent to find those persons whose names are here
writ, and can never find what names the writing
person hath here writ. I must to the learnèd. —
In good time. 45

22 **the store:** them

25 **Earth-treading stars:** many beautiful women
27 **well-apparelled:** beautifully dressed
29 **fennel:** a herb linked at the time to passion
30 **Inherit at:** be free to enjoy
31 **like her most whose merit most shall be:** see who you think is the most desirable
32 **mine:** my daughter
33 **May stand in number ... reckoning none:** may be one of them, although not among the most well-known beauties
34 **sirrah:** you, used to call a less important person
37 **stay:** wait

39 **meddle with:** busy himself with
40 **yard:** measuring stick used by a tailor (he confuses the various pieces of equipment and trades)
40 **last:** wooden foot used to measure shoes
43–4 **can never find ... hath here writ:** can't read

Enter Benvolio and Romeo, talking.

Benvolio
Tut, man, one fire burns out another's burning,
One pain is lessened by another's anguish.
Turn giddy, and be helped by backward turning.
One desperate grief cures with another's languish.
Take thou some new infection to thy eye,   50
And the rank poison of the old will die.

Romeo
Your plantain leaf is excellent for that.

Benvolio
For what, I pray thee?

Romeo
                                        For your broken shin.

Benvolio
Why, Romeo, art thou mad?

Romeo
Not mad, but bound more than a mad-man is: 55
Shut up in prison, kept without my food,
Whipped and tormented and—Good-e'en, good fellow.

Peter
God gi' good-e'en. I pray, sir, can you read?

Romeo
Ay, mine own fortune in my misery.

Peter
Perhaps you have learned it without book. But I pray,   60
can you read anything you see?

Romeo
Ay, if I know the letters and the language.

Peter
Ye say honestly, rest you merry!

Romeo
Stay, fellow; I can read.   *He reads the letter.*
Signior Martino and his wife and daughters; County   65
Anselme and his beauteous sisters; the lady widow of
Vitravio; Signior Placentio and his lovely nieces; Mercutio
and his brother Valentine; mine uncle Capulet, his wife and
daughters; my fair niece Rosaline; Livia; Signior Valentio
and his cousin Tybalt; Lucio and the lively Helena.   70
A fair assembly: whither should they come?

Peter
Up.

Romeo
Whither? To supper?

Peter
To our house.

Romeo
Whose house?   75

Peter
My master's.

Romeo
Indeed I should have asked you that before.

Peter
Now I'll tell you without asking. my master is the
great rich Capulet, and if you be not of the house of
Montagues, I pray, come and crush a cup of wine. Rest   80
you merry!   *Exit Peter.*

Benvolio
At this same ancient feast of Capulet's
Sups the fair Rosaline, whom thou so loves,
With all the admired beauties of Verona.
Go thither and with unattainted eye,   85
Compare her face with some that I shall show,
And I will make thee think thy swan a crow.

47 **another's anguish:** the pain that was there before
48 **backward turning:** turning the other way
49 **cures with another's languish:** is cured by the arrival of another
50 **Take thou some new infection to thy eye:** fall in love with someone else
51 **rank:** strong
52 **plantain leaf:** used to heal cuts
57 **Good-e'en:** a greeting used after midday
58 **gi':** give you
60 **without book:** off by heart
63 **rest you merry:** farewell
65 **County:** Count
71 **whither should they come?:** where are they invited?
80 **crush:** drink
83 **Sups:** has her supper
85 **thither:** there
85 **unattainted:** unprejudiced

Romeo	When the devout religion of mine eye
	Maintains such falsehood, then turn tears to fire,
	And these who often drowned could never die, 90
	Transparent heretics, be burnt for liars.
	One fairer than my love? The all-seeing sun
	Ne'er saw her match since first the world begun.
Benvolio	Tut, you saw her fair, none else being by,
	Herself poised with herself in either eye. 95
	But in that crystal scales let there be weighed
	Your lady's love against some other maid
	That I will show you shining at this feast,
	And she shall scant show well that now seems best.
Romeo	I'll go along, no such sight to be shown, 100
	But to rejoice in splendour of mine own. *Exit both.*

ACT 1 SCENE 3

Enter Lady Capulet and Nurse.

Lady Capulet	Nurse, where's my daughter? call her forth to me.
Nurse	Now, by my maidenhead at twelve year old
	I bade her come. What, lamb! What, ladybird!
	God forbid, where's this girl? What, Juliet!

Enter Juliet.

Juliet	How now, who calls? 5
Nurse	Your mother.
Juliet	Madam, I am here. What is your will?
Lady Capulet	This is the matter. — Nurse, give leave awhile,
	We must talk in secret. — Nurse, come back again,
	I have remembered me, thou's hear our counsel. 10
	Thou knowest my daughter's of a pretty age.
Nurse	Faith, I can tell her age unto an hour.
Lady Capulet	She's not fourteen.
Nurse	I'll lay fourteen of my teeth (and yet, to my teen be it
	spoken, I have but four), she's not fourteen. How long 15
	is it now to Lammas-tide?
Lady Capulet	A fortnight and odd days.
Nurse	Even or odd, of all days in the year, come Lammas-
	eve at night shall she be fourteen. Susan and she (God
	rest all Christian souls) were of an age. Well, Susan 20
	is with God, she was too good for me. But, as I said,
	on Lammas Eve at night shall she be fourteen, that
	shall she. Marry; I remember it well. 'Tis since the
	earthquake now eleven years, and she was weaned
	(I never shall forget it) of all the days of the year, upon 25
	that day, for I had then laid wormwood to my dug,
	sitting in the sun under the dove-house wall. My lord
	and you were then at Mantua (nay I do bear a brain).

87–8 **When the devout religion ... such falsehood:** when my loving eye tells me such a lie

90–1 **these who often drowned ... Transparent heretics:** these eyes that wept for love so often couldn't betray that love

94 **none else being by:** with no other beauties nearby

95 **poised with:** balanced against

96 **that crystal scales:** your eyes

97 **Your lady's love:** the love you have for Rosaline

99 **she shall scant show well that now seems best:** and the one you love best now will not seem anywhere near as beautiful

101 **splendour of mine own:** in how much more beautiful my love is than the rest

Director's Note, 1.2

✔ Paris asks permission to marry Juliet. Capulet asks him to wait, because she is too young, but gives him hope and invites him to the feast.

✔ Romeo and Benvolio find out the girl Romeo loves, Rosaline, is invited to the feast.

✔ Benvolio says they should go to the feast, to see that there are many more attractive women than Rosaline.

✔ How does Shakespeare mix humour and keep the story moving?

2 **maidenhead:** virginity

3 **bade:** told her to

7 **What is your will?:** what can I do for you?

8 **the matter:** what I want to discuss

8 **give leave:** leave us

10 **thou's hear our counsel:** you shall hear our discussion

11 **pretty age:** suitable age for marriage

14 **teen:** sorrow

15 **but:** only

16 **Lammas-tide:** a holy day, 1 August

19 **Susan:** the Nurse's daughter

20 **of an age:** the same age

24 **was weaned:** stopped breast-feeding

26 **laid wormwood to my dug:** put a bitter liquid on her nipple (to put the baby off breast-feeding)

28 **nay I do bear a brain:** haven't I got a good memory

A

B

C

The Nurse and Juliet, summer 2009.

1 One of these photos was taken at line 31, another at line 36, and the last at line 56.

Which do you think is which? Quote from the text to support your answer.

Penny Layden, Ellie Kendrick

SHAKESPEARE'S WORLD

Juliet's relationship with her mother and her Nurse

There were many different types of servants in Elizabethan households, both men and women. They had different status depending on their exact duties. Some worked for a family for many years (often all their lives). Others had a contract to work for a set period of time. Many of these servants were teenagers. Servants were given food and board in exchange for their work. Most were also paid a wage.

Although the Nurse is a servant, Shakespeare shows her as closer to Juliet than her mother is. This would not be unusual at the time. The Nurse's speech tells us she has been with the family at least since Juliet's birth. She helped raise Juliet from infancy. Aside from breast-feeding Juliet as a baby, the Nurse would have looked after Juliet's clothes and helped Juliet dress. She would have slept in Juliet's room at night. She also gave Juliet advice, and was her only trusted friend. Juliet spent more time with her than with the rest of her family. This level of friendship is not unusual amongst masters and servants in Shakespeare's plays. Desdemona and Emilia in *Othello* and Portia and Nerissa in *The Merchant of Venice* are close as well. Regardless of these friendships, however, servants were expected to respect and obey their masters. There was a hierarchy among servants too. Less important servants were expected to respect and obey more important ones. We see this in the play. Peter carries the Nurse's fan, although they are both servants.

But, as I said, when it did taste the wormwood on the
nipple of my dug and felt it bitter, pretty fool, to see it 30
tetchy and fall out with the dug. Shake quoth the dove-
house: 'twas no need, I trow, to bid me trudge. And
since that time it is eleven years, for then she could
stand alone. Nay, by th' rood, she could have run and
waddled all about. For even the day before, she broke 35
her brow: and then my husband (God be with his soul,
a' was a merry man) took up the child, "Yea", quoth he,
"dost thou fall upon thy face? Thou wilt fall backward
when thou hast more wit, Wilt thou not, Jule?" And, by
my holidam, the pretty wretch left crying and said "Ay". 40
To see now how a jest shall come about. I warrant, and
I should live a thousand years, I never should forget
it. "Wilt thou not, Jule?" quoth he, and, pretty fool it
stinted and said "Ay".

Lady Capulet   Enough of this, I pray thee, hold thy peace. 45

Nurse   Yes, madam, yet I cannot choose but laugh,
To think it should leave crying and say "Ay".
And yet, I warrant, it had upon its brow
A bump as big as a young cockerel's stone.
A perilous knock, and it cried bitterly. 50
"Yea", quoth my husband, "fall'st upon thy face?
Thou wilt fall backward when thou comest to age,
Wilt thou not, Jule?" It stinted and said "Ay".

Juliet   And stint thou too, I pray thee nurse, say I.

Nurse   Peace, I have done. God mark thee to his grace, 55
Thou wast the prettiest babe that e'er I nursed.
And I might live to see thee married once,
I have my wish.

Lady Capulet   Marry, that "marry" is the very theme
I came to talk of. Tell me, daughter Juliet, 60
How stands your disposition to be married?

Juliet   It is an honour that I dream not of.

Nurse   An honour! Were not I thine only nurse,
I would say thou hadst sucked wisdom from thy teat.

Lady Capulet   Well, think of marriage now. Younger than you 65
Here in Verona, ladies of esteem,
Are made already mothers. By my count
I was your mother much upon these years
That you are now a maid. Thus then in brief:
The valiant Paris seeks you for his love. 70

Nurse   A man, young lady. Lady, such a man
As all the world. Why, he's a man of wax.

Lady Capulet   Verona's summer hath not such a flower.

Nurse   Nay he's a flower, in faith a very flower.

Lady Capulet   What say you, can you love the gentleman? 75
This night you shall behold him at our feast.

29 **it:** the baby, Juliet
31 **tetchy and fall out with the dug:** cross and dislike feeding
31-2 **Shake quoth the dove-house:** the dove-house shook in the earthquake
32 **'twas no need, I trow, to bid me trudge:** in truth, it didn't need to do that just to make me move
34 **by th' rood:** by Christ's cross (a way of swearing you are telling the truth)
35-6 **broke her brow:** cut her forehead
37 **a':** he
38 **Thou wilt fall backward:** sexual double meaning
39 **thou hast more wit:** you're wiser
39-40 **by my holidam:** by my holy lady (a way of swearing you are telling the truth)
40 **left:** stopped
41 **come about:** come true
41 **warrant:** swear it's true
44 **stinted:** stopped (crying)
45 **hold thy peace:** that's enough talking
47 **it:** the baby, Juliet
49 **stone:** testicle
52 **comest to age:** are old enough

57 **And I might:** if I could just
57 **once:** one day

59 **Marry:** a mild oath – by Mary (Christ's mother)

61 **How stands your disposition:** how do you feel about …

64 **thy teat:** the breast that fed you

66 **ladies of esteem:** well-respected women of good social status
68-9 **much upon these years … now a maid:** at about your age

72 **a man of wax:** as perfect as a wax model of the perfect man

76 **behold:** see

FINDING A HUSBAND

In Act 1 Scene 3, the audience sees Juliet for the first time. Her mother, Lady Capulet, and her Nurse talk to her about marriage (lines 75–95).

- In pairs, read this text.
- Each person reads the line up to a punctuation mark. At the punctuation mark the other person takes over and reads to the following punctuation mark. Read to the end of line 95.

1 What reasons does Lady Capulet give Juliet for marrying Paris?
2 How does Juliet respond to the advice?

SHAKESPEARE'S WORLD

Arranged marriage and age at marriage

In Shakespeare's time, women typically married at age 24 to 26. Men usually waited until age 27 to 29. Many men had to finish an apprenticeship and save money to set up a home. People were encouraged to marry someone of a similar age and social class. So, children of wealthy, important people had fewer suitable choices. Their parents often arranged marriages for them, just as Capulet does. A woman had less choice over who she married than a man. Her father negotiated a marriage contract for her. This said how much he would give as a dowry (money or property given to her husband on the wedding day), and who would support her if her husband died. In Shakespeare's time, people had to announce their plans to marry in their local parish for three Sundays before the wedding. This was to make sure that no one objected. Weddings were public affairs that took place between 8am and 12pm. Secret marriages, such as that between Romeo and Juliet, were seen as shocking.

Director's Note, 1.3

- ✔ Lady Capulet tells Juliet about Paris' wish to marry her.
- ✔ Juliet is dutiful, and says she will look to like Paris, but only so far as her mother approves.
- ✔ This is the first time we see Juliet. What picture of her does Shakespeare present?

SHAKESPEARE'S WORLD

Boys and men playing women

During Shakespeare's lifetime, women were not allowed to act in public theatres. The leading female roles, like Juliet, were played by teenage boys before their voices broke. The acting companies only had a few such boys. Some female characters were played by men. They were usually the older, comic female parts, such as the Nurse (seen here played by a man, Bette Bourne). This gave Shakespeare the chance to write for the humorous possibility of a man dressed as a woman, which is a popular form of comedy to this day.

	Read o'er the volume of young Paris' face,	
	And find delight writ there with beauty's pen.	
	Examine every married lineament,	
	And see how one another lends content.	80
	And what obscured in this fair volume lies,	
	Find written in the margent of his eyes.	
	This precious book of love, this unbound lover,	
	To beautify him, only lacks a cover.	
	The fish lives in the sea, and 'tis much pride,	85
	For fair without, the fair within to hide.	
	That book in many's eyes doth share the glory,	
	That in gold clasps, locks in the golden story.	
	So shall you share all that he doth possess,	
	By having him, making yourself no less.	90
Nurse	No less? Nay, bigger! Women grow by men.	
Lady Capulet	Speak briefly, can you like of Paris' love?	
Juliet	I'll look to like, if looking liking move.	
	But no more deep will I endart mine eye	
	Than your consent gives strength to make it fly.	95

Enter Servant.

Peter	Madam, the guests are come, supper served up, you called, my young lady asked for, the nurse cursed in the pantry, and everything in extremity. I must hence to wait. I beseech you follow straight. *Exit Peter.*	
Lady Capulet	We follow thee. Juliet, the County stays.	100
Nurse	Go, girl, seek happy nights to happy days. *Exit all.*	

ACT 1 SCENE 4

Enter torch-bearers, Romeo, Mercutio, Benvolio, with five or six friends as masquers.

Romeo	What, shall this speech be spoke for our excuse?	
	Or shall we on without apology?	
Benvolio	The date is out of such prolixity.	
	We'll have no Cupid hoodwinked with a scarf,	
	Bearing a Tartar's painted bow of lath,	5
	Scaring the ladies like a crow-keeper;	
	Nor no without-book prologue, faintly spoke	
	After the prompter, for our entrance.	
	But let them measure us by what they will,	
	We'll measure them a measure, and be gone.	10
Romeo	Give me a torch, I am not for this ambling.	
	Being but heavy I will bear the light.	
Mercutio	Nay, gentle Romeo, we must have you dance.	
Romeo	Not I, believe me. You have dancing shoes	
	With nimble soles, I have a soul of lead	15
	So stakes me to the ground I cannot move.	

77 Read o'er the volume of young Paris' face: Lady Capulet uses a book metaphor throughout this speech; Juliet has to 'read' Paris' potential as a husband

79 married lineament: feature of his face

81 what obscured in this fair volume lies: what you can't tell from that

82 margent: margin (some people write comments in book margins)

83 unbound: double meaning: incomplete because unmarried; a book with no cover

86 For fair without, the fair within to hide: Juliet will complete him, she the beautiful cover, he the book inside

90 no less: as important as he is

91 grow: double meaning: grow in status; become pregnant

92 like of: accept

93 I'll look to like, if looking liking move: I'll go hoping to like him

94–5 no more deep will I endart ... to make it fly: I won't like him any more than you think I should

98 in extremity: needs doing at once

98–9 to wait: to serve the food and drink

99 straight: straight away

100 the County stays: the Count is waiting

SD masquers: masked entertainers

1 this speech be spoke for our excuse: we have a speech ready (masquers often gave a speech on arrival)

3 The date is out of such prolixity: it isn't fashionable to make speeches any more

4 hoodwinked: blindfolded

5 Tartar's painted bow of lath: a bow made from cheap wood, like a stage prop

6 crow-keeper: scarecrow

7 Nor no without-book prologue: nor any speech learned by heart

9 measure us: judge us

10 measure them a measure: give them a dance

11 I am not for this ambling: I don't want to dance

16 So stakes me: fixes me

23

Mercutio   You are a lover; borrow Cupid's wings
And soar with them above a common bound.

Romeo   I am too sore enpiercèd with his shaft
To soar with his light feathers, and so bound
I cannot bound a pitch above dull woe.
Under love's heavy burden do I sink.

Mercutio   And, to sink in it, should you burden love, Romeo
Too great oppression for a tender thing.

Romeo   Is love a tender thing? It is too rough,
Too rude, too boisterous, and it pricks like thorn.

Mercutio   If love be rough with you, be rough with love,
Prick love for pricking, and you beat love down.
Give me a case to put my visage in,
A visor for a visor. What care I
What curious eye doth quote deformities?
Here are the beetle brows shall blush for me.

Benvolio   Come, knock and enter; and no sooner in,
But every man betake him to his legs.

Romeo   A torch for me. Let wantons light of heart
Tickle the senseless rushes with their heels,
For I am proverbed with a grandsire phrase;
I'll be a candle-holder and look on,
The game was ne'er so fair, and I am done.

Mercutio   Tut, dun's the mouse, the constable's own word.
If thou art dun, we'll draw thee from the mire
Or, (save your reverence) love, wherein thou stickest
Up to the ears. Come, we burn daylight, ho!

Romeo   Nay, that's not so.

Mercutio   I mean, sir, in delay
We waste our lights in vain, like lamps by day.
Take our good meaning, for our judgement sits
Five times in that, ere once in our five wits.

Romeo   And we mean well in going to this masque,
But 'tis no wit to go.

Mercutio   Why, may one ask?

Romeo   I dreamt a dream to-night.

Mercutio   And so did I.

Romeo   Well, what was yours?

Mercutio   That dreamers often lie.

Romeo   In bed asleep, while they do dream things true.

Mercutio   O, then, I see Queen Mab hath been with you.

Benvolio   Queen Mab, what's she?

Mercutio   She is the fairies' midwife, and she comes
In shape no bigger than an agate-stone
On the fore-finger of an alderman,

20
25
30
35
40
45
50
55

18 **common bound:** normal limit
19 **sore enpiercèd with his shaft:** deeply in love, pierced by Cupid's arrow
20 **and so bound:** and held back like this
23–4 **to sink in it … for a tender thing:** be careful not to put too great a burden on something as easily damaged as love
28 **Prick love for pricking, and you beat love down:** act on your feelings and you will control love, not be controlled by it
29 **a case to put my visage in:** a mask to wear
30 **A visor for a visor:** a mask to hide my face
31 **What curious eye doth quote deformities:** if people gossip about how ugly I am
32 **beetle brows:** thick eyebrows (the mask)
34 **betake him to his legs:** start dancing
35 **wantons:** pleasure-seekers
36 **Tickle the senseless rushes with their heels:** dance
37 **proverbed with a grandsire phrase:** in the words of the proverb
39 **The game was ne'er so fair:** and see more of what's going on
40 **dun's the mouse:** be quiet and don't draw attention
40 **the constable's own word:** as a night watchman might say
41 **draw thee from the mire:** pull you out of the mud
42 **save your reverence:** excuse my rudeness
43 **burn daylight:** waste time
46 **good meaning:** the sense of what I say
46–7 **for our judgement sits … five wits:** because that's five times better than what our senses tell us
49 **'tis no wit to go:** it isn't wise to go
52 **while:** sometimes
53 **Queen Mab:** a powerful fairy
55 **fairies' midwife:** the fairy who delivers dreams to humans
56 **agate-stone:** agate was used to make rings carved with tiny pictures
57 **alderman:** an important town councillor

Drawn with a team of little atomies
Over men's noses as they lie asleep.
Her chariot is an empty hazel-nut   60
Made by the joiner squirrel or old grub,
Time out o' mind the fairies' coachmakers.
Her wagon-spokes made of long spinners' legs,
The cover of the wings of grasshoppers,
The traces of the smallest spider's web,   65
The collars of the moonshine's watery beams,
Her whip of cricket's bone, the lash of film,
Her wagoner a small grey-coated gnat,
Not so big as a round little worm
Pricked from the lazy finger of a maid;   70
And in this state she gallops night by night:
Through lovers' brains, and then they dream of love;
O'er courtiers' knees, that dream on curtsies straight;
O'er lawyers' fingers, who straight dream on fees;
O'er ladies' lips, who straight on kisses dream;   75
Which oft the angry Mab with blisters plagues,
Because their breaths with sweetmeats tainted are.
Sometime she gallops o'er a courtier's nose,
And then dreams he of smelling out a suit;
And sometime comes she with a tithe-pig's tail,   80
Tickling a parson's nose as 'a lies asleep,
Then he dreams of another benefice.
Sometime she driveth o'er a soldier's neck,
And then dreams he of cutting foreign throats,
Of breaches, ambuscadoes, Spanish blades,   85
Of healths five-fathom deep, and then anon
Drums in his ear, at which he starts and wakes,
And being thus frighted, swears a prayer or two
And sleeps again. This is that very Mab
That plaits the manes of horses in the night,   90
And bakes the elflocks in foul sluttish hairs,
Which once untangled, much misfortune bodes.
This is the hag, when maids lie on their backs,
That presses them and learns them first to bear,
Making them women of good carriage.   95
This is she—

Romeo   Peace, peace, Mercutio, peace,
Thou talk'st of nothing.

Mercutio   True, I talk of dreams,
Which are the children of an idle brain,
Begot of nothing but vain fantasy,
Which is as thin of substance as the air   100
And more inconstant than the wind, who woos
Even now the frozen bosom of the north.
And being angered, puffs away from thence,
Turning his side to the dew-dropping south.

Benvolio   This wind, you talk of blows us from ourselves,   105
Supper is done, and we shall come too late.

58 **atomies:** tiny creatures

61 **joiner:** carpenter
62 **Time out o' mind:** for as long as anyone can remember
63 **spinners:** spiders

65 **traces:** harness
66 **collars:** neck straps joined to the harness
67 **film:** very, very thin threads
68 **wagoner:** driver

71 **state:** magnificence
73 **courtiers:** socially important people who are part of a royal court
73 **curtsies:** bowing to the king or queen
76 **oft:** often
77 **sweetmeats:** sweet food
77 **tainted:** spoiled
79 **smelling out a suit:** finding someone who will reward him for taking their request to the king or queen
80 **tithe-pig:** people had to give a tenth of their income to the Church (tithe); poorer people paid in crops or animals
82 **benefice:** paid work for the Church
85 **breaches, ambuscadoes, Spanish blades:** breaking down castle walls, ambushes, the best Spanish swords
86 **healths five-fathom deep:** drinking toasts with a lot of wine
91 **bakes the elflocks in foul sluttish hairs:** tangles unbrushed hair
92 **much misfortune bodes:** means bad luck
94 **bear:** carry the weight of a man during sex or a baby in pregnancy. This is the start of a series of sexual double meanings
95 **of good carriage:** able to bear these weights
97 **nothing:** a double meaning: 1) nothing; 2) a slang reference to the vagina at the time, 'no-thing'
99 **Begot:** born of

104 **Turning his side:** changing direction
105 **blows us from ourselves:** distracts us

IMPROVISATION

In lines 48–50, and at the end of Act 1 Scene 4, before Capulet's feast (lines 107–114), Romeo shares his fears with his friends.

- In groups of three, select one person to be Romeo, one Mercutio, and one Benvolio.
- The person playing Romeo should take the last word of each line from Romeo's speech and use the words in a short improvised speech to explain why they should not go to Capulet's feast.
- In the improvisation, Mercutio and Benvolio should state whether they agree or disagree with Romeo's argument.

1 In the play, how do Romeo's friends respond to his dream?

2 What does the discussion reveal about their friendship?

Director's Note, 1.4

✔ Romeo, Benvolio, Mercutio and friends are on the way to Capulet's feast, disguised by their masks.
✔ Romeo is worried by a dream.
✔ Mercutio mocks him, telling him about Queen Mab.
✔ What does Shakespeare tell us in this scene about the characters of Romeo and Mercutio?

Capulet (far right) as Romeo and the masquers enter, spring 2009.

1 What have the director and designer done to show this scene is a party?

2 The director hasn't followed the stage directions at the end of Scene 4, and after line 13. What did he do that was different?

3 What effect do you think this moment had in the theatre? Explain your answer.

Romeo	I fear, too early, for my mind misgives,
	Some consequence yet hanging in the stars
	Shall bitterly begin his fearful date
	With this night's revels, and expire the term
	Of a despisèd life closed in my breast
	By some vile forfeit of untimely death.
	But he that hath the steerage of my course,
	Direct my sail. On, lusty gentlemen.
Benvolio	Strike drum.

107 **my mind misgives:** I have a bad feeling about this

108 **yet hanging in the stars:** fated to happen in the future

110

109–10 **Shall bitterly begin ... this night's revels:** will be set in motion at this party

110–2 **and expire the term ... untimely death:** ending with my death

115

113 **he that hath the steerage of my course:** God, who guides my life

They march about the stage, and stand to one side.

ACT 1 SCENE 5

Enter servingmen, including Peter, with dishclothes.

Peter	Where's Potpan, that he helps not to take away?
	He shift a trencher? He scrape a trencher!
First Servant	When good manners shall lie all in one or two men's hands and they unwashed too, 'tis a foul thing.
Peter	Away with the joint-stools, remove the court-cupboard, look to the plate. Good thou, save me a piece of marchpane, and, as thou lovest me, let the porter let in Susan Grindstone and Nell. — Anthony and Potpan!
Second Servant	Ay, boy, ready.
Peter	You are looked for and called for, asked for and sought for, in the great chamber.
First Servant	We cannot be here and there too. Cheerly boys, be brisk awhile, and the longer liver take all.

1 **take away:** clear the table
2 **trencher:** wooden plate

4 **foul:** dirty

5

5 **joint-stools:** stools
5 **court-cupboard:** sideboard
6 **look to the plate:** make sure no one steals the silver
6 **Good thou:** Do me a favour, will you
7 **marchpane:** marzipan

10

11 **great chamber:** main hall

13 **the longer liver take all:** whoever survives gets it all

Exit Peter and the servants.
Enter Capulet, Capulet's cousin, Lady Capulet, Juliet, Tybalt, all the guests and gentlewomen. Romeo and the masquers join them.

Capulet	Welcome, gentlemen. Ladies that have their toes
	Unplagued with corns will walk about with you.
	Ah, my mistresses, which of you all
	Will now deny to dance? She that makes dainty,
	She, I'll swear, hath corns. Am I come near ye now?
	Welcome, gentlemen! I have seen the day
	That I have worn a visor and could tell
	A whispering tale in a fair lady's ear,
	Such as would please. 'Tis gone, 'tis gone, 'tis gone.
	You are welcome, gentlemen! Come, musicians, play.

15

17 **deny to:** refuse to
17 **makes dainty:** holds back
18 **Am I come near ye now?:** have I hit on the truth?

20

15 **walk about:** dance

Music plays and they dance.

A hall, a hall, give room, and foot it, girls.
More light, you knaves, and turn the tables up,
And quench the fire, the room is grown too hot.
Ah, sirrah, this unlooked-for sport comes well.

25

24 **A hall:** (to the servants) make room (for the dancing)
24 **foot it:** dance
25 **turn the tables up:** put the tables away
27 **unlooked-for sport:** surprise entertainment (the masquers)

SHAKESPEARE'S WORLD

◇◇◇◇◇◇◇◇◇◇◇◇◇

Masques and masks

In the Tudor and Stuart periods, the upper classes held grand celebrations in their own houses. The family hired musicians and actors. They also took an active part themselves, often in masques. Masques could be anything from a simple fancy-dress party (where everyone wore a mask) to a full-scale theatrical show, with long speeches and elaborate special effects. Henry VIII was very fond of masques, and regularly acted in them. James I took a less active part, but enjoyed masques in his court. Shakespeare wrote both types of masque in his plays. The one in *The Tempest* is especially elaborate. In *Romeo and Juliet* only the younger characters wear masks and dance. This, then, is a simple masque. It is a chance for the youth of Verona to flirt with each other, whilst under the cover of disguise. Crucially, it gives Romeo and his friends the chance to enter the Capulet household without being detected.

Director's view

Dominic Dromgoole
Director, summer 2009

It is the essence of a lot of Shakespeare's writing – his ability to paint a broad social landscape as a backdrop, and then pick out moments of human drama and juggle three or four different stories very deftly and very quickly at the same time. I chose to leave the dance on stage when I did it, and then pull people forward to the front. You pull people down to the front, and they have a protracted period of nattering to each other, which Romeo and Juliet obviously have, because they speak that sonnet to each other. You have to choreograph the activity behind them, so that it goes from ebullient and noisy when everyone spills in at the beginning, to then being quite deliberate and stylised and uniform, just so that you are not pulling people's attention away.

Everyone is looking forward to Romeo and Juliet getting together. Everyone is hungry for the moment when they lock eyes on each other, and you can play on that. Tybalt is a wonderful spoiler, and he is a great energy – just as a sort of malevolent energy. Capulet, we have already got to know, we know that he is anxious, a slightly overzealous, over keen host. We work out very quickly there is some sort of dysfunction between him and his wife. So it is full of stories that have already been quite deftly built up, and they reach a very quick climax in that scene.

Tybalt (pushing his mask up) and Romeo, dancers behind, summer 2009.

Which line do you think Romeo was speaking when this photo was taken? Quote from the text to support your answer.

Ukweli Roach, Adetomiwa Edun

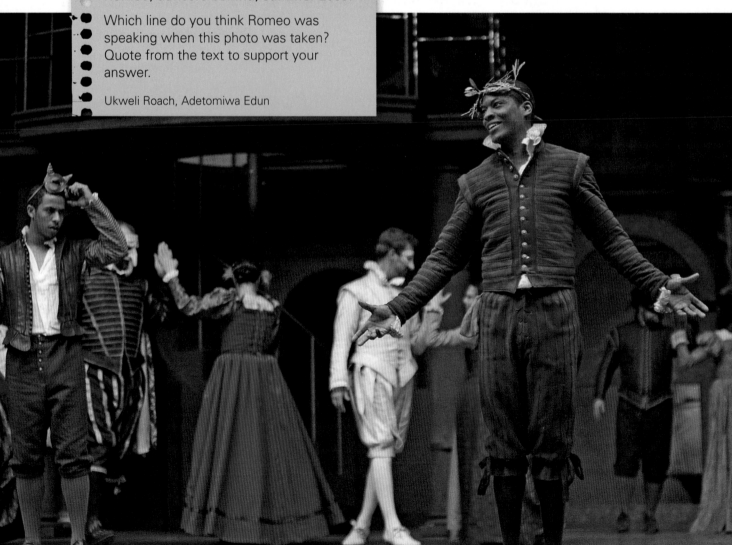

	Nay, sit, nay, sit, good cousin Capulet,	
	For you and I are past our dancing days.	
	How long is't now since last yourself and I	30
	Were in a masque?	

Capulet's Cousin   By'r lady, thirty years.

Capulet What, man! 'Tis not so much, 'tis not so much:
'Tis since the nuptial of Lucentio,
Come Pentecost as quickly as it will,
Some five and twenty years, and then we masked.   35

Capulet Cousin 'Tis more, 'tis more, his son is elder, sir.
His son is thirty.

Capulet   Will you tell me that?
His son was but a ward two years ago.

Romeo *[To a Servingman.]*
What lady is that which doth enrich the hand
Of yonder knight?   40

Servingman I know not, sir.

Romeo O, she doth teach the torches to burn bright!
It seems she hangs upon the cheek of night
As a rich jewel in an Ethiope's ear.
Beauty too rich for use, for earth too dear.   45
So shows a snowy dove trooping with crows,
As yonder lady o'er her fellows shows.
The measure done, I'll watch her place of stand,
And touching hers, make blessèd my rude hand.
Did my heart love till now? Forswear it sight,   50
For I ne'er saw true beauty till this night.

Tybalt This, by his voice, should be a Montague.
Fetch me my rapier, boy.   *[Exit Page.]*
               What, dares the slave
Come hither covered with an antic face,
To fleer and scorn at our solemnity?   55
Now, by the stock and honour of my kin,
To strike him dead I hold it not a sin.

Capulet Why, how now, kinsman, wherefore storm you so?

Tybalt Uncle, this is a Montague, our foe
A villain that is hither come in spite,   60
To scorn at our solemnity this night.

Capulet Young Romeo is it?

Tybalt 'Tis he, that villain Romeo.

Capulet Content thee, gentle coz, let him alone,
'A bears him like a portly gentleman,   65
And to say truth, Verona brags of him
To be a virtuous and well-governed youth.
I would not for the wealth of all the town
Here in my house do him disparagement,

---

31 **By'r lady:** by our lady (Christ's mother)
33 **nuptial:** wedding
34 **Come Pentecost as quickly as it will:** years pass so quickly

38 **a ward:** someone not old enough to run their own affairs, so has a guardian

44 **Ethiope:** a black African (from Ethiopia)
45 **Beauty too rich ... too dear:** too beautiful to live an ordinary life on earth
48 **The measure done:** now this dance is over
49 **rude:** rough, unworthy
50 **Forswear it sight:** deny it, my eyes

53 **rapier:** sword
53 **slave:** used as an insult
54 **hither:** here
54 **antic face:** mask
55 **fleer and scorn at our solemnity:** mock our celebration
56 **the stock and honour of my kin:** my family's honour
58 **wherefore storm you so?:** why are you so angry?

60 **in spite:** showing us no respect

64 **Content thee:** don't be so angry
65 **'A bears him like a portly gentleman:** he's behaving perfectly well
67 **well-governed:** well-behaved

69 **do him disparagement:** insult him

29

PALM TO PALM

In Act 1 Scene 5 Romeo and Juliet meet for the first time (lines 92–109).

- In pairs, one person read Romeo, and one read Juliet.
- After your first read-through, identify the last word of each line, and whether it is part of a rhyme.
- Now stand opposite each other to read the text aloud.
- Every time your line rhymes with another of your lines, take **one step** forward.
- Romeo, every time your line rhymes with Juliet's line, take **two steps** forward.
- Juliet, every time your line rhymes with Romeo's line, take **two steps** forward.

1 Which character makes the first move?
2 Is there a pattern in the movement?
3 What does this scene reveal about
   a) Juliet's personality?
   b) Romeo's personality?
4 What metaphors do the characters use to express their feelings and intentions?

CLUES IN THE PUNCTUATION

In this edition of the play, a dash is used when the speaker changes mid speech, and speaks to somebody else.

- In pairs, read Tybalt and Capulet's argument (lines 64–86). One reads Capulet, and the other reads Tybalt.
- Work out which parts are not part of Capulet's direct conversation with Tybalt.

1 What is Capulet doing in the lines not spoken to Tybalt?
- Now read the argument again, leaving out Capulet's lines not spoken to Tybalt. Does this change your view of the argument?
2 How is Tybalt disrespectful to Capulet?
3 How does Shakespeare enable Capulet to keep the argument private?

Romeo and Juliet, spring 2009.

Pick a line from the text on the opposite page which could be used as a caption for this photo. Give reasons for your choice.

James Alexandrou, Lorraine Burroughs

	Therefore be patient, take no note of him. It is my will, the which if thou respect, Show a fair presence and put off these frowns, An ill-beseeming semblance for a feast.
Tybalt	It fits, when such a villain is a guest. I'll not endure him.
Capulet	He shall be endured. What, goodman boy! I say he shall! Go to! Am I the master here or you? Go to! You'll not endure him? God shall mend my soul! You'll make a mutiny among my guests! You will set cock-a-hoop! You'll be the man!
Tybalt	Why, uncle, 'tis a shame.
Capulet	Go to, go to! You are a saucy boy. Is't so indeed? This trick may chance to scathe you. I know what, You must contrary me! Marry, 'tis time. — Well said, my hearts. — You are a princox, go, Be quiet, or — More light, more light for shame — I'll make you quiet. — What, cheerly my hearts!
Tybalt	Patience perforce with wilful choler meeting, Makes my flesh tremble in their different greeting. I will withdraw, but this intrusion shall Now seeming sweet, convert to bitter gall. *Exit*
Romeo	*[To Juliet.]* If I profane with my unworthiest hand This holy shrine, the gentle sin is this, My lips, two blushing pilgrims, ready stand To smooth that rough touch with a tender kiss.
Juliet	Good pilgrim, you do wrong your hand too much, Which mannerly devotion shows in this, For saints have hands, that pilgrims' hands do touch, And palm to palm is holy palmers' kiss.
Romeo	Have not saints lips, and holy palmers too?
Juliet	Ay, pilgrim, lips that they must use in prayer.
Romeo	O, then, dear saint, let lips do what hands do; They pray (grant thou) lest faith turn to despair.
Juliet	Saints do not move, though grant for prayers' sake.
Romeo	Then move not, while my prayer's effect I take.
	[They kiss.]
	Thus from my lips, by thine, my sin is purged.
Juliet	Then have my lips the sin that they have took.
Romeo	Sin from my lips? O trespass sweetly urged! Give me my sin again. *[They kiss.]*
Juliet	You kiss by th' book.

70

75

80

85

90

95

100

105

70 note: notice

72 Show a fair presence: be cheerful
73 An ill-beseeming semblance: which are not appropriate

76 goodman boy: an insult suggesting Tybalt isn't behaving like a gentleman
76 Go to!: that's enough of this
79 make a mutiny: disobey me
80 set cock-a-hoop: go wild
80 be the man: take the decisions
81 'tis a shame: it brings shame on us
82 saucy: disgracefully rude
83 trick may chance to scathe you: behaving like this won't do you any good
84 contrary: oppose
84 Marry, 'tis time ... : a mild oath – by Mary (Christ's mother). For the next few lines, Capulet is talking to his guests, his servants and Tybalt in quick succession
88–9 Patience perforce ... different greeting: this clash between enforced patience and my anger makes me shake
92 profane: mistreat a holy object
93 This holy shrine: Juliet's hand
94 pilgrims: travellers to holy places
96 you do wrong: you are unkind to
97 mannerly devotion shows in this: is acting with proper respect
99 palmers: name for pilgrims to the Holy Land, who came back with a palm leaf
99 palm to palm is holy palmers' kiss: it's more appropriate for palmers to touch hands in greeting, not kiss

104 grant for prayers' sake: they answer prayers
105 my prayer's effect: a kiss

106 purged: cleaned away

108 urged: argued for

109 You kiss by th' book: in just the right way

31

THE STRUCTURE OF THE SCENE

Act 1 Scene 5 is Capulet's feast. There is dancing throughout the scene.

- In groups, read through the *Working Cut*. Note or highlight all the stage directions.

- Read the *Working Cut* again, and this time note the language in the character's lines that suggests a change of focus.

- Now break the scene down into different sections. Within the whole scene give each section a name.

1 Make a table with two columns: *Section Name*, *Function in the scene*. Complete the table with the answers you have worked out.

Section Name	Function in the scene
Welcome	Shows Capulet wants to be a good host

For the director, staging this scene is a big challenge. Most people stay on stage all scene, but each section involves different people, and that is where you need the audience to focus.

- Draw several plans of the Globe stage (see page 3).

- For each section, plot onto a stage plan:

    a) where the action will take place

    b) where the other groups will be on the stage

    c) how groups will move as this section moves on to the next one.

- Using the *Working Cut* and all the decisions you have made, walk through the scene, reading the text aloud.

- Evaluate your decisions. Do you need to make changes to improve how it works?

2 Is the pace of the scene constant? In the text, can you identify when the pace alters?

3 How does Shakespeare create a scene with lots of people, where the audience focuses on just a couple of people at any one time?

4 What type of atmosphere does the scene generate?

Working Cut – text for experiment

Enter Servingmen, including Peter, with dishclothes.

Pet   Away with the joint-stools,— Anthony and Potpan!

2nd S.   Ay, boy, ready.

Pet   You are looked for and called for, asked for and sought for, in the great chamber.

1st S.   We cannot be here and there too.

Exit Peter and the servants.

Enter Capulet, Capulet's cousin, Lady Capulet, Juliet, Tybalt, all the guests and gentlewomen. Romeo and the masquers join them.

Cap   Welcome, gentlemen. Ladies that have their toes Unplagued with corns will walk about with you.

Music plays and they dance.

Rom   *[To a Servingman.]* What lady is that?

Serv.   I know not, sir.

Rom   O, she doth teach the torches to burn bright!

Tyb   This, by his voice, should be a Montague. Fetch me my rapier, boy. *[Exit Page.]* Uncle, this is a Montague, our foe

Cap   Young Romeo is it? Content thee, gentle coz, let him alone

Tyb   I'll not endure him.

Cap   Go to, go to!

Tyb   I will withdraw, but this intrusion shall Now seeming sweet, convert to bitter gall. *Exit.*

Rom   *[To Juliet.]* If I profane with my unworthiest hand This holy shrine, the gentle sin is this, My lips, two blushing pilgrims, ready stand To smooth that rough touch with a tender kiss.

Jul   Good pilgrim, you do wrong your hand too much, Which mannerly devotion shows in this, For saints have hands, that pilgrims' hands do touch, And palm to palm is holy palmers' kiss.

Rom   Have not saints lips, and holy palmers too?

Jul   Ay, pilgrim, lips that they must use in prayer.

Rom   O, then, dear saint, let lips do what hands do; They pray (grant thou) lest faith turn to despair.

Jul   Saints do not move, though grant for prayers' sake.

                    [They kiss.]

Nurse   Madam, your mother craves a word with you.

                    [Juliet moves away.]

Romeo   What is her mother?

Nurse   Her mother is the lady of the house.

Ben   Away, begone, the sport is at the best.

                    [They all exit, except Juliet and the Nurse.]

Juliet   Come hither, nurse. What is yond gentleman?

Nurse   I know not.

Juliet   Go ask his name. *[She goes.]*

Nurse   His name is Romeo, and a Montague;

Juliet   My only love sprung from my only hate!

                    [Someone calls within, 'Juliet!'.]

Nurse   Come let's away, the strangers all are gone.

Nurse	Madam, your mother craves a word with you.	110

[Juliet moves away.]

Romeo	What is her mother?	

111 **What:** who

Nurse	Marry, bachelor,
	Her mother is the lady of the house,
	And a good lady, and a wise and virtuous
	I nursed her daughter, that you talked withal.
	I tell you, he that can lay hold of her
	Shall have the chinks.

114 **withal:** with
115 **lay hold of:** marry

116 **the chinks:** the money
117 **dear account:** what a high price
117 **My life is my foe's debt:** an enemy holds my life in her hands

Romeo	*[Aside.]* Is she a Capulet?
	O dear account! My life is my foe's debt.
Benvolio	Away, begone, the sport is at the best.
Romeo	Ay, so I fear; the more is my unrest.

118 **the sport is at the best:** we've had the best of it
119 **the more is my unrest:** that's what bothers me

Capulet	Nay, gentlemen, prepare not to be gone,
	We have a trifling foolish banquet towards.
	Is it e'en so? Why then I thank you all.
	I thank you, honest gentlemen, good night.
	More torches here! — Come on then, let's to bed.
	Ah, sirrah, by my faith, it waxes late:
	I'll to my rest.

121 **We have a ... towards:** we're just going to have a bite to eat
122 **Is it e'en so?:** must you really go?

125 **it waxes:** it is getting
127 **yond:** over there

[They all exit, except Juliet and the Nurse.]

Juliet	Come hither, nurse. What is yond gentleman?
Nurse	The son and heir of old Tiberio.
Juliet	What's he that now is going out of door?
Nurse	Marry, that I think be young Petruchio.
Juliet	What's he that follows here, that would not dance?
Nurse	I know not.
Juliet	Go ask his name. *[She goes.]*
	If he be married.
	My grave is like to be my wedding bed.

134 **My grave is like to be my wedding bed:** two possible meanings: 1) I'll die unmarried, for I won't marry anyone else; 2) I'll die if I can't marry him
137 **sprung from my only hate:** born into my enemy's family
138 **Too early seen unknown ... too late:** I fell in love before I knew who he was
139 **Prodigious:** unlucky, ominous

143 **Anon:** I'm on my way
144 **strangers:** people who don't live in the house

Nurse	His name is Romeo, and a Montague;
	The only son of your great enemy.
Juliet	My only love sprung from my only hate!
	Too early seen unknown, and known too late.
	Prodigious birth of love it is to me,
	That I must love a lothèd enemy.
Nurse	What's this? what's this?
Juliet	A rhyme I learned even now
	Of one I danced withal.

[Someone calls within, 'Juliet!'.]

Nurse	Anon, anon!
	Come let's away, the strangers all are gone. *Exit all.* 144

Director's Note, 1.5

✔ Disguised, Romeo and his friends join the dancing.

✔ Tybalt recognises Romeo, is stopped from attacking him by Capulet, and swears vengeance.

✔ Romeo and Juliet meet, and start to fall in love. Later they both discover the other is from the 'enemy' family.

EXAMINER'S NOTES, 1.5

These questions help you to explore many aspects of *Romeo and Juliet*. At GCSE, your teacher will tell you which aspects are relevant to how your Shakespeare response will be assessed.

EXAMINER'S TIP

Voice

A character may speak in many different ways according to who they are speaking to, and how they feel. A character's language may show signs of attitude or of feeling, so that an audience can tell if the character is worried, angry, curious, challenging or trying to persuade.

Voice is the kind of speech behaviour which is so typical of a character that an audience can recognize who is speaking from a small extract. This may be because of accent, dialect or a personal language habit.

For example, Tybalt expresses a range of attitudes and feelings between lines 55 and 76:

'What, dares the slave
Come hither covered with an antic face,
To fleer and scorn at our solemnity?'
[This shows surprise at Romeo's presence followed by wounded honour at the assumed insult.]
'Uncle, this is a Montague, our foe'
[Urgent bringing of news to his senior.]
'It fits, when such a villain is a guest.'
[Sulky and defiant when his senior tells him that reacting would be 'ill-beseeming'.]
'Why, uncle, 'tis a shame.'
[Angry, sullen, reproachful.]
'I will withdraw, but this intrusion shall
Now seeming sweet, convert to bitter gall.'
[Reluctant and resentful, doing as he is told, but bitterly determined to have his revenge at a later date.]

❶ Character and plot development

So far, Romeo has been presented as one of a group of young men, sharing their banter but slightly apart because of his feelings about Rosaline. He joins the others in gatecrashing the Capulets' party because he's following his friends. In this scene he appears on his own, and we see him forget his friends (and Rosaline) when he sees Juliet. The scene is a mixture of party business, private talk and developing danger.

1. How does the opening of this scene contrast with the end of the preceding scene, lines 107–115?
2. What impressions does Shakespeare create in the 13 lines he gives to the four servants?
3. In what ways do the stage directions before and after the servants' lines help to create a particular setting?

❷ Characterisation and voice: dramatic language

Voice is an important part of character on stage. What we hear tells as much as what we see. Shakespeare's stage had no sound amplification, so Romeo's thoughts about Juliet had to be heard in an open-air theatre, even when he was talking to himself. What he says tells us about what he is thinking and how his feelings are developing.

4. What impression of Capulet is created by the lines between himself and his cousin (lines 14–38)?
5. How do Romeo's lines at 42–51 make Juliet seem more attractive than anyone else in the room?
6. What makes Romeo's speech here seem very formal and romantic compared with his previous speeches?
7. In what ways does Tybalt's speech following (lines 52–58) change the mood and express contrasting feelings?
8. What impressions of Capulet does Shakespeare create in lines 14–38?
9. How do the lines between Romeo and Juliet (98–116) make their relationship seem based on clever wit as well as romantic feeling?
10. Romeo and Juliet make several puns and references to religion in their first speeches. Do you think Shakespeare uses this religious language to make them seem religious? Or could you suggest any different purpose?

EXAMINER'S NOTES, 1.5

❸ Themes and ideas

The scene shows how suddenly and completely love can affect a person. It also shows how family honour and masculine pride can be equally powerful emotions.

11 How does Shakespeare show different effects of sudden strong feelings in Romeo and Tybalt in this scene?

12 How do Tybalt's remarks about Romeo show his feelings about respect and disrespect (lines 52–91)?

❹ Performance

The way the main characters speak is important in conveying the relationship between Romeo and Juliet and the dangers of the social world around them. The contrast between their private talk and the public scene about them is developed by Shakespeare through cutting between Tybalt's quarrel with Capulet, and Romeo and Juliet's gentle first encounter.

13 If you were directing the scene, would you have Romeo and Juliet speak alone on stage or would you have the other people at the ball still talking and dancing? What would be the advantages of either choice?

14 As the scene involves a masked ball, what do you think are the advantages and disadvantages of having actors wearing masks when they are speaking or listening?

15 How should Capulet's behaviour with Tybalt be played: as a host putting good manners before feelings or as a simple man enjoying the party and wanting no fuss?

❺ Contexts and responses

Audiences at different times and in different places may react differently to characters and to situations on stage.

16 What do you think may be a modern equivalent of the feud between the families that makes Tybalt hate Romeo?

17 How would modern parents react to being told that some uninvited people had turned up at a family celebration? Would they react in any different ways from Capulet and Tybalt?

❻ Reflecting on the scene

18 How does Shakespeare present young people in this scene?

19 What are the typical speech characteristics of Romeo, Capulet and Tybalt in this scene?

20 In what ways does Act 1 Scene 5 provide a variety of interest for the audience?

EXAMINER'S TIP

A good response

Show you are aware that the characters are not real people by mentioning their creator: e.g. 'Shakespeare makes Romeo seem afraid something bad may happen.'

Support your comment with a quotation: e.g. 'Shakespeare makes Romeo seem afraid something bad may happen when he says "Ay, so I fear; the more is my unrest".'

Show that you understand why Shakespeare uses dramatic devices: e.g., 'Shakespeare makes Romeo seem afraid something bad may happen when he says "Ay, so I fear; the more is my unrest". This reminds us of the Prologue's 'star-crossed lovers', creating dramatic irony when meeting Juliet makes him happy.'

USING THE VIDEO

Exploring interpretation and performance

If you have looked at the video extracts in Dynamic Learning, try these questions.

- Watch the rehearsal clip that shows this scene played to emphasise haste, and then a contrast between haste and slowness. Which do you think more appealing to an audience?

- How would you advise the actor to make it clear that he has a sweet tooth, and that he is asking someone else to steal some of the luxury treats from his master's table?

Romeo and Mercutio, spring 2009.

Why has the director decided to put Romeo up a ladder?

James Alexandrou, Shane Zaza

ACT 2

Enter Chorus

Chorus   Now old desire doth in his death-bed lie,
And young affection gapes to be his heir.
That fair for which love groaned for and would die,
With tender Juliet matched, is now not fair.
Now Romeo is beloved and loves again,   5
Alike bewitched by the charm of looks,
But to his foe supposed he must complain,
And she steal love's sweet bait from fearful hooks.
Being held a foe, he may not have access
To breathe such vows as lovers use to swear;   10
And she as much in love, her means much less
To meet her new-belovèd any where.
But passion lends them power, time means to meet,
Temp'ring extremities with extreme sweet.

[Exit]

ACT 2 SCENE 1

Enter Romeo alone.

Romeo   Can I go forward when my heart is here?
Turn back, dull earth, and find thy centre out.

Enter Benvolio with Mercutio. Romeo hides.

Benvolio   Romeo! My cousin Romeo! Romeo!

Mercutio   He is wise,
And on my life hath stol'n him home to bed.   5

Benvolio   He ran this way and leapt this orchard wall.
Call, good Mercutio.

Mercutio   Nay, I'll conjure too.
Romeo! Humours! Madman! Passion! Lover!
Appear thou in the likeness of a sigh,
Speak but one rhyme and I am satisfied;   10
Cry but "Ay me", pronounce but " love" and "dove";
Speak to my gossip Venus one fair word,
One nickname for her purblind son and heir,
Young Abraham Cupid, he that shot so trim,
When King Cophetua loved the beggar-maid. –   15
He heareth not, he stirreth not, he moveth not,
The ape is dead, and I must conjure him. –
I conjure thee by Rosaline's bright eyes,
By her high forehead and her scarlet lip,
By her fine foot, straight leg and quivering thigh,   20
And the demesnes that there adjacent lie,
That in thy likeness thou appear to us.

Benvolio   And if he hear thee, thou wilt anger him.

Mercutio   This cannot anger him. 'Twould anger him

---

1 **Now old desire doth in his death-bed lie:** Romeo's old love is dying and his new love waits eagerly to take over
3 **That fair:** Rosaline
4 **matched:** compared
5 **is beloved and loves again:** is in love and loved in return
6 **Alike:** both (Romeo and Juliet)
7 **his foe supposed:** someone who should be his enemy
7 **complain:** beg for love
10 **use to:** normally
11 **her means much less:** has even fewer chances
14 **Temp'ring extremities with extreme sweet:** making the difficulties lighter by the joy of meeting

1 **go forward:** walk away
2 **dull earth:** my body
2 **thy centre:** his heart, with Juliet

7 **conjure too:** magic him out of the air
8 **Humours:** moody one
9 **likeness:** shape
12 **my gossip:** my good friend (usually said by a woman about another woman)
12 **Venus:** the goddess of love
13 **purblind son and heir:** Venus' son, Cupid
14 **Abraham:** trickster, con-man
15 **King Cophetua:** a king who, in a song, fell in love with and married a socially very unsuitable beggar
17 **The ape is dead:** Romeo is playing dead like a performing monkey
17 **conjure him:** magic him back to life
21 **the demesnes:** places
21 **adjacent:** nearby

	To raise a spirit in his mistress' circle,
	Of some strange nature, letting it there stand
	Till she had laid it and conjured it down.
	That were some spite. My invocation
	Is fair and honest, and in his mistress' name
	I conjure only but to raise up him.
Benvolio	Come, he hath hid himself among these trees
	To be consorted with the humorous night.
	Blind is his love and best befits the dark.
Mercutio	If love be blind, love cannot hit the mark.
	Now will he sit under a medlar tree
	And wish his mistress were that kind of fruit
	As maids call medlars when they laugh alone.
	O Romeo that she were, O that she were
	An open arse and thou a poperin pear.
	Romeo, good night. I'll to my truckle-bed,
	This field-bed is too cold for me to sleep.
	Come, shall we go?
Benvolio	Go, then; for 'tis in vain
	To seek him here that means not to be found.

Exit Mercutio and Benvolio.

25 **raise a spirit:** magic up a spirit but also starts a series of sexual double meanings, in this case 'have an erection'

28 **That were some spite:** that would be infuriating

28 **invocation:** conjuring spell

32 **To be consorted:** be alone with

32 **humorous:** double meaning: damp; moody

34 **the mark:** what it aims at

35 **medlar:** an apple-like fruit, often compared to a vagina

39 **open arse:** nickname for a medlar

39 **poperin pear:** a type of pear shaped like a penis

40 **truckle-bed:** a small pull-out bed, often used by children

25
30
35
40

Director's Note, 2.1

✔ Romeo hides from his friends, climbing into the Capulet's orchard.

✔ Mercutio and Benvolio look for him, joking about Rosaline.

✔ They give up, and go away.

FROM THE REHEARSAL ROOM...

CONNECTING TO THE AUDIENCE

- In small groups, read Romeo's lines until you reach line 37. You can agree places where you change the person reading.

- Choose a place in the room to represent Juliet. It should be high up – for example, the top of the board.

- Now read the speech again, but this time every time Romeo speaks to Juliet or about Juliet, point to her position in the room and every time Romeo speaks directly to the audience, point to the rest of the group. (He can change for just part of a line.)

1 Can you identify the lines that Romeo directs to the audience in this scene?

2 How do you think the audience feels when Romeo speaks directly to them? Discuss the impact of this storytelling technique.

3 When a character speaks directly to the audience, he or she always tells the truth. How does Shakespeare move the story on very quickly in this section of this scene?

Romeo and Juliet, 2004.

Which lines do you think were being spoken when this photo was taken? Quote to support your answer.

Tom Burke, Kananu Kirimi

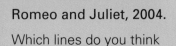

Romeo steps out.

Romeo	He jests at scars that never felt a wound.
	But, soft, what light through yonder window breaks?
	It is the east and Juliet is the sun.
	Arise fair sun and kill the envious moon,
	Who is already sick and pale with grief 5
	That thou, her maid, art far more fair than she.
	Be not her maid! Since she is envious
	Her vestal livery is but sick and green

[Enter Juliet above.]

	And none but fools do wear it. Cast it off!
	It is my lady, O it is my love! 10
	O that she knew she were!
	She speaks, yet she says nothing. What of that?
	Her eye discourses, I will answer it. –
	I am too bold, 'tis not to me she speaks.
	Two of the fairest stars in all the heaven, 15
	Having some business, do entreat her eyes
	To twinkle in their spheres till they return.
	What if her eyes were there, they in her head?
	The brightness of her cheek would shame those stars
	As daylight doth a lamp. Her eyes in heaven 20
	Would through the airy region stream so bright
	That birds would sing and think it were not night.
	See how she leans her cheek upon her hand.
	O that I were a glove upon that hand,
	That I might touch that cheek.
Juliet	Ay me.
Romeo	She speaks! 25
	O speak again, bright angel, for thou art
	As glorious to this night, being o'er my head,
	As is a wingèd messenger of heaven
	Unto the white-upturnèd wond'ring eyes
	Of mortals that fall back to gaze on him 30
	When he bestrides the lazy puffing clouds,
	And sails upon the bosom of the air.
Juliet	O Romeo, Romeo, wherefore art thou Romeo?
	Deny thy father and refuse thy name,
	Or if thou wilt not, be but sworn my love 35
	And I'll no longer be a Capulet.
Romeo	*[Aside.]* Shall I hear more, or shall I speak at this?
Juliet	'Tis but thy name that is my enemy.
	Thou art thyself, though not a Montague.
	What's Montague? it is nor hand, nor foot, 40
	Nor arm, nor face, nor any other part
	Belonging to a man. O be some other name!
	What's in a name? That which we call a rose
	By any other name would smell as sweet.

1 He jests at scars that never felt a wound: only someone who hasn't been in love can joke about the pain it gives

2 soft: hush

6 her maid: Juliet is a virgin and Diana, the moon goddess, also represents chastity

7 Be not her maid: give up your virginity

8 vestal livery: clothes worn by virgins who serve Diana in her temples

11 O that: if only

13 discourses: speaks volumes

16 some business: something they must do

16 do entreat: have begged

17 in their spheres: in their place in the sky

18 there: in the sky

18 they: the stars

21 through the airy region stream: shine in the sky

28 wingèd messenger of heaven: angel

33 wherefore art thou: why are you

34 Deny thy father and refuse thy name: say you are not a Montague

39 Thou art thyself, though not a Montague: change your name and you will be the same person

A

Juliet, spring 2009.

Look back at the photo on page 30 to see how Juliet in this production was dressed when she was last on stage. Explain why the director decided on this costume change.

James Alexandrou, Lorraine Burroughs

	So Romeo would, were he not Romeo called,	45
	Retain that dear perfection which he owes	
	Without that title. Romeo, doff thy name,	
	And for that name which is no part of thee	
	Take all myself.	
Romeo	I take thee at thy word.	
	Call me but love, and I'll be new baptized.	50
	Henceforth I never will be Romeo.	
Juliet	What man art thou that thus bescreened in night	
	So stumblest on my counsel?	
Romeo	By a name	
	I know not how to tell thee who I am.	
	My name, dear saint, is hateful to myself,	55
	Because it is an enemy to thee.	
	Had I it written, I would tear the word.	
Juliet	My ears have not yet drunk a hundred words	
	Of thy tongue's uttering, yet I know the sound.	
	Art thou not Romeo, and a Montague?	60
Romeo	Neither, fair maid, if either thee dislike.	
Juliet	How camest thou hither, tell me, and wherefore?	
	The orchard walls are high and hard to climb,	
	And the place death, considering who thou art,	
	If any of my kinsmen find thee here.	65
Romeo	With love's light wings did I o'erperch these walls,	
	For stony limits cannot hold love out,	
	And what love can do that dares love attempt.	
	Therefore thy kinsmen are no stop to me.	
Juliet	If they do see thee, they will murder thee.	70
Romeo	Alack, there lies more peril in thine eye	
	Than twenty of their swords. Look thou but sweet,	
	And I am proof against their enmity.	
Juliet	I would not for the world they saw thee here.	
Romeo	I have night's cloak to hide me from their eyes,	75
	And but thou love me, let them find me here.	
	My life were better ended by their hate,	
	Than death prorogued, wanting of thy love.	
Juliet	By whose direction found'st thou out this place?	
Romeo	By love, that first did prompt me to inquire,	80
	He lent me counsel and I lent him eyes.	
	I am no pilot, yet, wert thou as far	
	As that vast shore washed with the farthest sea,	
	I would adventure for such merchandise.	
Juliet	Thou know'st the mask of night is on my face,	85
	Else would a maiden blush bepaint my cheek	
	For that which thou hast heard me speak to-night.	
	Fain would I dwell on form, fain, fain deny	
	What I have spoke. But farewell compliment.	

46 **owes:** owns
47 **doff:** take off

52 **bescreened in:** hidden by
53 **counsel:** private exploration of my thoughts

59 **Of thy tongue's uttering:** you have spoken

61 **if either thee dislike:** if you don't like either of them

64–5 **the place death ... find thee here:** as you are a Montague, any Capulet who finds you here will kill you
66 **o'erperch:** fly over
67 **stony limits:** walls

71 **there lies more peril in thine eye:** your eyes are more dangerous
73 **proof against their enmity:** safe from their hatred

76 **but:** unless

78 **prorogued:** postponed
78 **wanting:** lacking
81 **lent me counsel:** advised me
82 **pilot:** navigator that guides ships into harbour
84 **I would adventure for such merchandise:** I'd take the risks with you as the reward
86 **Else:** otherwise
88 **Fain would I dwell on form:** I wish we could follow the usual rules of courtship
89 **farewell compliment:** it's too late for those social conventions now

FROM THE REHEARSAL ROOM...

POINTING ON PRONOUNS

- In pairs, read the *Working Cut* of Act 2 Scene 2.
- Decide who will read each part.
- Stand opposite each other.
- Read through the scene and each time your character says a pronoun or proper name, point at who or what you are talking to or about. Make sure that you really do point at a definite person or place.

1 Are there any patterns in the pointing?

2 What does this scene tell us about how Juliet feels about Romeo?

3 How does Romeo respond to Juliet in this scene?

Romeo and Juliet, 2004.

Compare this scene in this production with the spring 2009 production on page 40. What are the similarities and differences? Explain your answer.

Tom Burke, Kananu Kirimi

Working Cut – text for experiment

Rom	I take thee at thy word.
	Call me but love, and I'll be new baptized.
	Henceforth I never will be Romeo.
Jul	What man art thou that thus bescreened in night
	So stumblest on my counsel?
Rom	By a name
	I know not how to tell thee who I am.
	My name, dear saint, is hateful to myself,
	Because it is an enemy to thee.
Jul	Art thou not Romeo, and a Montague?
	How camest thou hither, tell me, and wherefore?
	The orchard walls are high and hard to climb.
Rom	With love's light wings did I o'erperch these walls,
	For stony limits cannot hold love out.
Jul	If they do see thee, they will murder thee.
Rom	Alack, there lies more peril in thine eye
	Than twenty of their swords.
Jul	I would not for the world they saw thee here.
Rom	I have night's cloak to hide me from their eyes,
	And but thou love me, let them find me here.
	My life were better ended by their hate,
	Than death proroguèd, wanting of thy love.
Jul	Thou know'st the mask of night is on my face,
	Else would a maiden blush bepaint my cheek
	For that which thou hast heard me speak to-night.
	Fain would I dwell on form, fain, fain deny
	What I have spoke. But farewell compliment.
	Dost thou love me? I know thou wilt say "Ay",
	And I will take thy word. Yet if thou swear'st,
	Thou mayst prove false.
Rom	Lady, by yonder blessed moon I vow,
Jul	O, swear not by the moon, th' inconstant moon,
Rom	What shall I swear by?
Jul	Do not swear at all.
	Or, if thou wilt, swear by thy gracious self,
	Which is the god of my idolatry,
	And I'll believe thee. Good night, good night
Rom	O wilt thou leave me so unsatisfied?
Jul	What satisfaction canst thou have tonight?
Rom	Th' exchange of thy love's faithful vow for mine.
Jul	I gave thee mine before thou didst request it.
	And yet I would it were to give again.
Rom	Wouldst thou withdraw it? For what purpose love?
Jul	But to be frank, and give it thee again.
	And yet I wish but for the thing I have:
	My bounty is as boundless as the sea,
	My love as deep, the more I give to thee
	The more I have, for both are infinite.
	I hear some noise within. Dear love, adieu.

Dost thou love me? I know thou wilt say "Ay", 90
And I will take thy word. Yet if thou swear'st,
Thou mayst prove false. At lovers' perjuries
They say Jove laughs. O gentle Romeo,
If thou dost love, pronounce it faithfully.
Or if thou think'st I am too quickly won, 95
I'll frown and be perverse and say thee nay,
So thou wilt woo. But else, not for the world.
In truth, fair Montague, I am too fond,
And therefore thou mayst think my haviour light.
But trust me, gentleman, I'll prove more true 100
Than those that have more coying to be strange.
I should have been more strange, I must confess,
But that thou overheard'st, ere I was ware,
My true love's passion. Therefore pardon me,
And not impute this yielding to light love 105
Which the dark night hath so discoverèd.

Romeo   Lady, by yonder blessed moon I vow,
That tips with silver all these fruit-tree tops —

Juliet   O, swear not by the moon, th' inconstant moon,
That monthly changes in her circled orb, 110
Lest that thy love prove likewise variable.

Romeo   What shall I swear by?

Juliet   Do not swear at all.
Or, if thou wilt, swear by thy gracious self,
Which is the god of my idolatry,
And I'll believe thee.

Romeo   If my heart's dear love — 115

Juliet   Well, do not swear. Although I joy in thee,
I have no joy of this contract to-night.
It is too rash, too unadvised, too sudden,
Too like the lightning, which doth cease to be
Ere one can say "It lightens." Sweet, good night. 120
This bud of love, by summer's ripening breath,
May prove a beauteous flower when next we meet.
Good night, good night, as sweet repose and rest
Come to thy heart as that within my breast.

Romeo   O wilt thou leave me so unsatisfied? 125

Juliet   What satisfaction canst thou have tonight?

Romeo   Th' exchange of thy love's faithful vow for mine.

Juliet   I gave thee mine before thou didst request it.
And yet I would it were to give again.

Romeo   Wouldst thou withdraw it? For what purpose love? 130

Juliet   But to be frank, and give it thee again.
And yet I wish but for the thing I have:
My bounty is as boundless as the sea,
My love as deep, the more I give to thee
The more I have, for both are infinite. 135

---

92 **perjuries:** broken oaths
93 **Jove:** king of the gods in Roman myths
93 **laughs:** doesn't take them seriously, won't punish them
94 **pronounce it faithfully:** tell me so truthfully
96 **say thee nay:** turn you away
97 **So thou wilt woo:** to keep you courting me
98 **fond:** infatuated
97 **haviour light:** behaviour too easy
101 **have more coying to be strange:** act more distant just to draw you in
102 **strange:** reserved
103 **ere I was ware:** before I realised you were there
105–6 **And not impute this ... discoverèd:** and don't think I'm immoral because of what I've said when I thought I was alone

109 **inconstant:** ever changing
110 **in her circled orb:** as she moves through the sky

114 **of my idolatry:** I worship

117 **this contract:** these promises we are making
118 **too unadvised:** not thought through

125 **unsatisfied:** double meaning: without having sorted things out; sexually unsatisfied

129 **I would it were to give again:** I wish I still had it to give as I choose

131 **frank:** open and generous

133 **my bounty:** my willingness to give

Director's view

Bill Buckhurst
Director, spring 2009

Juliet has a kind of maturity that Romeo lacks. I'm thinking about the Balcony Scene, she controls the events in a way that he doesn't. He allows himself to get carried away with his feelings. If you look at his language in the Balcony Scene he uses huge imagery, he is a king of using big images to describe his feelings. When he is in the orchard, and he looks up at the balcony: 'the moon' and 'the sun' and 'the stars'; he uses the biggest images he can think of to describe his feelings, which is very lovely. It has actually been quite an interesting thing to explore in rehearsals, because the temptation with that kind of language is to get all flowery with it, but actually it's the danger and the pitfall you don't want to fall into. So he's using this large, rather metaphorical language and Juliet's quite practical really. I mean she does say, 'you were the God of my idolatry', which is a massive image to think about. But she's really practical, like, 'if you really love me, let's get married tomorrow'. She takes control in a way that Romeo seems unable to. And whether that says something about her understanding of life and the way one is responsible for one's actions, I'm not sure.

SHAKESPEARE'S WORLD

◇◇◇◇◇◇◇◇◇◇◇◇◇

Upper Level

The actors in the open air playhouses used more than just the stage. A trapdoor gave them access to the stage from underneath. There was also an upper level, at the same height as the middle gallery of audience members.

The upper level was small and often crowded. The most expensive seats in the playhouse were up there and the musicians also used it. For this reason, scenes in the upper level are usually very short, and have no more than three actors. Despite these restrictions, Shakespeare and his contemporaries often wrote action for the upper level. This scene is longer than usual, but Juliet is alone and barely has to move. The use of the upper level means that she is both safe at home and at the same time visible to Romeo, who refers to her as 'being o'er my head'. In this way, the upper level allows for an extended moment of intimacy.

Juliet and Romeo. *Left:* summer 2009; *right:* spring 2009.

Both photos were taken at about the same point in the text on page 45. Which lines do you think were being spoken? As well as giving the line or lines, explain why you chose them.

l Ellie Kendrick, Adetomiwa Edun; *r* Lorraine Burroughs, James Alexandrou

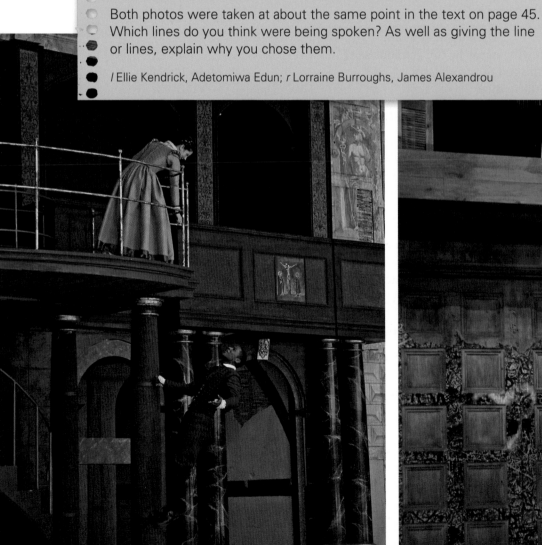

I hear some noise within. Dear love, adieu. —

[Nurse calls within.]

Anon, good nurse! – Sweet Montague, be true.
Stay but a little, I will come again.   *[Exit Juliet above.]*

Romeo O blessèd, blessèd night! I am afeard
Being in night, all this is but a dream,   140
Too flattering-sweet to be substantial.

[Enter Juliet above.]

Juliet Three words, dear Romeo, and good night indeed,
If that thy bent of love be honourable,
Thy purpose marriage, send me word tomorrow,
By one that I'll procure to come to thee,   145
Where and what time thou wilt perform the rite,
And all my fortunes at thy foot I'll lay
And follow thee my lord throughout the world.

Nurse *[Within.]* Madam!

Juliet I come, anon.— But if thou mean'st not well,   150
I do beseech thee —
Nurse *[Within.]* Madam!

Juliet   By and by, I come.—
To cease thy strife, and leave me to my grief,
Tomorrow will I send.

Romeo   So thrive my soul —

Juliet A thousand times good night!   155

Romeo A thousand times the worse to want thy light.

Exit Juliet, above.

Love goes toward love as schoolboys from their books,
But love from love, toward school with heavy looks.

Enter Juliet, above, again.

Juliet Hist, Romeo, hist! O, for a falc'ner's voice,
To lure this tassel-gentle back again.   160
Bondage is hoarse and may not speak aloud,
Else would I tear the cave where Echo lies
And make her airy tongue more hoarse than mine,
With repetition of my Romeo.

Romeo It is my soul that calls upon my name.   165
How silver-sweet sound lovers' tongues by night,
Like softest music to attending ears.

Juliet Romeo.

Romeo   My nyas.

Juliet   What o'clock tomorrow
Shall I send to thee?

Romeo   By the hour of nine.

---

137 **Anon:** I'm on my way
138 **Stay but a little:** wait just a minute

141 **flattering-sweet:** perfectly in tune with what I want
141 **substantial:** real

143 **thy bent of love:** your intentions
144 **Thy purpose:** your aim
145 **procure:** set up
146 **the rite:** the wedding ceremony

150 **thou mean'st not well:** you don't mean marriage, just seduction
151 **beseech:** beg
152 **By and by:** right away
153 **thy strife:** trying to make me love you
153 **leave me to my grief:** grief because he doesn't mean to marry her

156 **the worse to want thy light:** darker without you to light it

159 **Hist:** an attention-getting noise, used by a falconer to attract his birds. This starts a series of comparisons with falconry
160 **tassel-gentle:** male falcon
161 **Bondage is hoarse:** prisoners (she's shut in her father's house) must whisper
162 **Echo:** a nymph in Greek mythology who, when her love was rejected, lived in a cave, only able to 'echo' the last words of anything said to her
167 **attending:** listening
168 **nyas:** a young hawk, not yet trained

MAGNETS

Using the *Working Cut* text, explore how Romeo and Juliet feel about each other in this scene.

- In pairs, read the exchange aloud.
- Now stand opposite each other. Read the extract again, but this time take one step forward if you feel your character is leading, one step backwards if you feel your character is retreating or two steps forwards if you feel your character is following.
- Repeat the exercise several times before discussing what you have discovered about the character's intentions in this scene.

1 Which character is leading in this scene? Find evidence in the text to support your opinion.

2 What does this scene reveal about Romeo and Juliet's feelings for each other?

3 What impact does the Nurse have? How do her interruptions affect the audience?

Actor's view

Colin Hurley
The Friar, spring 2009.

I find it helpful to look at the story just from my character's point of view. I was in my cell; Romeo turned up and asked me to marry him to Juliet. Because, quite often we don't take into account what we don't know. I didn't witness their meeting. I don't know whether it's true love or an infatuation, and that's quite important. Having spent what seems like quite a long time trying to talk Romeo down, just calm him down a bit, suddenly I turn and say 'do you know what, I am going to marry you'. A lecture we had was so enlightening in terms of how high the stakes are. What they are doing is a criminal act. The Friar is saying, 'yeah, let's break the law'.

Friar Lawrence, spring 2009.

This photo was taken during the first 30 lines of Act 2 Scene 3 (some of which are on page 49).
Which line or lines would you choose as a caption for the photo? Quote, and give reasons for your choice.

Colin Hurley

Working Cut – text for experiment

Jul	I hear some noise within. Dear love, adieu. — *[Nurse calls.]* Anon, good nurse! — Sweet Montague, be true. Stay but a little, I will come again. *[Exit Juliet above.]*
Rom	O blessèd, blessèd night! *[Enter Juliet above.]*
Jul	Three words, dear Romeo, and good night indeed, If that thy bent of love be honourable, Thy purpose marriage, send me word tomorrow, And all my fortunes at thy foot I'll lay And follow thee my lord throughout the world.
Nur	*[Within.]* Madam!
Jul	I come, anon. — But if thou mean'st not well, I do beseech thee —
Nurse	*[Within.]* Madam!
Jul	By and by, I come. — To cease thy strife, and leave me to my grief, To-morrow will I send. A thousand times good night!
Rom	A thousand times the worse to want thy light.
Jul	Hist, Romeo, hist! Romeo. What o'clock tomorrow Shall I send to thee?
Rom	By the hour of nine.
Jul	I will not fail, 'tis twenty years till then.

Juliet	I will not fail, 'tis twenty years till then.	170
	I have forgot why I did call thee back.	
Romeo	Let me stand here till thou remember it.	
Juliet	I shall forget, to have thee still stand there,	
	Rememb'ring how I love thy company.	
Romeo	And I'll still stay, to have thee still forget,	175
	Forgetting any other home but this.	
Juliet	'Tis almost morning, I would have thee gone.	
	And yet no further than a wanton's bird,	
	Who lets it hop a little from his hand,	
	Like a poor prisoner in his twisted gyves,	180
	And with a silken thread plucks it back again,	
	So loving-jealous of his liberty.	
Romeo	I would I were thy bird.	
Juliet	Sweet, so would I,	
	Yet I should kill thee with much cherishing.	
	Good night, good night! Parting is such sweet sorrow,	185
	That I shall say good night till it be morrow.	
Romeo	*[Exit Juliet, above.]*	
	Sleep dwell upon thine eyes, peace in thy breast,	
	Would I were sleep and peace, so sweet to rest.	
	Hence will I to my ghostly Friar's close cell,	
	His help to crave, and my dear hap to tell.	190

ACT 2 SCENE 3

Enter Friar Lawrence, with a basket.

Friar Lawrence	The grey-eyed morn smiles on the frowning night,	
	Check'ring the eastern clouds with streaks of light,	
	And fleckled darkness, like a drunkard, reels	
	From forth day's pathway made by Titan's wheels.	
	Now, ere the sun advance his burning eye,	5
	The day to cheer and night's dank dew to dry,	
	I must upfill this osier cage of ours	
	With baleful weeds and precious-juicèd flowers.	
	The earth, that's nature's mother, is her tomb.	
	What is her burying grave, that is her womb.	10
	And from her womb children of divers kind	
	We sucking on her natural bosom find.	
	Many for many, virtues excellent,	
	None but for some, and yet all different.	
	O mickle is the powerful grace that lies	15
	In plants, herbs, stones, and their true qualities.	
	For nought so vile that on the earth doth live	
	But to the earth some special good doth give.	
	Nor aught so good but strained from that fair use,	
	Revolts from true birth, stumbling on abuse.	20
	Virtue itself turns vice, being misapplied,	
	And vice sometime by action dignified.	

Enter Romeo.

178 **wanton's bird:** spoilt child's pet bird
180 **gyves:** chains that bind his feet
183 **I would:** I wish
184 **much cherishing:** too much attention
189 **Hence will I:** I'll go from here
189 **ghostly Friar's close cell:** the private place of Friar Lawrence, Romeo's 'spiritual' father
190 **crave:** ask for
190 **my dear hap:** my good luck

Director's Note, 2.2

✔ Romeo hides in the Capulets' garden.
✔ He overhears Juliet declare her love for him, and tells he her loves her.
✔ They talk, and despite Juliet's worry that things are moving so fast, agree to marry the next day.
✔ Romeo is to arrange it, and Juliet will send somebody for a message at nine o'clock.
✔ How does Shakespeare show the intensity of their feelings for each other?

2 **Check'ring:** patterning
3 **fleckled darkness, like a drunkard:** the darkness, streaked with red like a drunkard's face
4 **From forth day's pathway … wheels:** out of the way of the sun god's chariot and the arrival of day
5 **ere:** before
7 **upfill this osier cage:** fill my willow basket
8 **baleful weeds:** poisonous herbs
9-10 **The earth, that's nature's mother … is her womb:** the earth is both a burying place and a place that gives plants life
11 **divers kind:** different sorts
13-4 **Many for many … all different:** many have many uses; none have no use at all
15 **mickle:** great
15 **grace:** healing qualities
17-8 **For nought … special good doth give:** there's nothing that doesn't have some good to it
19 **aught:** different sorts
19 **strained from that fair use:** used wrongly
20 **Revolts from … stumbling on abuse:** has a bad effect far from its natural effect
22 **by action dignified:** can be used for a good purpose

47

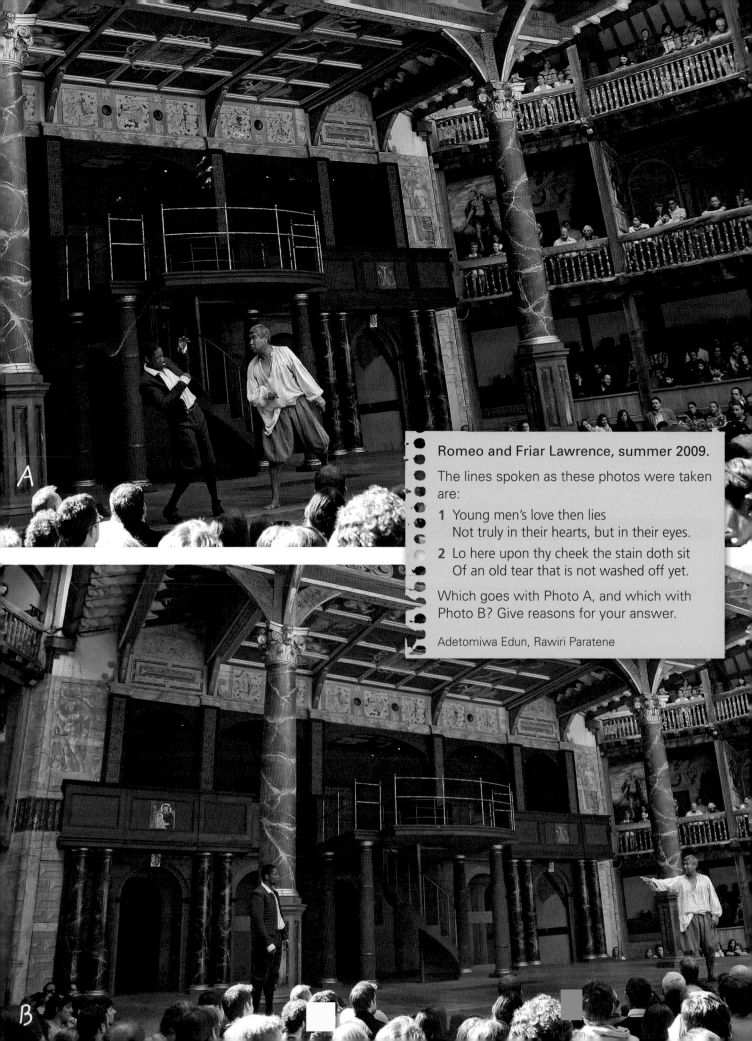

A

Romeo and Friar Lawrence, summer 2009.

The lines spoken as these photos were taken are:

1 Young men's love then lies
Not truly in their hearts, but in their eyes.

2 Lo here upon thy cheek the stain doth sit
Of an old tear that is not washed off yet.

Which goes with Photo A, and which with Photo B? Give reasons for your answer.

Adetomiwa Edun, Rawiri Paratene

B

Within the infant rind of this weak flower	23 **infant rind:** undeveloped skin
Poison hath residence and medicine power.	
For this, being smelt, with that part cheers each part, 25	25 **with that part:** with its smell
Being tasted, slays all senses with the heart.	26 **slays all senses with the heart:** kills you
Two such opposèd kings encamp them still	28 **grace:** goodness
In man as well as herbs, grace and rude will.	28 **rude will:** selfish actions
And where the worser is predominant,	
Full soon the canker death eats up that plant. 30	30 **canker:** plant-destroying worm

Romeo   Good morrow, father.

Friar Lawrence   *Benedicite.*

What early tongue so sweet saluteth me?	31 **Benedicite:** God bless you
Young son, it argues a distempered head	33 **argues a distempered head:** suggests something is troubling you
So soon to bid good morrow to thy bed.	
Care keeps his watch in every old man's eye, 35	35 **Care keeps his watch ... old man's eye:** it is usually the old who lie awake worrying
And where care lodges, sleep will never lie,	
But where unbruisèd youth with unstuffed brain	37 **unbruisèd:** as yet unharmed by life
Doth couch his limbs, there golden sleep doth reign.	37 **unstuffed:** not yet over-filled
Therefore thy earliness doth me assure	38 **couch his limbs:** sleep
Thou art up-roused by some distemp'rature. 40	39 **assure:** convince
Or if not so, then here I hit it right,	40 **up-roused by some distemp'rature:** out of bed because you're troubled
Our Romeo hath not been in bed tonight.	

Romeo   That last is true, the sweeter rest was mine.

43 **the sweeter rest was mine:** I was doing something better than sleeping

Friar Lawrence   God pardon sin! Wast thou with Rosaline?

Romeo With Rosaline, my ghostly father? No, 45	45 **ghostly father:** spiritual father, religious teacher
I have forgot that name and that name's woe.	46 **that name's woe:** the misery it gave me

Friar Lawrence   That's my good son, but where hast thou been then?

Romeo I'll tell thee, ere thou ask it me again.	
I have been feasting with mine enemy,	
Where on a sudden one hath wounded me 50	
That's by me wounded. Both our remedies	51-2 **Both our remedies ... holy physic lies:** you can cure us both by helping us and using your religious powers
Within thy help and holy physic lies.	
I bear no hatred, blessèd man, for lo,	54 **intercession:** the thing I ask for
My intercession likewise steads my foe.	54 **likewise steads:** also helps

Friar Lawrence Be plain, good son, and homely in thy drift, 55	55 **Be plain:** make your meaning clear
Riddling confession finds but riddling shrift.	55 **homely in thy drift:** use simple language
	56 **Riddling confession finds but riddling shrift:** your confession has to be properly understood to be properly pardoned

Romeo Then plainly know my heart's dear love is set	
On the fair daughter of rich Capulet.	
As mine on hers, so hers is set on mine,	
And all combined, save what thou must combine 60	
By holy marriage. When and where and how	
We met, we wooed and made exchange of vow,	
I'll tell thee as we pass. But this I pray,	63 **pass:** walk along
That thou consent to marry us today.	

Friar Lawrence Holy Saint Francis, what a change is here! 65	
Is Rosaline, that thou didst love so dear,	
So soon forsaken? Young men's love then lies	67 **forsaken:** abandoned
Not truly in their hearts, but in their eyes.	
Jesu Maria, what a deal of brine	69 **brine:** tears
Hath washed thy sallow cheeks for Rosaline! 70	70 **sallow** sickly-looking

FAIR CONTEST?

Act 2 Scene 4 opens with Mercutio and Benvolio believing Tybalt has challenged Romeo to a duel (lines 1–35).

- In pairs, read the *Working Cut*.
- Read the *Working Cut* again, but this time note or highlight all the words or phrases that describe how good Tybalt and Romeo might be in a fight.

1 Who would win if Romeo and Tybalt fought a duel?

2 What does Mercutio think of Tyablt's sword fighting style? Explain why.

Working Cut – text for experiment

Mer	Alas poor Romeo, he is already dead: stabbed with a white wench's black eye, run through the ear with a love song. And is he a man to encounter Tybalt?
Ben	Why, what is Tybalt?
Mer	More than prince of cats. O he's the courageous captain of compliments. He fights as you sing prick-song, keeps time, distance and proportion. Rests me his minim rests, one, two, and the third in your bosom. The very butcher of a silk button, a duellist, a gentleman of the very first house. Ah, the immortal *passado*, the *punto reverso*, the *hay*.
Ben	The what?
Mer	The pox of such antic, lisping, affecting fantasticoes, these new tuners of accent! "By Jesu, a very good blade! A very tall man! A very good whore!" Why, is not this a lamentable thing, grandsire, that we should be thus afflicted with these fashion-mongers, who stand so much on the new form.

Director's Note, 2.3

✔ Romeo goes straight to Friar Lawrence.

✔ Friar Lawrence assumes Romeo has been with Rosaline, so Romeo tells him he now loves Juliet, and the couple want the Friar to marry them.

✔ Friar Lawrence points out Romeo's love changes very quickly, but agrees to marry them.

✔ Why does Friar Lawrence agree to marry them?

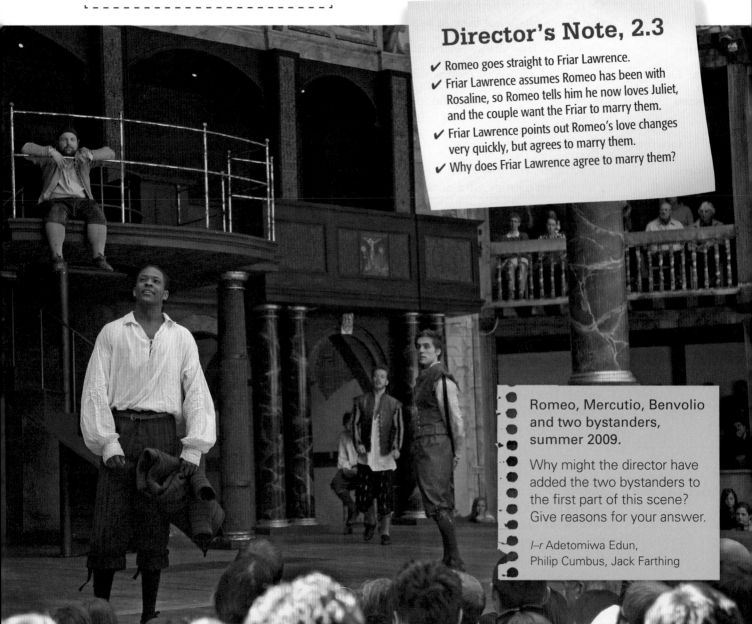

Romeo, Mercutio, Benvolio and two bystanders, summer 2009.

Why might the director have added the two bystanders to the first part of this scene? Give reasons for your answer.

l–r Adetomiwa Edun, Philip Cumbus, Jack Farthing

How much salt water thrown away in waste
To season love, that of it doth not taste.
The sun not yet thy sighs from heaven clears,
Thy old groans yet ringing in my ancient ears.
Lo here upon thy cheek the stain doth sit
Of an old tear that is not washed off yet.
If e'er thou wast thyself, and these woes thine,
Thou and these woes were all for Rosaline.
And art thou changed? Pronounce this sentence then,
Women may fall, when there's no strength in men.

Romeo   Thou chid'st me oft for loving Rosaline.

Friar Lawrence   For doting, not for loving, pupil mine.

Romeo   And bad'st me bury love.

Friar Lawrence   Not in a grave,
To lay one in, another out to have.

Romeo   I pray thee, chide me not. Her I love now
Doth grace for grace, and love for love allow.
The other did not so.

Friar Lawrence   O she knew well
Thy love did read by rote, that could not spell.
But come young waverer, come, go with me,
In one respect I'll thy assistant be.
For this alliance may so happy prove,
To turn your households' rancour to pure love.

Romeo   O let us hence. I stand on sudden haste.

Friar Lawrence   Wisely and slow, they stumble that run fast.   *Exit both.*

ACT 2 SCENE 4

Enter Benvolio and Mercutio.

Mercutio   Where the devil should this Romeo be?
Came he not home tonight?

Benvolio   Not to his father's, I spoke with his man.

Mercutio   Why that same pale hard-hearted wench, that Rosaline,
Torments him so, that he will sure run mad.

Benvolio   Tybalt, the kinsman of old Capulet,
Hath sent a letter to his father's house.

Mercutio   A challenge, on my life.

Benvolio   Romeo will answer it.

Mercutio   Any man that can write may answer a letter.

Benvolio   Nay, he will answer the letter's master how he dares,
being dared.

Mercutio   Alas poor Romeo, he is already dead: stabbed with a
white wench's black eye, run through the ear with a
love song, the very pin of his heart cleft with the blind
bow-boy's butt-shaft. And is he a man to encounter Tybalt?

72 season: give flavour
75 Lo: look
77 thou wast thyself, and these woes thine: you were telling the truth about how you felt
79 Pronounce this sentence then: then this is my verdict
80 Women may fall ... strength in men: when men are weak, what chance do women have
81 chid'st: were angry with me
82 doting: being infatuated
84 To lay one in, another out to have: to bury one love in and take another from
86 grace for grace, and love for love allow: loves me equally
88 read by rote, that could not spell: just going through the motions, not real
90 In one respect: for one reason
91 this alliance: their marriage
92 rancour: deep-rooted enmity
93 I stand on sudden haste: I'm in a hurry
1 should: can
7 his father's: Romeo's father's
8 A challenge, on my life: I bet it is a challenge to a duel
9 answer: accept
11 how he dares, being dared: if he really will fight having issued the challenge
15 pin of his heart: heart's centre
15 cleft: split
15–6 the blind bow-boy's: Cupid's
16 butt-shaft: blunt, target practice arrow
16 encounter: fight a duel with

Benvolio	Why, what is Tybalt?
Mercutio	More than prince of cats. O he's the courageous captain of compliments. He fights as you sing prick-song, keeps time, distance and proportion. Rests me his minim rests, one, two, and the third in your bosom. The very butcher of a silk button, a duellist, a duellist, a gentleman of the very first house, of the first and second cause. Ah, the immortal *passado*, the *punto reverso*, the *hay*.
Benvolio	The what?
Mercutio	The pox of such antic, lisping, affecting fantasticoes, these new tuners of accent! "By Jesu, a very good blade! A very tall man! A very good whore!" Why, is not this a lamentable thing, grandsire, that we should be thus afflicted with these strange flies, these fashion-mongers, these pardon-me's, who stand so much on the new form, that they cannot sit at ease on the old bench? O their bones, their bones!

Enter Romeo.

Benvolio	Here comes Romeo, here comes Romeo.
Mercutio	Without his roe, like a dried herring. O flesh, flesh, how art thou fishified? Now is he for the numbers that Petrarch flowed in: Laura to his lady was but a kitchen wench (marry, she had a better love to be-rhyme her), Dido a dowdy; Cleopatra a gipsy; Helen and Hero hildings and harlots; Thisbe a grey eye or so, but not to the purpose. Signior Romeo, *bonjour*. There's a French salutation to your French slop. You gave us the counterfeit fairly last night.
Romeo	Good morrow to you both. What counterfeit did I give you?
Mercutio	The slip, sir, the slip. Can you not conceive?
Romeo	Pardon, good Mercutio, my business was great, and in such a case as mine a man may strain courtesy.
Mercutio	That's as much as to say, such a case as yours constrains a man to bow in the hams.
Romeo	Meaning, to courtesy.
Mercutio	Thou hast most kindly hit it.
Romeo	A most courteous exposition.
Mercutio	Nay, I am the very pink of courtesy.
Romeo	Pink for flower.
Mercutio	Right.
Romeo	Why, then is my pump well flowered.
Mercutio	Sure wit, follow me this jest now till thou hast worn out thy pump, that when the single sole of it is worn, the jest may remain after the wearing, soley singular.

52

Glossary notes:

17 **what is:** what kind of a man is
18 **prince of cats:** refers to Tybert, prince of cats in a well-known story at the time
19 **captain of compliments:** master of all the latest rules of fighting
19–20 **sing prick-song:** sight read sheet music; start of a run of comparisons between duelling and singing.
22 **The very butcher of a silk button:** he could cut your coat buttons off
23 **of the very first house:** from the best school of fencing
23–4 **of the first and second cause:** the two acceptable reasons for duelling
24–5 *passado ... hay:* fencing terms
27–8 **the pox of ... tuners of accent:** curse these affected people with their put on accents (he then imitates them)
29 **tall:** brave
30 **grandsire:** grandfather
31 **strange flies:** foreign insects
31 **fashion-mongers:** slaves to the latest thing in speech and dress
32 **pardon-me's:** over-polite people
32 **stand so:** insist on
33 **form:** double meaning: bench; behaviour
33 **old bench:** old ways of behaving
36 **roe:** double meaning: female deer; semen. The start of a run of double meanings implying Romeo has had sex
37–8 **for the numbers ... flowed in:** he'll write classical love poetry, like the Roman poet Petrarch to his mistress Laura
40–1 **Dido ... Cleopatra ... Helen ... Hero ... Thisbe:** all women in great love stories
43 **French slop:** baggy breeches
43–4 **gave us the counterfeit:** tricked us
47 **the slip:** double meaning: fake coin; avoiding them
47 **conceive:** work out what I mean
49 **strain courtesy:** be rude
50–1 **such a case ... in the hams:** you're so tired from sex you're weak at the knees
53 **Thou hast most kindly hit it:** that's right
56 **Pink:** a garden flower; 'flower' was used to refer to virginity, male and female
58 **is my pump well flowered:** double meaning: well decorated dancing shoe; loss of virginity (deflowering)
60 **single:** only; Romeo and Mercutio start a battle of puns about wearing out shoes and sex being wearing

Romeo	O single-soled jest, solely singular for the singleness.
Mercutio	Come between us, good Benvolio, my wits faint.
Romeo	Switch and spurs, switch and spurs, or I'll cry a match.
Mercutio	Nay, if our wits run the wild-goose chase, I am done. 65 For thou hast more of the wild-goose in one of thy wits than, I am sure, I have in my whole five. Was I with you there for the goose?
Romeo	Thou wast never with me for anything when thou wast not there for the goose. 70
Mercutio	I will bite thee by the ear for that jest.
Romeo	Nay, good goose, bite not.
Mercutio	Thy wit is a very bitter sweeting, it is a most sharp sauce.
Romeo	And is it not then well served into a sweet goose?
Mercutio	O here's a wit of cheveril, that stretches from an inch 75 narrow to an ell broad!
Romeo	I stretch it out for that word "broad", which added to the goose, proves thee far and wide a broad goose.
Mercutio	Why, is not this better now than groaning for love? Now art thou sociable, now art thou Romeo, now art 80 thou what thou art, by art as well as by nature. For this drivelling love is like a great natural that runs lolling up and down to hide his bauble in a hole.
Benvolio	Stop there, stop there.
Mercutio	Thou desirest me to stop in my tale against the hair. 85
Benvolio	Thou wouldst else have made thy tale large.
Mercutio	O, thou art deceived; I would have made it short, for I was come to the whole depth of my tale, and meant, indeed, to occupy the argument no longer.

Enter Nurse and Peter.

Romeo	Here's goodly gear. A sail, a sail! 90
Mercutio	Two, two, a shirt and a smock.
Nurse	Peter!
Peter	Anon.
Nurse	My fan, Peter.
Mercutio	Good Peter, to hide her face! For her fan's the fairer face! 95
Nurse	God you good morrow, gentlemen.
Mercutio	God you good e'en, fair gentlewoman.
Nurse	Is it good e'en?
Mercutio	'Tis no less, I tell you, for the bawdy hand of the dial is now upon the prick of noon. 100
Nurse	Out upon you! What a man are you?

63 Come between us: stop us punning
64 Switch and spurs … cry a match: you have to try harder, as a rider forces a horse on with a whip and spurs, or I've won
65 wild-goose chase: triple meaning: the horse racing equivalent of follow-my-leader; 'goose' was slang for both 'prostitute' and 'fool'
67-8 Was I with you there for the goose?: did I keep up now I've started goose puns?

73 sweeting: apple used for apple sauce

75-6 here's a wit … an ell broad: you can make your small wit stretch a long way
77 broad: double meaning: wide; indecent

81 by art: because you're quick witted again
82 drivelling: talking nonsense
82 a great natural: a simple-minded person
83 bauble: double meaning: jester's blown-up pig's bladder; penis
85 tale: double meaning: story; sounds like 'tail', slang for penis. More puns on this follow
85 against the hair: double meaning: against my wish; sounds like 'hare', slang for prostitute

90 goodly gear: new material for joking
90 a sail!: a sailor's cry on seeing a ship
91 a shirt and a smock: a man and a woman

96 God you good morrow: Good morning
97 e'en: any time after noon

99 bawdy: sexually explicit
99 dial: sundial
101 Out upon you: for shame
101 What a man: what kind of a man

53

Romeo	One, gentlewoman, that God hath made, himself to mar.	102 **mar:** ruin
Nurse	By my troth, it is well said; "for himself to mar", quoth a? Gentlemen, can any of you tell me where I may find the young Romeo? 105	103 **By my troth:** truly 103–4 **quoth a?:** he says
Romeo	I can tell you. But young Romeo will be older when you have found him than he was when you sought him. I am the youngest of that name, for fault of a worse.	108 **for the fault of a worse:** for lack of anything worse
Nurse	You say well.	
Mercutio	Yea, is the worst well? Very well took, i' faith, wisely, wisely. 110	110 **took:** understood 112 **confidence:** private conversation; Shakespeare has the Nurse misuse words as part of the comedy of the scene – she may mean for 'conference'
Nurse	If you be he, sir, I desire some confidence with you.	
Benvolio	She will endite him to some supper.	113 **endite:** deliberate mistake for 'invite'
Mercutio	A bawd, a bawd, a bawd. So ho!	114 **bawd:** woman who runs a brothel
Romeo	What hast thou found? 115	114 **So ho!:** a hunting call
Mercutio	No hare, sir; unless a hare, sir, in a Lenten pie that is something stale and hoar ere it be spent. [Sings.] An old hare hoar, And an old hare hoar, Is very good meat in Lent. 120 But a hare that is hoar Is too much for a score, When it hoars ere it be spent. Romeo, will you come to your father's? We'll to dinner thither. 125	116–23 **No hare, sir ... ere it be spent:** Mercutio mocks the nurse, obscenely punning on her age, the similarity in sound between 'hoar' and 'whore' and the fact 'hare' was slang for prostitute 124 **dinner:** the midday meal
Romeo	I will follow you.	
Mercutio	Farewell, ancient lady. Farewell lady, lady, lady.	

Exit Mercutio and Benvolio.

Nurse	I pray you, sir, what saucy merchant was this, that was so full of his ropery?	128 **saucy merchant:** rude, un-gentlemanly man 129 **ropery:** spiteful and sexual jokes
Romeo	A gentleman, nurse, that loves to hear himself talk and 130 will speak more in a minute than he will stand to in a month.	131 **stand to:** put up with
Nurse	An a speak anything against me, I'll take him down, and a' were lustier than he is, and twenty such jacks. And if I cannot, I'll find those that shall. Scurvy knave, 135 I am none of his flirt-gills; I am none of his skains-mates. [To Peter.] And thou must stand by too, and suffer every knave to use me at his pleasure?	133 **An a:** and if he 133 **take him down:** take him down a peg or two 134 **lustier:** stronger 134 **jacks:** yobs 135 **Scurvy knave:** discourteous villain 136–7 **flirt-gills, skains-mates:** whores 138 **suffer:** allow
Peter	I saw no man use you at his pleasure. If I had, my weapon should quickly have been out, I warrant you, I dare 140 draw as soon as another man, if I see occasion in a good quarrel, and the law on my side.	138 **use me at his pleasure:** take advantage of me (unintentional double meaning)
Nurse	Now, afore God, I am so vexed that every part about me quivers. Scurvy knave! [To Romeo.] Pray you, sir, a word. And as I told you, my young lady bid me enquire 145 you out. What she bid me say, I will keep to myself.	

54

| | But first let me tell ye, if ye should lead her into a fool's paradise, as they say, it were a very gross kind of behaviour, as they say. For the gentlewoman is young, and therefore, if you should deal double with her, truly 150 it were an ill thing to be offered to any gentlewoman, and very weak dealing. |

Romeo Nurse, commend me to thy lady and mistress. I protest unto thee —

Nurse Good heart, and i' faith, I will tell her as much. Lord, 155 Lord, she will be a joyful woman.

Romeo What wilt thou tell her, nurse? Thou dost not mark me.

Nurse I will tell her, sir, that you do protest which, as I take it, is a gentlemanlike offer.

Romeo Bid her devise some means to come to shrift this 160 afternoon, and there she shall at Friar Lawrence' cell be shrived and married. *[He offers her money.]* Here is for thy pains.

Nurse No truly sir; not a penny.

Romeo Go to, I say you shall. 165

Nurse This afternoon, sir? Well, she shall be there.

Romeo And stay, good nurse, behind the abbey wall.
Within this hour my man shall be with thee
And bring thee cords made like a tackled stair,
Which to the high topgallant of my joy 170
Must be my convoy in the secret night.
Farewell, be trusty and I'll quit thy pains.
Farewell, commend me to thy mistress.

Nurse Now God in heaven bless thee. Hark you, sir.

Romeo What sayest thou, my dear nurse? 175

Nurse Is your man secret? Did you ne'er hear say,
Two may keep counsel putting one away?

Romeo Warrant thee, my man's as true as steel.

Nurse Well, sir; my mistress is the sweetest lady. Lord,
Lord, when 'twas a little prating thing. — O, there is a 180
nobleman in town, one Paris, that would fain lay knife
aboard. But she, good soul, had as lief see a toad, a very
toad, as see him. I anger her sometimes and tell her
that Paris is the properer man, but I'll warrant
you, when I say so, she looks as pale as any clout in 185
the 'versal world. Doth not rosemary and Romeo begin
both with a letter?

Romeo Ay, nurse, what of that? Both with an R.

Nurse Ah, mocker, that's the dog's name. R is for the — No, I
know it begins with some other letter, and she hath the 190
prettiest sententious of it, of you and rosemary, that it
would do you good to hear it.

147–8 **lead her into a fool's paradise:** promise marriage only to seduce her
148 **gross:** monstrous
150 **deal double:** deceive
152 **weak dealing:** shameful behaviour
153 **commend me:** give my greetings to
153–4 **I protest unto thee:** I assure you

157 **mark:** listen to

160 **devise some means:** find a way to
160 **shrift:** confession, where she tells her sins to a Catholic priest or friar
161–2 **be shrived:** have her sins forgiven

169 **cords made like a tackled stair:** a rope ladder
170 **the high topgallant of my joy:** Juliet's balcony
171 **convoy:** way up
172 **quit thy pains:** reward your efforts

176 **secret:** able to keep a secret
177 **Two may keep counsel … away:** Proverb: two can keep a secret; three can't
178 **Warrant thee:** I promise
180 **prating:** chattering
181–2 **would fain lay knife aboard:** wants to marry her
182 **as lief:** rather

184 **properer:** handsomer
185 **as pale as any clout:** a common saying
186 **'versal:** whole
186 **rosemary:** herb of remembrance, used at weddings and funerals

189 **dog's name:** 'r' sounds like growling
191 **sententious:** she means 'sentence', for saying

Ellie Kendrick
Juliet, summer 2009

I think this scene is lovely. The soliloquy at the beginning is fantastic because it is just a 13-year-old girl speaking. Obviously, for Juliet it is multiplied a million times, all teenagers remember that time when they are desperately waiting for a call, or really excited about the person they have got a crush on. But, obviously, with Juliet it is really quite exaggerated. And, so I think it is a really lovely soliloquy, and it is very humorous as well, when she is mocking old folks being, 'slow, heavy, and pale as lead'.

It is a classic teenagers' speech, not sympathising with the elders, and resenting the Nurse for failing to come quick enough to deliver the message from her loved one. And I think it is very clear that she knows the Nurse very well in this scene, because she is very frustrated with her, we can see that in lines when she says:

'How art thou out of breath, when thou hast breath
To say to me that thou art out of breath?'

(Which in itself is a line which is very difficult to say with enough breath.) So she is clearly irritated with her, but there is a huge amount of affection there, and she also knows that she has to flatter the Nurse in order to get the information she wants out of her. So she says, throughout the scene, 'Sweet, sweet, sweet nurse,' 'honey nurse' and really sucks up to her. So on the one side there is that, on the other side she is getting really frustrated with her for failing to tell her the news that she wants to hear.

Working Cut – text for experiment

Jul Now good sweet nurse — O Lord, why look'st thou sad?

Nur I am a-weary, give me leave awhile.

Jul Nay, come I pray thee, speak good, good nurse, speak.

Nur Do you not see that I am out of breath?

Jul How art thou out of breath, when thou hast breath
To say to me that thou art out of breath?
Is thy news good, or bad? Answer to that.

Nur Well, you have made a simple choice. You know not how to choose a man. Romeo? No, not he. —What, have you dined at home?

Jul No, no. But all this I did know before.
What says he of our marriage? What of that?

Nur Lord, how my head aches! What a head have I!
My back a' t' other side. Ah, my back, my back!

Jul Sweet, sweet, sweet nurse, tell me what says my love?

Nur Your love says, like an honest gentleman,
And a courteous, and a kind, and a handsome,
And I warrant a virtuous — Where is your mother?

Jul Where is my mother? How oddly thou repliest.

Nur Henceforward do your messages yourself.

Jul Here's such a coil. Come, what says Romeo?

Director's Note, 2.4

✔ Benvolio tells Mercutio that Tybalt has sent a challenge to Romeo.

✔ They meet the now happy Romeo who wins a battle of words with Mercutio.

✔ The Nurse arrives. Romeo gives her the message for Juliet – find a way to go to Friar Lawrence's cell in the afternoon and they shall be married.

✔ The Nurse is to wait for Romeo's servant to bring her a ladder.

FROM THE REHEARSAL ROOM...

TACTICS

Get into pairs. Label yourselves **A** and **B**.

- **A**, think of something you desperately want **B** to tell you. It must be very important. Your job is to get **B** to do this. However, you can only use one word to achieve your goal – 'Yes'.

- **B**, you do not want to tell **A**. You have one word to let **A** know – 'No'.

- **A** and **B**: You should say your words in as many different ways and tones of voice as possible to persuade your partner to agree with you.

1 List the different tactics that you both used in the improvisation.

2 Which did you think was the most successful (and why)?

3 Compare your answers with other groups. What are the similarities and differences?

- Now read the *Working Cut* text between Juliet and the Nurse.

4 List all the range of tactics used by both characters. Do they use any of the tactics that you used in your improvisations?

5 Which character applied the most successful tactics? Find evidence in the text to support your opinion.

Romeo	Commend me to thy lady.	*[Exit Romeo.]*
Nurse	Ay, a thousand times. — Peter.	
Peter	Anon.	195
Nurse	Before and apace.	*Exit Nurse and Peter.*

196 **Before and apace:** go in front and hurry

ACT 2 SCENE 5

Enter Juliet.

Juliet
The clock struck nine when I did send the nurse,
In half an hour she promised to return.
Perchance she cannot meet him. That's not so.
O, she is lame. Love's heralds should be thoughts,
Which ten times faster glide than the sun's beams   5
Driving back shadows over louring hills.
Therefore do nimble-pinioned doves draw Love,
And therefore hath the wind-swift Cupid wings.
Now is the sun upon the highmost hill
Of this day's journey, and from nine till twelve   10
Is three long hours, yet she is not come.
Had she affections and warm youthful blood,
She would be as swift in motion as a ball.
My words would bandy her to my sweet love,
And his to me.   15
But old folks, many feign as they were dead,
Unwieldy, slow, heavy, and pale as lead.

Enter Nurse and Peter.

O God, she comes! O honey nurse, what news?
Hast thou met with him? Send thy man away.

Nurse
Peter, stay at the gate.   *[Exit Peter.]* 20

Juliet
Now good sweet nurse —O Lord, why look'st thou sad?
Though news be sad, yet tell them merrily.
If good, thou shamest the music of sweet news
By playing it to me with so sour a face.

Nurse
I am a-weary, give me leave awhile.   25
Fie, how my bones ache! What a jaunce have I had!

Juliet
I would thou hadst my bones, and I thy news.
Nay, come I pray thee, speak good, good nurse, speak.

Nurse
Jesu, what haste! Can you not stay awhile?
Do you not see that I am out of breath?   30

Juliet
How art thou out of breath, when thou hast breath
To say to me that thou art out of breath?
The excuse that thou dost make in this delay
Is longer than the tale thou dost excuse.
Is thy news good, or bad? Answer to that.   35
Say either, and I'll stay the circumstance.
Let me be satisfied, is't good or bad?

Nurse
Well, you have made a simple choice. You know
not how to choose a man. Romeo? No, not he, though

3 **Perchance:** perhaps
4 **heralds:** messengers

6 **louring:** dark, threatening
7 **Therefore do .... draw Love:** that's why swift-winged doves pull the chariot of Venus (the goddess of love)

14 **bandy:** hit her (like a tennis ball)

16 **feign as:** act as if

20 **stay:** wait

25 **give me leave awhile:** just wait a minute
26 **jaunce:** exhausting trip

34 **thou dost excuse:** you say you have no breath to tell

36 **stay the circumstance:** wait for the details

38 **simple:** foolish

A

B

C

Juliet and the Nurse during Act 2 Scene 5.

Top left: spring 2009; *right and lower left*: summer 2009.

For each photo answer these questions:

1 Was the photo taken before or after the Nurse tells Juliet Romeo's message (lines 68–9)? Give reasons for your answer.

2 Which line would you pick as a caption for the photo? Explain your reasons.

Top left: Lorraine Burroughs, Jane Bertish; *right and lower left*: Penny Layden (Nurse), Ellie Kendrick (Juliet)

Director's Note, 2.5

✔ Juliet waits impatiently for the Nurse to return.

✔ The Nurse teases Juliet, complaining about how tired the errand has made her.

✔ She finally tells Juliet the arrangements to meet Romeo and be married.

✔ What moods does Shakespeare create in this scene?

	his face be better than any man's, yet his leg excels all men's, and for a hand, and a foot, and a body, though they be not to be talked on, yet they are past compare. He is not the flower of courtesy, but I'll warrant him as gentle as a lamb. Go thy ways, wench. Serve God. — What, have you dined at home?	40 45
Juliet	No, no. But all this did I know before. What says he of our marriage? What of that?	
Nurse	Lord, how my head aches! What a head have I! It beats as it would fall in twenty pieces. My back a' t' other side. Ah, my back, my back! Beshrew your heart for sending me about To catch my death with jauncing up and down.	50
Juliet	I' faith, I am sorry that thou art not well. Sweet, sweet, sweet nurse, tell me what says my love?	
Nurse	Your love says, like an honest gentleman, And a courteous, and a kind, and a handsome, And I warrant a virtuous — Where is your mother?	55
Juliet	Where is my mother? Why, she is within, Where should she be? How oddly thou repliest. "Your love says, like an honest gentleman, Where is your mother?"	60
Nurse	O God's lady dear, Are you so hot? Marry, come up, I trow. Is this the poultice for my aching bones? Henceforward do your messages yourself.	
Juliet	Here's such a coil. Come, what says Romeo?	65
Nurse	Have you got leave to go to shrift to-day?	
Juliet	I have.	
Nurse	Then hie you hence to Friar Lawrence's cell, There stays a husband to make you a wife. Now comes the wanton blood up in your cheeks, They'll be in scarlet straight at any news. Hie you to church, I must another way, To fetch a ladder by the which your love Must climb a bird's nest soon when it is dark. I am the drudge and toil in your delight, But you shall bear the burden soon at night. Go, I'll to dinner, hie you to the cell.	70 75
Juliet	Hie to high fortune! Honest nurse, farewell.	

Exit Juliet and Nurse.

42 **be not to be talked on:** aren't worth talking about
43 **the flower of courtesy:** perfect in his manners
44 **Go thy ways, wench. Serve God:** but that's enough of that, be a good girl

50 **a' t' other side:** on the other side
51 **Beshrew:** curse
52 **jauncing:** prancing like a horse

55 **honest:** honourable

58 **within:** indoors

61 **God's lady dear:** Mary, Christ's mother
62 **hot:** impatient
62 **Marry, come up, I trow:** exclamation of impatience
63 **poultice:** soothing warm pack of herbs
64 **Henceforward:** from now on
65 **coil:** fuss
66 **shrift:** confession, where she tells her sins to a Catholic priest
68 **hie you hence:** go

70 **wanton:** passionate

75 **drudge:** poor, unimportant servant
76 **bear the burden:** carry the weight of Romeo during sex

Juliet and Romeo kiss during Act 2 Scene 6, 2004.

1 There is no stage direction for a kiss in this scene. Why do you think the director and actors chose to add one? Explain your reasons, quoting from the text to support your answer if you can.

2 If you were the director, when would you have Juliet and Romeo kiss? Explain why.

Kananu Kirimi, Tom Burke

ACT 2 SCENE 6

Enter Friar Lawrence and Romeo.

Friar Lawrence   So smile the heavens upon this holy act,
That after hours with sorrow chide us not!

Romeo   Amen, amen. But come what sorrow can,
It cannot countervail the exchange of joy
That one short minute gives me in her sight.   5
Do thou but close our hands with holy words,
Then love-devouring death do what he dare,
It is enough I may but call her mine.

Friar Lawrence   These violent delights have violent ends
And in their triumph, die like fire and powder,   10
Which as they kiss consume. The sweetest honey
Is loathsome in his own deliciousness,
And in the taste confounds the appetite.
Therefore love moderately, long love doth so,
Too swift arrives as tardy as too slow.   15

Juliet runs in and embraces Romeo.

Here comes the lady. O so light a foot
Will ne'er wear out the everlasting flint.
A lover may bestride the gossamers
That idles in the wanton summer air,
And yet not fall, so light is vanity.   20

Juliet   Good even to my ghostly confessor.

Friar Lawrence   Romeo shall thank thee, daughter, for us both.

Juliet   As much to him, else is his thanks too much.

Romeo   Ah, Juliet, if the measure of thy joy
Be heaped like mine, and that thy skill be more   25
To blazon it, then sweeten with thy breath
This neighbour air, and let rich music's tongue
Unfold the imagined happiness that both
Receive in either by this dear encounter.

Juliet   Conceit, more rich in matter than in words,   30
Brags of his substance, not of ornament.
They are but beggars that can count their worth,
But my true love is grown to such excess
I cannot sum up sum of half my wealth.

Friar Lawrence   Come, come with me, and we will make short work.   35
For, by your leaves, you shall not stay alone
Till holy church incorporate two in one.

[Exit Friar, Romeo and Juliet.]

2 **after hours with sorrow chide us not:** we aren't punished by sorrow in the future
4 **countervail:** equal
6 **Do thou but ... holy words:** Just marry us
10 **powder:** gunpowder
11 **as they kiss consume:** burn each other up on touching
12 **Is loathsome in his own deliciousness:** can be sickly because it is so delicious
13 **confounds:** spoils
15 **tardy:** late
17 **ne'er:** never
17 **the everlasting flint:** the ground
18 **bestride the gossamers:** walk so lightly on spiders' webs
19 **idles:** drift
20 **vanity:** the delights of the world
21 **ghostly:** spiritual
21 **confessor:** priest or friar who hears a person confess their sins
24–5 **the measure of thy joy Be heaped like mine:** if you're as happy as I am
25 **that:** if
26 **blazon:** describe
27 **This neighbour air:** the air around us
28 **Unfold:** tell
28–9 **both Receive in either:** we both will have
30–1 **Conceit, more rich ... of ornament:** understanding boasts about what it really has, it doesn't dress it up in fancy words
32 **They are but beggars ... worth:** only beggars can list all they have
34 **sum up sum:** calculate
35 **make short work:** quickly marry you
37 **incorporate two in one:** has made you husband and wife

Director's Note, 2.6

✔ Friar Lawrence and Romeo wait for Juliet.
✔ She arrives, and Friar Lawrence takes then off to marry them.

Working Cut – text for experiment

Enter Benvolio, Mercutio, his page, & Montague servants.

Ben   I pray thee, good Mercutio, let's retire,
The day is hot, the Capels are abroad,
And if we meet we shall not 'scape a brawl.

Enter Tybalt, Petruchio, and others.

        By my head, here comes the Capulets.

Mer   By my heel, I care not.

Tyb   *[To his men.]* Follow me close, for I will speak to them.
       – Gentlemen, good-e'en, a word with one of you.

Mer   And but one word with one of us? Couple it with
something, make it a word and a blow.

Tyb   You shall find me apt enough to that, sir, and you
will give me occasion.

Mer   Could you not take some occasion without giving?

Tyb   Mercutio, thou consortest with Romeo.

Mer   Consort? What, dost thou make us minstrels? And
thou make minstrels of us, look to hear nothing
but discords. *[Moving his hand to his sword.]*
Here's my fiddlestick, here's that shall make you
dance. 'Zounds, consort!

Ben   We talk here in the public haunt of men.
Either withdraw unto some private place,
Or reason coldly of your grievances,
Or else depart. Here all eyes gaze on us.

Mer   Men's eyes were made to look, and let them gaze.
I will not budge for no man's pleasure, I.

[Enter Romeo.]

Tyb   Well, peace be with you, sir, here comes my man.

Mer   But I'll be hanged, sir, if he wear your livery.

Tyb   Romeo, the love I bear thee can afford
No better term than this: thou art a villain.

Rom   Tybalt, the reason that I have to love thee
Doth much excuse the appertaining rage
To such a greeting. Villain am I none,
Therefore farewell, I see thou knowest me not.

Tyb   Boy, this shall not excuse the injuries
That thou hast done me, therefore turn and draw.

Rom   I do protest I never injured thee,
But love thee better than thou canst devise

Mer   O calm, dishonourable, vile submission!
Alla stoccata carries it away. *[Drawing his sword.]*
Tybalt, you rat-catcher, will you walk?

Tyb   What wouldst thou have with me?

Mer   Good king of cats, nothing but one of your nine
lives. Will you pluck your sword out of his pilcher
by the ears? Make haste, lest mine be about your
ears ere it be out.

Tyb   I am for you. *[Drawing his sword.]*

Rom   Gentle Mercutio, put thy rapier up.

Mer   Come sir, your *passado. [They fight.]*

Rom   Draw, Benvolio; beat down their weapons.
Gentlemen, for shame, forbear this outrage!

FROM THE REHEARSAL ROOM...

WORDS AS WEAPONS

In groups of four, read the *Working Cut*, each person taking one part.

- As each person reads their lines, the others should listen for any words that sound like insults and then repeat the word aloud.
- Write down or highlight all the words or phrases that you repeated.
- Discuss how Tybalt and Mercutio use the words in this exchange.

1 Which words are the most effective?

2 What are the characteristics of an effective 'weapon word'? (For example, word length, word sound, use of vowels and consonants, meaning.)

3 How does Mercutio use words to taunt Tybalt?

Benvolio and Mercutio, touring production 2008.

Do you think this photo was taken before or after Tybalt enters (line 34)?

Michael Cox, Nitzan Sharron

Enter Benvolio, Mercutio, his page, and servants of the Montagues.

Benvolio
I pray thee, good Mercutio, let's retire,
The day is hot, the Capels are abroad,
And if we meet we shall not 'scape a brawl,
For now these hot days is the mad blood stirring.

Mercutio
Thou art like one of those fellows, that when he enters   5
the confines of a tavern, claps me his sword upon the
table and says "God send me no need of thee"; and
by the operation of the second cup, draws him on the
drawer, when indeed there is no need.

Benvolio
Am I like such a fellow?   10

Mercutio
Come, come, thou art as hot a Jack in thy mood as any
in Italy, and as soon moved to be moody, and as soon
moody to be moved.

Benvolio
And what to?

Mercutio
Nay, and there were two such, we should have none   15
shortly, for one would kill the other. Thou? Why thou
wilt quarrel with a man that hath a hair more, or a hair
less, in his beard than thou hast. Thou wilt quarrel with
a man for cracking nuts, having no other reason but
because thou hast hazel eyes. What eye but such an eye,   20
would spy out such a quarrel? Thy head is as full of
quarrels as an egg is full of meat, and yet thy head hath
been beaten as addle as an egg for quarrelling. Thou
hast quarrelled with a man for coughing in the street,
because he hath wakened thy dog that hath lain asleep   25
in the sun. Didst thou not fall out with a tailor for
wearing his new doublet before Easter? With another,
for tying his new shoes with old ribbon? And yet thou
wilt tutor me from quarrelling?

Benvolio
And I were so apt to quarrel as thou art, any man   30
should buy the fee-simple of my life for an hour and a
quarter.

Mercutio
The fee-simple? O simple!

Enter Tybalt, Petruchio, and others.

Benvolio
By my head, here comes the Capulets.

Mercutio
By my heel, I care not.   35

Tybalt
[To his men.]   Follow me close, for I will speak to them.
[To Benvolio and Mercutio.]
Gentlemen, good-e'en, a word with one of you.

Mercutio
And but one word with one of us? Couple it with
something, make it a word and a blow.

Tybalt
You shall find me apt enough to that, sir, and you will   40
give me occasion.

1 **retire:** go home
2 **Capels:** Capulets
2 **abroad:** somewhere around
3 **'scape a brawl:** be able to avoid a fight
6 **the confines of a tavern:** a pub
6 **claps me his sword:** bangs his sword
8 **the operation of the second cup:** the time he's had his second drink
8 **draws him:** draws his sword
9 **drawer:** man serving the drink

11 **hot:** quick-tempered
11 **Jack:** fellow
12–3 **as soon moved to be moody ... moved:** as quickly made angry as you are made angry that it has happened
15 **and there were:** if there were

20 **hazel:** double meaning: eye colour; type of nut

22 **meat:** something edible
23 **addle:** rotten (so an egg that won't produce a chick)

27 **doublet:** jacket

29 **tutor me from:** advise me to avoid
30 **And I were so apt:** if I was so given to
31 **fee-simple:** complete ownership

33 **simple:** fool

34 **By my head:** a common exclamation
35 **By my heel:** Mercutio makes up this exclamation, which hints at running away

38 **Couple:** join

41 **occasion:** a good reason

A

B

SHAKESPEARE'S WORLD

Swordfighting

A sword was part of an Elizabethan gentleman's elaborate dress. Most gentlemen carried swords in public, and many had a dagger too. The weapons were more a sign of status than for defence. However, young gentlemen, or gallants as they were known, did fight in the streets. The fact that even the servants in *Romeo and Juliet* carry swords, and shields too (not normally carried at all), is a sign of just how extreme the old feud has become.

Gentlemen were taught the art of fencing. In this scene, Mercutio uses fencing terms and also complains that Tybalt 'fights by the book'. The fights themselves were governed by a strict set of rules that they were honour bound to obey. Tybalt breaks these rules by thrusting under Romeo's arm.

The open air playhouses did more than just show plays. They staged exhibitions of sword fighting, tournaments and prize fights between duellers. Some theatres including The Curtain, where *Romeo and Juliet* was probably first played, became well known for these fights. With the exciting swordplay of the first half of the play, Shakespeare is giving his audience the action they expect, as well as the main plot of the love story.

C

Tybalt and Mercutio fight, summer 2009.

1 These are in the order they were taken during the fight. What has changed between Photos A and B, and Photo C?

2 Is it possible to tell who seems to be winning? Explain your answer.

Ukweli Roach, Philip Cumbus

Mercutio	Could you not take some occasion without giving?	
Tybalt	Mercutio, thou consortest with Romeo.	
Mercutio	Consort? What, dost thou make us minstrels? And thou make minstrels of us, look to hear nothing but discords. *[Moving his hand to his sword.]* Here's my fiddlestick, here's that shall make you dance. 'Zounds, consort!	45
Benvolio	We talk here in the public haunt of men. Either withdraw unto some private place, Or reason coldly of your grievances, Or else depart. Here all eyes gaze on us.	50
Mercutio	Men's eyes were made to look, and let them gaze. I will not budge for no man's pleasure, I. *[Enter Romeo.]*	
Tybalt	Well, peace be with you, sir, here comes my man.	
Mercutio	But I'll be hanged, sir, if he wear your livery. Marry, go before to field, he'll be your follower. Your worship in that sense may call him "man."	55
Tybalt	Romeo, the love I bear thee can afford No better term than this: thou art a villain.	
Romeo	Tybalt, the reason that I have to love thee Doth much excuse the appertaining rage To such a greeting. Villain am I none, Therefore farewell, I see thou knowest me not.	60
Tybalt	Boy, this shall not excuse the injuries That thou hast done me, therefore turn and draw.	65
Romeo	I do protest I never injured thee, But love thee better than thou canst devise Till thou shalt know the reason of my love. And so, good Capulet, which name I tender As dearly as my own, be satisfied.	70
Mercutio	O calm, dishonourable, vile submission! *Alla stoccata* carries it away. *[Drawing his sword.]* Tybalt, you rat-catcher, will you walk?	
Tybalt	What wouldst thou have with me?	
Mercutio	Good king of cats, nothing but one of your nine lives, that I mean to make bold withal, and as you shall use me hereafter, drybeat the rest of the eight. Will you pluck your sword out of his pilcher by the ears? Make haste, lest mine be about your ears ere it be out.	75
Tybalt	I am for you. *[Drawing his sword.]*	80
Romeo	Gentle Mercutio, put thy rapier up.	
Mercutio	Come sir, your *passado*. *[They fight.]*	
Romeo	Draw, Benvolio; beat down their weapons. Gentlemen, for shame, forbear this outrage! Tybalt, Mercutio, the Prince expressly hath Forbidden bandying in Verona streets: Hold, Tybalt! good Mercutio!	85

43 **consortest with:** are a friend of
44 **minstrels:** music makers – 'consort' is a name of a small group of musicians
44 **And thou:** if you
46 **fiddlestick:** he means his sword
47 **'Zounds:** an oath, from 'God's wounds'
48 **the public haunt of men:** a public place
50 **reason coldly of:** calmly talk through
53 **I will not budge for no man's pleasure:** I won't move for any man's convenience
54 **my man:** the man I'm looking for
55 **I'll be hanged, sir, if he wear your livery:** he's certainly not a Capulet's servant ('man' can mean 'servant' who wears his master's 'livery' or uniform)
56 **go before to field:** lead the way to the duelling place
56 **follower:** another word for 'servant' but meaning that Romeo will follow to fight
61-2 **the appertaining rage To such a greeting:** the anger I should feel at such an insult
64 **Boy:** an insult to a young man
65 **turn and draw:** come back and fight
67 **devise:** imagine
69 **tender:** value
70 **be satisfied:** don't push this challenge
72 ***Alla stoccata:*** another reference to fancy fencing terms
73 **will you walk:** will you fight me
76 **to make bold withal:** to take
77 **drybeat:** beat up, rather than fight with swords, like gentlemen
78 **pilcher:** scabbard
78 **by the ears:** right now, with no formality
79 **lest:** in case
82 ***passado:*** fencing term
84 **forbear:** stop
86 **bandying:** fighting

65

A

Above: The fight, summer 2009.

l–r Philip Cumbus, Adetomiwa Edun, Ukweli Roach

Below: Benvolio and Mercutio, spring 2009.

l–r Ben Aldridge, Shane Zaza

Pick a stage direction or line which could be used as a caption for Photo A and Photo B. Give reasons for your choice.

B

[During the fight, Romeo tries to part them, and Tybalt stabs Mercutio under Romeo's arm. Tybalt runs offstage.]

Mercutio   I am hurt.
A plague on both your houses! I am sped.
Is he gone and hath nothing?

Benvolio   What, art thou hurt?   90

Mercutio   Ay, ay, a scratch, a scratch. Marry, 'tis enough.
Where is my page? Go, villain, fetch a surgeon. *[Exit Page.]*

Romeo   Courage man, the hurt cannot be much.

Mercutio   No, 'tis not so deep as a well, nor so wide
as a church door; but 'tis enough, 'twill serve. Ask for   95
me tomorrow, and you shall find me a grave man. I
am peppered, I warrant, for this world. A plague o'
both your houses! 'Zounds, a dog, a rat, a mouse, a
cat to scratch a man to death, a braggart, a
rogue, a villain, that fights by the book of   100
arithmetic! — Why the devil came you between us? I
was hurt under your arm.

Romeo   I thought all for the best.

Mercutio   Help me into some house, Benvolio,
Or I shall faint. A plague o' both your houses!   105
They have made worms' meat of me.
I have it, and soundly too. Your houses!

Exit Mercutio, helped by Benvolio and the servants.

Romeo   This gentleman, the Prince's near ally,
My very friend, hath got his mortal hurt
In my behalf. My reputation stained   110
With Tybalt's slander, — Tybalt, that an hour
Hath been my cousin. O sweet Juliet,
Thy beauty hath made me effeminate
And in my temper softened valour's steel.

Enter Benvolio.

Benvolio   O Romeo, Romeo, brave Mercutio is dead.   115
That gallant spirit hath aspired the clouds,
Which too untimely here did scorn the earth.

Romeo   This day's black fate on more days doth depend,
This but begins the woe others must end.

Benvolio   Here comes the furious Tybalt back again. *Enter Tybalt.*   120

Romeo   Alive in triumph and Mercutio slain?
Away to heaven respective lenity,
And fire and fury be my conduct now.
Now, Tybalt, take the "villain" back again
That late thou gav'st me, for Mercutio's soul   125
Is but a little way above our heads,
Staying for thine to keep him company.
Either thou, or I, or both, must go with him.

88 **A plague on both your houses:** curse both Montagues and Capulets
88 **sped:** fatally wounded
89 **Is he gone and hath nothing?:** has Tybalt got away unwounded?
91 **'tis enough:** it's enough to kill me
95 **'twill serve:** it's enough to kill me
96 **grave:** double meaning: serious; dead
97 **peppered:** ruined, finished off
100-1 **by the book of arithmetic:** 'by numbers', by the rules of fencing
106 **worms' meat:** a corpse
107 **I have it, and soundly too:** I'm certainly fatally wounded
108 **near ally:** close relative
109 **very:** true
110 **In my behalf:** defending me
111 **that an hour:** that for an hour
113 **effeminate:** weak, not manly
114 **temper:** double meaning: hardening (as in steel for a sword); nature
114 **softened valour's steel:** made me cowardly
116-7 **That gallant spirit hath aspired ... the earth:** his soul has scorned the earth and flown to Heaven too soon
118 **on more days doth depend:** will have an effect on the future
119 **others:** other days
122 **Away to heaven respective lenity:** no more treating him like a relative
123 **be my conduct:** drive my actions
125 **late:** just now
127 **Staying:** waiting

The fight between Romeo and Tybalt, summer 2009.

At this point Romeo has slashed and stabbed Tybalt with his sword, thrown the sword aside, and he turns to kick the dying Tybalt. This is an interpretation of the fight developed by this production.

1 What impression does this give of Romeo's state of mind?
2 Do you agree with this interpretation? Explain your answer.

Adetomiwa Edun, Ukweli Roach

The Prince, Capulet, Lady Capulet, Tybalt (dead) and Benvolio, spring 2009.

Benvolio is speaking. Which line do you think he was saying when this photo was taken? Quote to support your answer.

l–r Nick Khan, Vincent Brimble, Golda Rosheuvel, Marshall Griffin, Ben Aldridge

Tybalt	Thou wretched boy, that didst consort him here,	129	**that didst consort him:** who was with him
	Shalt with him hence.		
Romeo	This shall determine that.	130	130 **Shalt with him hence:** will leave with him
			130 **This:** Romeo's sword

They fight. Tybalt falls.

Benvolio	Romeo, away, be gone!		
	The citizens are up, and Tybalt slain.		
	Stand not amazed, the Prince will doom thee death	133	**amazed:** stunned
	If thou art taken. Hence, be gone, away!	133	**doom thee:** sentence you to
Romeo	O! I am fortune's fool!		
Benvolio	Why dost thou stay?	135	135 **fortune's fool:** the puppet of Fortune, the goddess of luck

Exit Romeo, then enter citizens from another door.

Citizen	Which way ran he that killed Mercutio?		
	Tybalt, that murderer, which way ran he?		
Benvolio	There lies that Tybalt.		
Citizen	Up, sir, go with me.		
	I charge thee in the Prince's name, obey.	139	**charge:** order

Enter the Prince, Montague, Capulet, their wives and others.

Prince	Where are the vile beginners of this fray?	140	140 **the vile beginners of this fray:** those who started this fight
Benvolio	O noble Prince, I can discover all	141	**discover:** tell
	The unlucky manage of this fatal brawl.	142	**manage:** events
	There lies the man, slain by young Romeo,		
	That slew thy kinsman, brave Mercutio.		
Lady Capulet	Tybalt, my cousin! O my brother's child!	145	
	O Prince! O cousin! Husband! O, the blood is spilled		
	Of my dear kinsman. Prince, as thou art true,	147	**true:** fair
	For blood of ours, shed blood of Montague.		
	O cousin, cousin!		
Prince	Benvolio, who began this bloody fray?	150	
Benvolio	Tybalt, here slain, whom Romeo's hand did slay.		
	Romeo that spoke him fair, bid him bethink	152	**spoke him fair:** was polite
	How nice the quarrel was, and urged withal	152	**bethink:** consider
	Your high displeasure. All this uttered	153	**nice:** trivial
		153	**withal:** as well
	With gentle breath, calm look, knees humbly bowed,	155	
	Could not take truce with the unruly spleen	156	**take truce with:** pacify
	Of Tybalt, deaf to peace, but that he tilts	156	**unruly spleen:** hot temper
	With piercing steel at bold Mercutio's breast.	157	**but that he tilts:** so that he thrusts
	Who all as hot, turns deadly point to point		
	And, with a martial scorn, with one hand beats	160	160 **martial:** war-like
	Cold death aside and with the other sends		
	It back to Tybalt, whose dexterity	162	**dexterity:** skill
	Retorts it. Romeo, he cries aloud,		
	"Hold, friends! Friends, part!" And swifter than his tongue		
	His agile arm beats down their fatal points,	165	
	And 'twixt them rushes, underneath whose arm	166	**'twixt:** between
	An envious thrust from Tybalt hit the life	167	**envious:** malicious
		167	**hit the life:** killed

WORDS FAILING

- In groups of four read through the *Working Cut*, each taking one part.
- Look carefully at Benvolio's description of events to the Prince. Note words and phrases that depict each stage of the fight.
- Compare Benvolio's step-by-step account of the fight with Tybalt and Romeo's lines at the beginning of the *Working Cut*.

1 Is Benvolio telling the truth?

2 What role does Benvolio play in the scene between Romeo and Tybalt?

3 How does Romeo react after Tybalt's death?

4 Who is to blame for Tybalt's death? Find evidence in the text to support your opinion.

Director's view

Dominic Dromgoole
Director, summer 2009

It is hard to deny that attachment to Tybalt. I think you can overplay it, and sometimes you see it overplayed in the Ball scene. And even though the actress playing Lady Capulet was always very enthusiastic to get her hands on the actor playing Tybalt, we tried to tamp it down a little bit in that scene. It is very clear the extremity of the reaction is so enormous when Tybalt is dead, and then the degree of her grief is so extended, and so absolute afterwards, it does seem there is more than a familial attachment there. And it is set up very delicately and very well, the fact that there is a dysfunction in the relationship between Capulet and his wife and that that is not as vigorous or as healthy or active as it might be, so it seems that Tybalt is there to step in.

Actor's view

Yolanda Vazquez
Lady Capulet, 2008
(not a Globe production)

I don't think Lady Capulet's reaction to Tybalt's death means she has been having an affair with him. Tybalt is a young man, her brother's son, who she is very close to and loves very much. I have three nephews, if anything would happen to them ... I think that for Lady Capulet, losing Tybalt is like losing the son she never had. She is looking after him. He is part of her household, she is looking after him, which is what they used to do with young men and young women, so she's looking after her brother's son, and he dies in her care.

Working Cut – text for experiment

Ben	O Romeo, Romeo, brave Mercutio is dead.
	Here comes the furious Tybalt back again.
[Enter Tybalt.]	
Rom	Alive in triumph and Mercutio slain?
	Now, Tybalt, take the "villain" back again
	That late thou gav'st me, for Mercutio's soul
	Is but a little way above our heads,
	Staying for thine to keep him company.
Tyb	Thou wretched boy, that didst consort him here,
	Shalt with him hence.
Rom	This shall determine that.
	They fight. Tybalt falls.
Ben	Romeo, away, be gone!
	Stand not amazed, the Prince will doom thee death
	If thou art taken. Hence, be gone, away!
Rom	O! I am fortune's fool! *Exit Romeo. Enter Prince.*
Prin	Where are the vile beginners of this fray?
Ben	O noble Prince, I can discover all
Prin	Benvolio, who began this bloody fray?
Ben	Tybalt, here slain, whom Romeo's hand did slay.
	Romeo that spoke him fair, bid him bethink
	How nice the quarrel was. All this uttered
	With gentle breath, calm look, knees humbly bowed,
	Could not take truce with the unruly spleen
	Of Tybalt, deaf to peace, but that he tilts
	With piercing steel at bold Mercutio's breast.
	Who all as hot, turns deadly point to point
	And, with a martial scorn, with one hand beats
	Cold death aside and with the other sends
	It back to Tybalt, whose dexterity
	Retorts it. Romeo, he cries aloud,
	"Hold, friends! Friends, part!" And swifter than his tongue
	His agile arm beats down their fatal points,
	And 'twixt them rushes, underneath whose arm
	An envious thrust from Tybalt hit the life
	Of stout Mercutio, and then Tybalt fled.
	But by and by comes back to Romeo,
	And to 't they go like lightning, for ere I
	Could draw to part them, was stout Tybalt slain.
	And as he fell, did Romeo turn and fly.

Capulet restrains his wife, summer 2009.

Does the text support the interpretation that Lady Capulet is much more upset than her husband? Quote from the text to support your answer.

Miranda Foster, Ian Redford

Of stout Mercutio, and then Tybalt fled.
But by and by comes back to Romeo,
Who had but newly entertained revenge,
And to 't they go like lightning, for ere I
Could draw to part them, was stout Tybalt slain.
And as he fell, did Romeo turn and fly.
This is the truth, or let Benvolio die.

Lady Capulet   He is a kinsman to the Montague,
Affection makes him false he speaks not true.
Some twenty of them fought in this black strife,
And all those twenty could but kill one life.
I beg for justice, which thou, Prince, must give.
Romeo slew Tybalt, Romeo must not live.

Prince   Romeo slew him, he slew Mercutio.
Who now the price of his dear blood doth owe?

Montague   Not Romeo, Prince, he was Mercutio's friend.
His fault concludes but what the law should end,
The life of Tybalt.

Prince   And for that offence
Immediately we do exile him hence.
I have an interest in your hate's proceeding,
My blood for your rude brawls doth lie a-bleeding.
But I'll amerce you with so strong a fine
That you shall all repent the loss of mine.
I will be deaf to pleading and excuses;
Nor tears nor prayers shall purchase out abuses.
Therefore use none. Let Romeo hence in haste,
Else, when he is found, that hour is his last.
Bear hence this body and attend our will.
Mercy but murders, pardoning those that kill.

Exit all, some carrying Tybalt's body.

170
175
180
185
190
195

169 **by and by:** at that moment
170 **but newly entertained:** just decided on
171 **ere:** before
172 **draw:** draw my sword
172 **stout:** brave
173 **fly:** run away
176 **Affection makes him false:** he's biased in their favour
177 **black strife:** evil attack
182 **Who now the price of his dear blood doth owe?:** So who should pay for that?
184 **His fault concludes ... should end:** his action (killing Tybalt) was only what your punishment would have been anyway, for killing Mercutio
186 **exile him hence:** send him away from Verona
187 **an interest in your hate's proceeding:** I've become personally involved in your quarrels
188 **My blood:** Mercutio
189 **amerce:** punish
190 **the loss of mine:** the death of my relative
192 **purchase out abuses:** by pardons for these crimes
194 **Else:** otherwise
194 **that hour is his last:** he will be executed
195 **attend our will:** come with me to hear your punishment
196 **Mercy but murders ... kill:** if I pardon murder it will just lead to more killing

Director's Note, 3.1

✔ Tybalt, determined to fight Romeo, meets Mercutio and Benvolio. Romeo arrives, but refuses to fight.
✔ Shocked at Romeo's refusal, Mercutio fights Tybalt and is fatally wounded.
✔ Romeo now wants revenge, and fights and kills Tybalt.
✔ Romeo flees. The Prince arrives and banishes Romeo.

EXAMINER'S NOTES, 3.1

These questions help you to explore many aspects of *Romeo and Juliet*. At GCSE, your teacher will tell you which aspects are relevant to how your Shakespeare response will be assessed.

EXAMINER'S TIP

A good response

A good response may include more than one way of interpreting a scene. The key word is 'or'. For example, in this scene, Mercutio's death may make an audience feel sympathy for a witty and amusing young man who has tragically died. Or it could make an audience feel that this is what you can expect when a young man can't control his mouth and temper.

USING THE VIDEO

Exploring interpretation and performance

If you have looked at the video extracts in Dynamic Learning, try these questions.

- Tybalt's manner in the opening of this scene (2009 production) is less aggressive than in Act 1 Scene 5. How does this show in his response to Mercutio's three attempts to provoke him?

- Mercutio is seemingly a better swordsman than Tybalt. What effect does this have on his attitude when Romeo's intervention results in Tybalt's stabbing him?

❶ Character and plot development

This scene is full of dramatic action – insults, fights and deaths. It develops the plot by making Romeo even more an enemy of the Capulets because he has killed Tybalt, and by isolating him from Juliet because he is banished from Verona, under penalty of death if he returns. All this has the effect of making Romeo and Juliet seek some desperate means of solving their problems.

Romeo's character is developed in the scene by showing him torn between keeping the peace and being angry at the death of his friend.

1 How do Benvolio's opening words suggest some potential danger?
2 From what we have seen of Benvolio so far, do you think Mercutio's description of him is realistic (lines 11–29)?
3 Despite his comments about how Benvolio has been quick-tempered in the past, Mercutio has learned nothing about avoiding trouble. How does Shakespeare show this in Mercutio's talk with Tybalt (lines 35–47)?

❷ Characterisation and voice: dramatic language

In the play so far, we have heard voices of tender passion and voices of mocking taunts. The voices in the scene are harsh, provocative and loud, expressing alarm and warning, anger and abuse.

4 How does Shakespeare show the young men's attitudes in the way they speak?
5 How does Benvolio's speech attempt to calm things down (lines 48–51)?
6 How does Romeo try to calm things down?
7 Mercutio's angry feelings change after he has been wounded. How does Shakespeare show this?
8 The action changes Romeo, too. How does his attitude show a change of feelings following Mercutio's wounding?

❸ Themes and ideas

The scene creates a realistic sense of the feelings which keep the family feud alive. Shakespeare never bothers to give details of what caused the feud in the first place, but he shows that the feud influences even the youngest members of the families and their friends.

9 Which main characters do you think are driven by feelings of honour and respect in this scene?
10 How does Shakespeare show that Romeo is attempting to deal with conflicting loyalties in this scene?
11 How far is Fate represented as the cause of events in this scene, compared with young men's attitudes and feelings?
12 Shakespeare shows that some of the attitudes which have caused the trouble in the scene are not just the attitudes of young men. How does Lady Capulet's speech (lines 145–149) suggest this?
13 How does Benvolio's speech (lines 151–174) try to give a fair and balanced summary of events rather than blame any single person?

EXAMINER'S NOTES, 3.1

4 Performance

This scene follows the quiet scene in Friar Lawrence's cell where Romeo and Juliet are married, and provides a contrast in place, characters, mood and action. There is plenty in this scene to create noise and movement on stage, as the young men exchange insults and events become more serious and tragic.

14 Romeo's part in this scene requires the actor to use several kinds of voice. What kinds of voice do you think the actor should use for lines 60–70, lines 83–87, lines 108–114 and lines 121–128?

15 What do you think are the thoughts in Romeo's head after he has killed Tybalt, and Benvolio is urging him to get away?

16 Would you advise the other actors in this scene to watch Romeo and Tybalt fight or attempt to stop them – or join in a general brawl?

5 Contexts and responses

One of the things that makes an audience take a play seriously is the belief that what it sees on stage could happen in real life. If we don't believe that what we see on stage could happen in real life, we are not likely to feel pity or fear, happiness or relief. Our responses are based on seeing the context on stage as similar to contexts we are familiar with in our own lives.

17 Mercutio lists various ways in which Benvolio has been easily provoked to anger. Do these reasons for quarrelling seem exaggerated and unrealistic to you – or do you think that similar reasons may cause people to quarrel today?

6 Reflecting on the scene

18 Which of the following do you think Shakespeare makes most influential in developing the tragic situation:
- the family feud
- young men's tempers
- Fate?

19 How does Shakespeare convey Romeo's different feelings and attitudes in this scene?

20 In what ways has your response to this scene been influenced by a stage or screen performance?

EXAMINER'S TIP

Writing about drama

An audience watching a play must be gripped by what happens on stage, without reading the script.

Writing about a drama text needs to show how the plot is constructed to keep an audience interested, with shifts of scene and changes of character on stage, and lines which an actor can not only speak but perform with visible and audible emphasis.

EXAMINER'S TIP

Reflecting on the scene

Make sure you consider Shakespeare's skill in characterisation – making characters believable and seeming real in performance on stage – representing important themes and ideas.

This will help you treat them as imaginary characters created by Shakespeare, rather than real people.

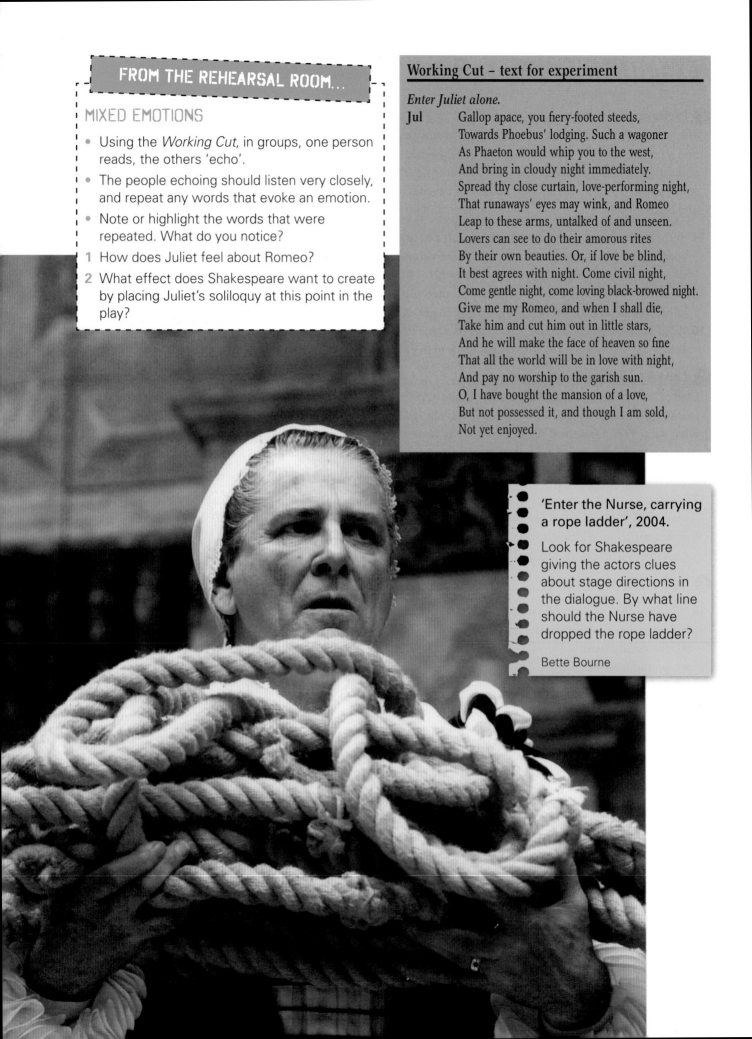

FROM THE REHEARSAL ROOM...

MIXED EMOTIONS

- Using the *Working Cut*, in groups, one person reads, the others 'echo'.
- The people echoing should listen very closely, and repeat any words that evoke an emotion.
- Note or highlight the words that were repeated. What do you notice?

1 How does Juliet feel about Romeo?
2 What effect does Shakespeare want to create by placing Juliet's soliloquy at this point in the play?

Working Cut – text for experiment

Enter Juliet alone.

Jul   Gallop apace, you fiery-footed steeds,
         Towards Phoebus' lodging. Such a wagoner
         As Phaeton would whip you to the west,
         And bring in cloudy night immediately.
         Spread thy close curtain, love-performing night,
         That runaways' eyes may wink, and Romeo
         Leap to these arms, untalked of and unseen.
         Lovers can see to do their amorous rites
         By their own beauties. Or, if love be blind,
         It best agrees with night. Come civil night,
         Come gentle night, come loving black-browed night.
         Give me my Romeo, and when I shall die,
         Take him and cut him out in little stars,
         And he will make the face of heaven so fine
         That all the world will be in love with night,
         And pay no worship to the garish sun.
         O, I have bought the mansion of a love,
         But not possessed it, and though I am sold,
         Not yet enjoyed.

'Enter the Nurse, carrying a rope ladder', 2004.

Look for Shakespeare giving the actors clues about stage directions in the dialogue. By what line should the Nurse have dropped the rope ladder?

Bette Bourne

Enter Juliet alone.

Juliet   Gallop apace, you fiery-footed steeds,
Towards Phoebus' lodging. Such a wagoner
As Phaeton would whip you to the west,
And bring in cloudy night immediately.
Spread thy close curtain, love-performing night,   5
That runaways' eyes may wink, and Romeo
Leap to these arms, untalked of and unseen.
Lovers can see to do their amorous rites
By their own beauties. Or, if love be blind,
It best agrees with night. Come civil night,   10
Thou sober-suited matron all in black,
And learn me how to lose a winning match,
Played for a pair of stainless maidenhoods.
Hood my unmanned blood, bating in my cheeks
With thy black mantle, till strange love grow bold,   15
Think true love acted simple modesty.
Come night, come Romeo, come, thou day in night;
For thou wilt lie upon the wings of night
Whiter than new snow on a raven's back.
Come gentle night, come loving black-browed night.   20
Give me my Romeo, and when I shall die,
Take him and cut him out in little stars,
And he will make the face of heaven so fine
That all the world will be in love with night,
And pay no worship to the garish sun.   25
O, I have bought the mansion of a love,
But not possessed it, and though I am sold,
Not yet enjoyed. So tedious is this day
As is the night before some festival
To an impatient child that hath new robes   30
And may not wear them. O, here comes my nurse.

Enter the Nurse, carrying a rope ladder.

And she brings news, and every tongue that speaks
But Romeo's name speaks heavenly eloquence.
Now, nurse, what news? What hast thou there, the cords
That Romeo bid thee fetch?

Nurse   Ay, ay, the cords.   35

Juliet   Ay me, what news? Why dost thou wring thy hands?

Nurse   Ah, welladay! He's dead, he's dead, he's dead!
We are undone, lady, we are undone!
Alack the day, he's gone, he's killed, he's dead.

Juliet   Can heaven be so envious?

Nurse   Romeo can,   40
Though heav'n cannot. O Romeo, Romeo!
Who ever would have thought it? Romeo!

Juliet   What devil art thou that dost torment me thus?
This torture should be roared in dismal hell.

1-4 Gallop apace ... night immediately: Juliet is urging the day to pass quickly using images of Phoebus' (the sun god's) chariot driven by his son, Phaeton

5 close: concealing

6 runaways' eyes may wink: the eyes of those who are still out may not notice

8 do their amorous rites: make love

10 best agrees: is most suited to

10 civil: respectable

11 sober-suited matron: older woman dressed respectably

12 learn me: teach me

12 how to lose a winning match: how to lose my virginity and win my husband

13 a pair of stainless maidenheads: the virginities of Romeo and Juliet

14 Hood my unmanned ... cheeks: hide my blushes (falcon imagery of putting a hood over a young, untrained hawk's head to calm it)

15 black mantle: the darkness of night

15 strange: unfamiliar

16 Think true love ... modesty: see sex between true lovers as respectable

25 garish: vulgar, over-bright

26-8 bought the mansion ... Not yet enjoyed: I'm married in name but not yet a proper wife

33 But: only

33 heavenly eloquence: the most beautiful language

34 the cords: the rope ladder

37 welladay: expression of misery

38 undone: ruined

40 envious: malicious, spiteful

40 Romeo can: the nurse knows he's killed Tybalt

44 this torture: the nurse's rambling

Juliet, listening to the Nurse, summer 2009.

Look closely at the expression on her face. Which part of which of the Nurse's speeches do you think she is listening to? Quote from the text and explain your answer.

Ellie Kendrick

Actor's view

Ellie Kendrick
Juliet, summer 2009

Yes, Juliet really goes through a whirlwind of emotions in this scene. She starts with immense joy, very happy, because she is going to be seeing her husband, and that is really exciting for her. And then she goes from that immense joy to sudden, desperate, sadness because she thinks the Nurse is telling her Romeo is dead. But then the Nurse finally says it, very plainly, after going round the houses. She says, 'Tybalt is gone and Romeo banished,/Romeo that killed him, he is banishèd.' And then for Juliet, her instant first reaction is one of immense shock: 'Did Romeo's hand shed Tybalt's blood?' And I played that as her being really shocked and appalled by that, and then she very interestingly manifests this cognitive dissonance which she is feeling, in her speech that follows, when she uses a series of antitheses – 'Beautiful tyrant, fiend angelical ... Despisèd substance of divinest show!' And she is using lots of opposites which represent the opposites of feeling that she is having – hate and love for Romeo. But it is not until she hears criticism of Romeo in the Nurse's mouth, 'Shame come to Romeo!' that she suddenly realises how wrong she is, and instantly regrets that huge well of anger that she had against him. And she says, 'Blistered be thy tongue/For such a wish!' to the Nurse, and then goes on to realise that Romeo is everything to her, that she would not care if all her family were dead as long as he is still around.

Actor's view

Lorraine Burroughs
Juliet, spring 2009

Why Juliet chooses Romeo's banishment as more important than Tybalt's death is raw emotion. Tybalt is her cousin and she loves him – it's awful what has happened and her first initial reaction is utter disgrace at Romeo for what he has done and she feels completely betrayed of the love she has given him and how she has opened up to him and said that she is going to give her life to him and he has done that to her and her family. She tries to hate him but she can't, she loves him and the fact that he's banished, everything that they have just gone through is ruined, is going to be worthless if she stays angry with Romeo and that's it, over. She has to address this and find him and figure out how she is going to see him again because he now is her life. Tybalt being alive or dead isn't an issue in comparison to her and Romeo, Romeo is her life, without him she is dead.

Hath Romeo slain himself? Say thou but "Ay",   45
And that bare vowel "I" shall poison more
Than the death-darting eye of cockatrice.
I am not I, if there be such an ay.
Or those eyes shut, that make thee answer "Ay."
If he be slain, say "Ay"; or if not, "No."   50
Brief sounds determine of my weal or woe.

Nurse

I saw the wound, I saw it with mine eyes,
God save the mark, here on his manly breast.
A piteous corse, a bloody piteous corse.
Pale, pale as ashes, all bedaubed in blood,   55
All in gore-blood; I swoonèd at the sight.

Juliet

O break my heart, poor bankrupt, break at once!
To prison, eyes, ne'er look on liberty.
Vile earth to earth resign, end motion here.
And thou and Romeo press one heavy bier.   60

Nurse

O Tybalt, Tybalt, the best friend I had.
O courteous Tybalt, honest gentleman,
That ever I should live to see thee dead!

Juliet

What storm is this that blows so contrary?
Is Romeo slaughtered? And is Tybalt dead?   65
My dearest cousin, and my dearer lord?
Then dreadful trumpet sound the general doom,
For who is living, if those two are gone?

Nurse

Tybalt is gone and Romeo banished,
Romeo that killed him, he is banishèd.   70

Juliet

O God! Did Romeo's hand shed Tybalt's blood?

Nurse

It did, it did, alas the day, it did!

Juliet

O serpent heart, hid with a flowering face.
Did ever dragon keep so fair a cave?
Beautiful tyrant, fiend angelical,   75
Ravenous dove-feathered raven! Wolvish-ravening lamb,
Despisèd substance of divinest show!
Just opposite to what thou justly seem'st,
A damnèd saint, an honourable villain.
O nature! What hadst thou to do in hell   80
When thou didst bower the spirit of a fiend
In mortal paradise of such sweet flesh?
Was ever book containing such vile matter
So fairly bound? O that deceit should dwell
In such a gorgeous palace!

Nurse

                  There's no trust,   85
No faith, no honesty in men. All perjured,
All forsworn, all naught, all dissemblers.
Ah, where's my man? Give me some *aqua vitae*!
These griefs, these woes, these sorrows make me old.
Shame come to Romeo!

Juliet

                  Blistered be thy tongue   90
For such a wish! He was not born to shame.

---

45 **Ay:** triple meaning: yes; the pronoun 'I'; sounds like 'eye' (Juliet uses all these in the next few lines)

47 **cockatrice:** a mythical creature whose looks could kill

51 **determine of my weal or woe:** will decide if I am to be happy or miserable

53 **God save the mark:** God forgive me for saying so

54 **piteous corse:** corpse that would fill you with pity

56 **gore-blood:** congealing blood

56 **swoonèd:** fainted

57 **bankrupt:** her heart has lost all it had, as a bankrupt has lost all his money and has to go to prison

59 **Vile earth ... end motion here:** I must die too and be buried in the earth

60 **And thou ... heavy bier:** my body will be carried to the grave with Romeo's

62 **honest:** honourable

64 **so contrary:** in different directions

66 **lord:** husband

67 **dreadful trumpet sound the general doom:** the world has ended, it is the Day of Judgement

73 **serpent:** the serpent that tempted Eve in the Bible story

73 **flowering:** handsome, smiling

74 **keep:** own, live in

76 **Ravenous dove-feathered raven:** greedy raven dressed in a dove's white feathers

76 **Wolvish-ravening lamb:** lamb that behaves like a wolf

77 **Despisèd substance of divinest show:** vile thing that appears so beautiful

78 **justly:** truly, actually

81 **bower the spirit of a fiend:** hide a devil's soul

84 **fairly:** beautifully

86–7 **perjured, forsworn, dissemblers:** liars

88 **man:** servant

88 *aqua vitae:* strong alcoholic drink, like brandy

ECHOING EMOTIONS

- Working in pairs, **A** reads Juliet's lines and **B** acts as Juliet's echo.
- Read the *Working Cut*. The person echoing should listen very closely and repeat any words that are connected to an emotion.

1 Note or highlight the words that were repeated. What do you notice?

- Repeat the activity. This time, **B** reads Juliet's lines and **A** echoes any words that are connected to an action or an decision that needs to be made.

2 Note or highlight the repeated words. What do you notice about this list?

3 Describe Juliet's state of mind in this exchange with the Nurse.

4 How does Juliet feel about Romeo at the end of this scene?

5 Compare Juliet's reaction to Tybalt's death to Romeo's reaction. What do you notice?

Working Cut – text for experiment

Jul
Ah, poor my lord, what tongue shall smooth thy name
When I, thy three-hours wife, have mangled it?
But, wherefore, villain, didst thou kill my cousin?
That villain-cousin would have killed my husband.
Back foolish tears, back to your native spring,
Your tributary drops belong to woe,
Which you mistaking offer up to joy.
My husband lives, that Tybalt would have slain;
And Tybalt's dead, that would have slain my husband.
All this is comfort, wherefore weep I then?
Some word there was, worser than Tybalt's death,
That murdered me. I would forget it fain,
But O, it presses to my memory
Like damnèd guilty deeds to sinners' minds.
"Tybalt is dead, and Romeo banishèd",
That "banishèd", that one word "banishèd",
Hath slain ten thousand Tybalts. Tybalt's death
Was woe enough if it had ended there.
Or if sour woe delights in fellowship
Why followed not, when she said "Tybalt's dead",
Thy father or thy mother, nay, or both,
Which modern lamentations might have moved?
But with a rear-ward following Tybalt's death,
"Romeo is banishèd". To speak that word
Is father, mother, Tybalt, Romeo, Juliet,
All slain, all dead. "Romeo is banishèd!"
There is no end, no limit, measure, bound,
In that word's death. No words can that woe sound.

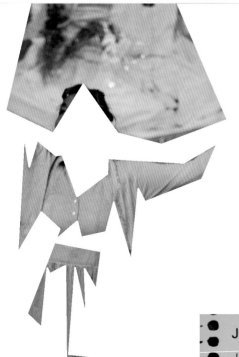

Director's Note, 3.2

✔ Juliet longs for night and the arrival of Romeo.
✔ The Nurse arrives, grieving for Tybalt's death.
✔ At first Juliet is confused, and fears Romeo is dead.
✔ When she understands Romeo is banished, she despairs for her marriage.
✔ The Nurse goes to make arrangements for Juliet and Romeo to spend the night together.

Juliet, spring 2009.

Juliet goes through a range of emotions in this scene. Looking at the whole of the scene, from page 75, during which part of the scene do you think this photo was taken? Quote from the text to support your answer.

Lorraine Burroughs

	Upon his brow shame is ashamed to sit;		
	For 'tis a throne where honour may be crowned		
	Sole monarch of the universal earth.		**94 Sole monarch:** absolute ruler
	O what a beast was I to chide at him!	95	**95 chide at him:** speak badly of him
Nurse	Will you speak well of him that killed your cousin?		
Juliet	Shall I speak ill of him that is my husband?		
	Ah, poor my lord, what tongue shall smooth thy name		**98 smooth thy name:** restore your reputation
	When I, thy three-hours wife, have mangled it?		
	But, wherefore, villain, didst thou kill my cousin?	100	**100 wherefore:** why
	That villain-cousin would have killed my husband.		
	Back foolish tears, back to your native spring,		**102 native spring:** source, her eyes
	Your tributary drops belong to woe,		**103 tributary drops:** tears
	Which you mistaking offer up to joy.		
	My husband lives, that Tybalt would have slain;	105	
	And Tybalt's dead, that would have slain my husband.		
	All this is comfort, wherefore weep I then?		
	Some word there was, worser than Tybalt's death,		
	That murdered me. I would forget it fain,		**109 forget it fain:** gladly forget it
	But O, it presses to my memory	110	
	Like damnèd guilty deeds to sinners' minds.		
	"Tybalt is dead, and Romeo banished",		
	That "banishèd", that one word "banishèd",		
	Hath slain ten thousand Tybalts. Tybalt's death		
	Was woe enough if it had ended there.	115	
	Or if sour woe delights in fellowship		**116 sour woe delights in fellowship:** misery loves company
	And needly will be ranked with other griefs,		**117 needly will be ranked:** must be part of
	Why followed not, when she said "Tybalt's dead",		**118 she:** the nurse
	Thy father or thy mother, nay, or both,		**120 modern lamentations might have moved:** would just have caused normal, ordinary grief
	Which modern lamentations might have moved?	120	
	But with a rear-ward following Tybalt's death,		
	"Romeo is banishèd". To speak that word		
	Is father, mother, Tybalt, Romeo, Juliet,		
	All slain, all dead. "Romeo is banishèd!"		
	There is no end, no limit, measure, bound,	125	
	In that word's death. No words can that woe sound.		**126 that word's death:** the death that word brings
	Where is my father and my mother, Nurse?		**126 sound:** measure
Nurse	Weeping and wailing over Tybalt's corse.		
	Will you go to them? I will bring you thither.		
Juliet	Wash they his wounds with tears, mine shall be spent,	130	**130 spent:** shed
	When theirs are dry, for Romeo's banishment.		
	Take up those cords. Poor ropes, you are beguiled,		**132 beguiled:** cheated
	Both you and I, for Romeo is exiled.		
	He made you for a highway to my bed,		
	But I, a maid, die maiden-widowèd.	135	**135 maid:** virgin
	Come cords, come nurse, I'll to my wedding-bed,		**135 maiden-widowèd:** a virgin and a widow
	And death, not Romeo, take my maidenhead.		**137 maidenhead:** virginity
Nurse	Hie to your chamber. I'll find Romeo		**138 Hie:** go straight
	To comfort you, I wot well where he is.		**139 wot:** know
	Hark ye, your Romeo will be here at night.	140	
	I'll to him, he is hid at Lawrence' cell.		
Juliet	O find him! Give this ring to my true knight,		
	And bid him come to take his last farewell. *Exit both.*		

Friar Lawrence and Romeo, spring 2009.

This production is set in modern dress and the graffiti on the back wall of the stage suggests a modern urban setting.

1 What are the director and designer suggesting by the use of flowers on the pillar?

2 Do you think this is appropriate for this play?

Colin Hurley, James Alexandrou

ACT 3 SCENE 3

Enter Friar Lawrence.

Lawrence	Romeo, come forth, come forth thou fearful man.
	Affliction is enamoured of thy parts,
	And thou art wedded to calamity. *[Enter Romeo.]*
Romeo	Father, what news? What is the Prince's doom?
	What sorrow craves acquaintance at my hand
	That I yet know not?
Friar Lawrence	Too familiar
	Is my dear son with such sour company.
	I bring thee tidings of the Prince's doom.
Romeo	What less than doomsday is the Prince's doom?
Friar Lawrence	A gentler judgement vanished from his lips,
	Not body's death, but body's banishment.
Romeo	Ha, banishment? Be merciful, say "death".
	For exile hath more terror in his look,
	Much more than death. Do not say "banishment."
Friar Lawrence	Hence from Verona art thou banishèd.
	Be patient, for the world is broad and wide.
Romeo	There is no world without Verona walls
	But purgatory, torture, hell itself.
	Hence "banishèd" is banished from the world,
	And world's exile is death. Then banishèd
	Is death mistermed. Calling death "banishèd,"
	Thou cutt'st my head off with a golden axe
	And smil'st upon the stroke that murders me.
Friar Lawrence	O deadly sin, O rude unthankfulness!
	Thy fault our law calls death, but the kind Prince,
	Taking thy part, hath rushed aside the law,
	And turned that black word "death" to "banishment."
	This is dear mercy, and thou seest it not.
Romeo	'Tis torture, and not mercy. Heav'n is here
	Where Juliet lives, and every cat and dog
	And little mouse, every unworthy thing,
	Live here in heaven and may look on her,
	But Romeo may not. More validity,
	More honourable state, more courtship lives
	In carrion-flies than Romeo. They may seize
	On the white wonder of dear Juliet's hand
	And steal immortal blessing from her lips,
	Who even in pure and vestal modesty,
	Still blush, as thinking their own kisses sin.
	But Romeo may not, he is banishèd.
	This may flies do, when I from this must fly.
	They are free men, but I am banishèd.
	And say'st thou yet that exile is not death?
	Hadst thou no poison mixed, no sharp-ground knife,
	No sudden mean of death, though ne'er so mean,

Line numbers: 5, 10, 15, 20, 25, 30, 35, 40, 45

1 **fearful:** frightened
2 **Affliction is enamoured of thy parts:** misery is attracted to you
3 **calamity:** disaster
4 **doom:** judgement
5 **craves acquaintance at my hand:** is waiting to be introduced
6–7 **Too familiar Is my dear son … company:** you are miserable enough as it is
8 **tidings:** news
9 **doomsday:** the Day of Judgement (death)
10 **vanished:** came
17 **without Verona walls:** outside Verona
18 **But:** except
18 **purgatory:** where Catholics believe the souls of the dead suffered for sin before being allowed into Heaven
19 **Hence "banishèd":** to be banished from Verona
20 **world's exile:** to be exiled from the world
21 **mistermed:** under the wrong name
24 **O deadly sin, O rude unthankfulness!:** such ingratitude in wishing for death will damn your soul to Hell
25 **Thy fault our law calls death:** the punishment for your crime is death
26 **rushed:** forced
28 **dear:** a valuable
33 **validity:** value
34 **honourable state:** respect
34 **courtship:** double meaning: the chance to woo; gentlemanly behaviour
34–5 **lives In carrion-flies:** is possible for flies that live on rotting flesh
38 **vestal:** virginal
43 **say'st thou yet:** do you still say
44 **Hadst thou no:** haven't you any
45 **No sudden mean of death:** any quick way to kill myself
45 **though ne'er so mean:** no matter how unpleasant

Romeo and Friar Lawrence, 2004.

Pick one of the following three lines, which you think Romeo is most likely to have been saying when this photo was taken. Give reasons for your answer.

a) But "banishèd" to kill me? "Banishèd"? (line 46)

b) It helps not, it prevails not. Talk no more. (line 60)

c) Mist-like, enfold me from the search of eyes. (line 74)

Tom Burke, John McEnery

	But "banishèd" to kill me? "Banishèd"?	
	O Friar, the damnèd use that word in hell.	
	Howlings attend it. How hast thou the heart,	
	Being a divine, a ghostly confessor,	
	A sin-absolver, and my friend professed,	50
	To mangle me with that word "banishèd"?	
Friar Lawrence	Thou fond mad man, hear me a little speak.	
Romeo	O thou wilt speak again of banishment.	
Friar Lawrence	I'll give thee armour to keep off that word,	
	Adversity's sweet milk, philosophy,	55
	To comfort thee, though thou art banishèd.	
Romeo	Yet "banishèd"? Hang up philosophy,	
	Unless philosophy can make a Juliet,	
	Displant a town, reverse a prince's doom,	
	It helps not, it prevails not. Talk no more.	60
Friar Lawrence	O then I see that mad men have no ears.	
Romeo	How should they, when that wise men have no eyes?	
Friar Lawrence	Let me dispute with thee of thy estate.	
Romeo	Thou canst not speak of that thou dost not feel.	
	Wert thou as young as I, Juliet thy love,	65
	An hour but married, Tybalt murderèd,	
	Doting like me and like me banishèd.	
	Then mightst thou speak.	
	Then mightst thou tear thy hair,	
	And fall upon the ground, as I do now,	70
	Taking the measure of an unmade grave.	

Knocking within.

Friar Lawrence	Arise, one knocks, good Romeo, hide thyself.	
Romeo	Not I, unless the breath of heartsick groans,	
	Mist-like, enfold me from the search of eyes. *Knocking.*	
Friar Lawrence	Hark, how they knock! — Who's there?— Romeo, arise!	75
	Thou wilt be taken. — Stay awhile! — Stand up.	

Knocking.

	Run to my study. — By and by! — God's will,	
	What simpleness is this? — I come, I come! *Knocking.*	
	Who knocks so hard?	
	Whence come you? What's your will?	80
Nurse	*[Within.]* Let me come in, and you shall know my	
	errand.	
	I come from Lady Juliet.	
Friar Lawrence	Welcome then. *Enter Nurse.*	
Nurse	O holy Friar, O tell me holy Friar,	
	Where is my lady's lord? Where's Romeo?	85
Friar Lawrence	There on the ground, with his own tears made drunk.	
Nurse	O, he is even in my mistress' case,	

Glosses:

48 **Howlings attend it:** they howl as they do so
49 **divine:** churchman
49 **ghostly:** spiritual
50 **my friend professed:** someone who says he's my friend
51 **mangle me:** mutilate me
52 **fond:** foolish
55 **Adversity's sweet milk, philosophy:** the best addition to trouble: the ability to think through the problem and accept it
57 **Yet:** still
57 **Hang up:** put away
59 **Displant:** move
60 **it prevails not:** it doesn't convince me
62 **when that:** when
63 **Let me dispute with thee of thy estate:** let's discuss your situation
66 **An hour but married:** only married an hour ago
67 **Doting:** deeply in love
71 **Taking the measure of:** measuring out
72 **one:** someone
73–4 **the breath of heartsick groans ... search of eyes:** my groaning makes a mist that hides me from sight
76 **taken:** arrested
76 **Stay awhile!:** wait a minute (to the person knocking)
77 **By and by!:** I'm on my way (to the person knocking)
78 **simpleness:** stupidity
80 **What's your will?:** what do you want?
87 **even in my mistress' case:** in the same state as my mistress

83

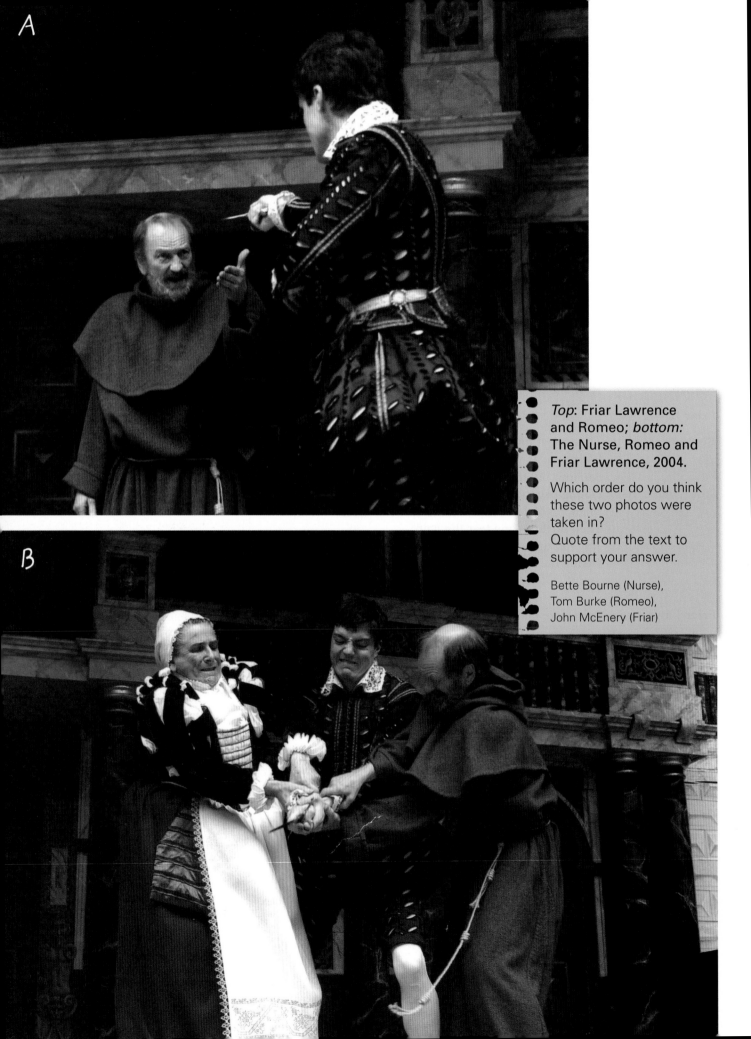

A

B

Top: Friar Lawrence and Romeo; *bottom:* The Nurse, Romeo and Friar Lawrence, 2004.

Which order do you think these two photos were taken in?
Quote from the text to support your answer.

Bette Bourne (Nurse),
Tom Burke (Romeo),
John McEnery (Friar)

Just in her case. O woeful sympathy!
Piteous predicament! Even so lies she,
Blubbering and weeping, weeping and blubbering. 90
Stand up, stand up, stand and you be a man:
For Juliet's sake, for her sake, rise and stand.
Why should you fall into so deep an O?

Romeo   Nurse.

Nurse   Ah sir, ah sir, death's the end of all.

Romeo   Speak'st thou of Juliet? How is it with her? 95
Doth she not think me an old murderer,
Now I have stained the childhood of our joy
With blood removed but little from her own?
Where is she? And how doth she? And what says
My concealed lady to our cancelled love? 100

Nurse   O, she says nothing, sir, but weeps and weeps,
And now falls on her bed, and then starts up,
And Tybalt calls, and then on Romeo cries,
And then down falls again.

Romeo   As if that name,
Shot from the deadly level of a gun, 105
Did murder her; as that name's cursed hand
Murdered her kinsman. O tell me, Friar, tell me,
In what vile part of this anatomy
Doth my name lodge? Tell me, that I may sack
The hateful mansion.   *[Drawing his dagger.]*

Friar Lawrence   Hold thy desperate hand. 110
Art thou a man? Thy form cries out thou art.
Thy tears are womanish, thy wild acts denote
The unreasonable fury of a beast.
Unseemly woman in a seeming man,
And ill-beseeming beast in seeming both, 115
Thou hast amazed me. By my holy order,
I thought thy disposition better tempered.
Hast thou slain Tybalt? Wilt thou slay thyself?
And slay thy lady that in thy life lies,
By doing damnèd hate upon thyself? 120
Why rail'st thou on thy birth, the heav'n and earth?
Since birth, and heav'n, and earth, all three do meet
In thee at once, which thou at once wouldst lose.
Fie, fie, thou sham'st thy shape, thy love, thy wit,
Which like a usurer abound'st in all. 125
And usest none in that true use indeed
Which should bedeck thy shape, thy love, thy wit.
Thy noble shape is but a form of wax,
Digressing from the valour of a man,
Thy dear love sworn but hollow perjury, 130
Killing that love which thou hast vowed to cherish.
Thy wit, that ornament to shape and love,
Misshapen in the conduct of them both,
Like powder in a skilless soldier's flask,
Is set afire by thine own ignorance, 135

88 **woeful sympathy:** how alike in misery
89 **Piteous predicament:** you pity their situation
91 **and you be:** if you are

93 **so deep an O:** such wailing

96 **old:** clever, skilful
97 **the childhood of our joy:** our newly-made relationship
98 **removed … her own:** of a close relative
100 **My concealed lady:** my secret wife
100 **cancelled:** ended, removed
103 **on Romeo cries:** calls out for Romeo
104 **that name:** Romeo
105 **level:** aim
108 **this anatomy:** my body
109 **lodge:** live
109–10 **sack … mansion:** destroy its home
111 **Thy form cries out thou art:** you look like one
112 **denote:** show
113 **unreasonable:** not thought through
114–5 **Unseemly woman … seeming both:** your womanish behaviour isn't right for the man you appear to be; your animal behaviour suits neither man nor woman
117 **disposition:** character, nature
119 **thy lady that in thy life lies:** your wife whose life depends on yours
120 **doing damnèd hate upon thyself:** committing suicide (which Catholics at the time believed damned you to Hell)
121 **rail'st thou on:** do you abuse
121 **heav'n and earth:** your soul and body
123 **at once wouldst lose:** now want to destroy
124 **thy shape:** your body
124 **thy wit:** your intelligence
125–7 **like a usurer … thy wit:** like a money-lender with money, you have so much of and aren't using properly
128–9 **form of wax … of a man:** not a living, thinking man capable of bravery
130 **Thy dear love … perjury:** the love you have sworn is nothing but lies
133 **Misshapen … them both:** is thinking wrongly about killing both of them

85

SHAKESPEARE'S WORLD

Clandestine marriage

Romeo and Juliet's marriage ceremony was *clandestine* because they married secretly, and without going through the proper procedures. Since they were both under twenty-one, they needed their parents' consent to marry. Romeo, Juliet and Friar Lawrence all put themselves at risk by this secret marriage. All of them had broken the law. Courts wanted to make sure that all marriages were legal, so they punished priests who performed weddings under irregular circumstances. Other people, including the parents, could challenge a marriage that they did not think was lawful, and have it declared void. All three could be forced to pay a fine or serve public penance for their actions.

Here, Friar Lawrence encourages Romeo to go to Juliet before he leaves Verona for exile. This gives them an opportunity to consummate their marriage. Once a marriage was consummated, the courts were much less likely to declare it void. By encouraging Romeo to consummate his marriage, Friar Lawrence tries to prevent the courts from acting against it.

Actor's view

Colin Hurley
Friar Lawrence, spring 2009

So, what's actually happened is he's killed someone and he is in hiding at my place. I've gone out to find out what the word on the street is, come back, call him out:

'come forth, come forth, thou fearful man.'

And then I tell him that there's good news and there's bad news. Strictly speaking, he should be killed of course, because that's what the Prince said but he says 'No, no, you're going to be banished' so, that's a good thing. Romeo, being a young man in love and a bit on the melodramatic side, goes on about it being torture not mercy. I have to talk him out of his despair, with a lot of talk of his unthankfulness being a sin. I mean we kind of had a bit of a spat. I love that:

'[Friar] O then I see that mad men have no ears.

[Romeo] How should they, when that wise men have no eyes?

[Friar] Let me dispute with thee of thy estate.

[Romeo] Thou canst not speak of that thou dost not feel.'

and I found that very interesting. That this young guy goes 'What do you know about where I am emotionally? How would you know? You're an old bloke, you're fiddling about with your flowers and your herbs, you're a virgin, and you try to tell me' and so he is. I find that with youth now, they can say 'You don't understand, there's no way you understand.' And it's sort of true and it sort of isn't.

FROM THE REHEARSAL ROOM...

ROMEO'S REACTION TO THE NEWS

This activity is part of a pair with the one about Juliet's reaction to the news on page 78. Both activities have the same structure, and you should think about your answers to the questions about Juliet before answering Question 5.

- Working in small groups, take one of the sections below and decide who will read each part. Some of you will be 'echoers'.
- The sections are lines 1–23, 24–51, 52–71, 72–92, 93–109, 109–159 and 160–176.
- Read your section. The echoers should listen very closely and repeat any words that are connected to an emotion.

1 Note or highlight the words that were repeated. What do you notice?

- Repeat the activity. This time the echoers repeat any words that are connected to an action or a decision that needs to be made.

2 Note down or highlight the repeated words. What do you notice about this list?

- Go through the sections in order as a class, building up a whole class list of the two sets of words.

3 Describe Romeo's state of mind in this exchange with Friar Lawrence and the Nurse.

4 How does Romeo feel about Juliet and the situation at the end of this scene?

5 Compare Romeo's reaction in this scene to Juliet's reaction. What do you notice?

Director's Note, 3.3

✔ Friar Lawrence tells Romeo his punishment is banishment, not death.

✔ Romeo insists banishment from Juliet is worse than death. He falls to the ground, weeping.

✔ The Nurse arrives, saying Juliet is in a similar state.

✔ Romeo fears Juliet must hate him for killing Tybalt, and tries to stab himself, but is stopped by the Friar (and, perhaps, the Nurse).

✔ The Friar sends Romeo to spend the night with Juliet, telling him he must go to Mantua before daybreak.

✔ Does Shakespeare show Romeo acting like a teenager in love?

And thou dismembered with thine own defence.
What, rouse thee man, thy Juliet is alive,
For whose dear sake thou wast but lately dead.
There art thou happy. Tybalt would kill thee,
But thou slew'st Tybalt. There art thou happy
The law that threatened death becomes thy friend
And turns it to exile. There art thou happy.
A pack of blessings light upon thy back,
Happiness courts thee in her best array,
But like a mishavèd and sullen wench,
Thou pouts upon thy fortune and thy love.
Take heed, take heed, for such die miserable.
Go get thee to thy love as was decreed,
Ascend her chamber, hence and comfort her.
But look thou stay not till the watch be set,
For then thou canst not pass to Mantua,
Where thou shalt live, till we can find a time
To blaze your marriage, reconcile your friends,
Beg pardon of the Prince, and call thee back
With twenty hundred thousand times more joy
Than thou went'st forth in lamentation.
Go before nurse, commend me to thy lady,
And bid her hasten all the house to bed,
Which heavy sorrow makes them apt unto.
Romeo is coming.

Nurse O Lord, I could have stayed here all the night
To hear good counsel. O what learning is!
— My lord, I'll tell my lady you will come.

Romeo Do so, and bid my sweet prepare to chide.

Nurse Here sir, a ring she bid me give you sir.
Hie you, make haste, for it grows very late. *Exit Nurse.*

Romeo How well my comfort is revived by this,

Friar Lawrence Go hence, good night, and here stands all your state:
Either be gone before the watch be set,
Or by the break of day disguised from hence.
Sojourn in Mantua, I'll find out your man,
And he shall signify from time to time
Every good hap to you that chances here.
Give me thy hand, 'tis late. Farewell, good night.

Romeo But that a joy past joy calls out on me,
It were a grief so brief to part with thee.
Farewell. *They exit.*

ACT 3 SCENE 4

Enter Capulet, Lady Capulet, and Paris.

Capulet Things have fallen out, sir, so unluckily,
That we have had no time to move our daughter.
Look you, she loved her kinsman Tybalt dearly,
And so did I. Well, we were born to die.
'Tis very late, she'll not come down to-night.

136 dismembered with thine own defence: blown apart by the thing meant to protect you
138 but lately dead: trying to kill yourself over
139 happy: fortunate
143 light: land
144 array: clothes and jewels
145 mishavèd: badly behaved
145 sullen wench: sulky girl
147 such: people who behave like that
148 as was decreed: as you planned
150 look: make sure that
150 till the watch be set: until the watchmen go on guard at night
151 pass: go out of the city gates
153 blaze: tell everyone about
153 reconcile your friends: get your families to accept it
156 lamentation: sorrow
157 before: ahead
159 apt unto: likely to do
164 chide: tell me I should not have killed Tybalt
168 here stands all your state: your future depends on your remembering this
170 disguised from hence: leave well disguised
171 Sojourn: stay for a while
172 signify: bring you news
173 good hap to you that chances here: everything that's happening in Verona
175 calls out on me: calls me away
176 It were a grief ... part with thee: I'd be sorry to leave you in such a hurry
1 fallen out: turned out
2 to move: to persuade

SHAKESPEARE'S WORLD

Arranged marriages

Most marriages, especially in wealthy and important families, were arranged by the couple's parents. They tried to match social status and age. In church, the couple had to agree to marry, but the pressure for them to accept a marriage arranged by their parents was great. Both Romeo and Juliet came from such families. Arranged marriages let the parents make the most advantageous matches. At the time, marriages were only legal if conducted by the Church. The Church taught children to obey their parents, even in choice of husband or wife. However, in practice, parents tried to chose someone their child liked and was happy to marry. If a young person fell in love with someone suitable, their parents might well try to arrange the marriage their child wanted. Certainly many children might feel they had the right to refuse at least one suggested partner that they disliked. Some people would have sympathised with Juliet in this scene. Her father's behaviour would seem extreme, even at a time when parents arranged marriages.

Director's Note, 3.4

- ✔ Capulet suddenly changes his mind, and tells Paris he can marry Juliet in three days' time.
- ✔ Capulet says it will be a quiet wedding because of the death of Tybalt.
- ✔ He tells his wife to prepare Juliet.
- ✔ How has Capulet changed since Act 1 Scene 2?

Left: Juliet and Romeo, 2004.

Kananu Kirimi, Tom Burke

Right: Juliet and Romeo (in the audience), spring 2009.

Lorraine Burroughs, James Alexandrou

Photos A and B, and C (page 90), are from different productions. They show moments during the first 59 lines of this scene. Pick one or two lines that you think were being spoken when each photo was taken, and give reasons for your choice.

A

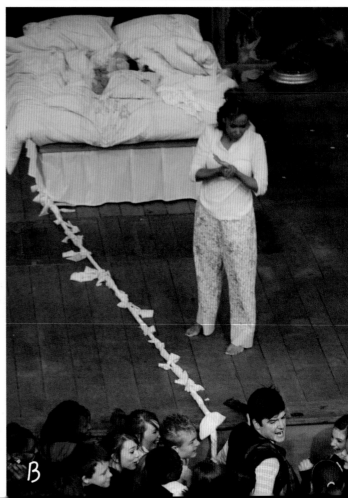

B

	I promise you, but for your company,
	I would have been a-bed an hour ago.
Paris	These times of woe afford no time to woo.
	Madam, good night, commend me to your daughter.
Lady Capulet	I will, and know her mind early tomorrow,
	To-night she is mewed up to her heaviness.
Capulet	Sir Paris, I will make a desperate tender
	Of my child's love. I think she will be ruled
	In all respects by me. Nay, more, I doubt it not.
	Wife, go you to her ere you go to bed,
	Acquaint her here of my son Paris' love,
	And bid her, mark you me, on Wednesday next —
	But soft, what day is this?
Paris	Monday, my lord.
Capulet	Monday! Ha, Ha! Well, Wednesday is too soon,
	O' Thursday let it be. O' Thursday, tell her,
	She shall be married to this noble earl.
	Will you be ready? Do you like this haste?
	We'll keep no great ado, a friend or two,
	For hark you, Tybalt being slain so late,
	It may be thought we held him carelessly,
	Being our kinsman, if we revel much.
	Therefore we'll have some half a dozen friends,
	And there an end. But what say you to Thursday?
Paris	My lord, I would that Thursday were tomorrow.
Capulet	Well, get you gone, o' Thursday be it, then.
	— Go you to Juliet ere you go to bed,
	Prepare her wife, against this wedding day.
	— Farewell, my lord. — Light to my chamber, ho!
	Afore me, it is so very late, that we
	May call it early by and by. Good night. *They exit.*

Line numbers: 10, 15, 20, 25, 30, 35

Glossary:
- 8 **afford:** give
- 10 **know her mind:** I'll make her decide
- 11 **mewed up to her heaviness:** shut up in her misery
- 12 **desperate tender:** bold offer
- 15 **ere:** before
- 16 **son:** Capulet has accepted the marriage, so already treats Paris as his son-in-law
- 17 **bid her:** tell her
- 17 **mark you me:** listen carefully now
- 18 **soft:** wait a minute
- 24 **We'll keep no great ado:** we won't have a big fussy wedding
- 25 **hark you:** listen
- 25 **so late:** so recently
- 26-7 **held him carelessly ... revel much:** a big celebration may look as if we didn't care about his death, even though he's family
- 29 **And there an end:** no more
- 30 **I would:** I wish
- 33 **against:** for
- 35 **Afore me:** double meaning: an exclamation (e.g. well, well); an instruction to the servant to go in front with the light
- 36 **by and by:** soon

ACT 3 SCENE 5

Enter Romeo and Juliet aloft.

Juliet	Wilt thou be gone? It is not yet near day.
	It was the nightingale, and not the lark,
	That pierced the fearful hollow of thine ear,
	Nightly she sings on yon pomegranate tree.
	Believe me, love, it was the nightingale.
Romeo	It was the lark, the herald of the morn,
	No nightingale. Look, love, what envious streaks
	Do lace the severing clouds in yonder east.
	Night's candles are burnt out, and jocund day
	Stands tiptoe on the misty mountain tops.
	I must be gone and live, or stay and die.
Juliet	Yond light is not daylight, I know it, I.
	It is some meteor that the sun exhales
	To be to thee this night a torch-bearer
	And light thee on thy way to Mantua.

Line numbers: 5, 10, 15

Glossary:
- 2 **nightingale/lark:** nightingales sing in the evening, larks sing at dawn
- 3 **fearful:** frightened
- 7-8 **what envious streaks ... yonder east:** dawn is coming, making the clouds pink, envious of our love
- 9 **Night's candles:** the stars
- 9 **jocund:** cheerful
- 13 **exhales:** breathes out

Romeo and Juliet, summer 2009.

1 If you were directing this scene in a theatre like the Globe, how would you stage it? Explain your answer.

2 If you were directing this scene in a film, how would you do it differently?

Adetomiwa Edun, Ellie Kendrick

FROM THE REHEARSAL ROOM...

TACTICS

- In pairs, label yourselves **A** and **B**.
- In this short activity, **A** must say to **B** 'Go'. **B** can only reply 'Peace'.
- **A**, say your word in as many different ways and tones of voice as possible to make **B** do what you want.
- **B**, find as many different ways as you can to refuse.

1 List the different tactics that both **A** and **B** used as verbs; e.g. pleaded, charmed.

- **A**, this time you can say either 'Stay' or 'Go'. **B**, you can still just say 'Peace'.
- Repeat the activity, with **A** changing the word some of the time.
- Now, read the *Working Cut* several times using the different tactics and reactions you have just developed.

2 In what way was the activity you did before the *Working Cut* similar to the dialogue between Juliet and Romeo?

3 What makes Juliet change her mind? Quote from the text to support your answer.

Working Cut – text for experiment

Jul	Wilt thou be gone? It is not yet near day.
Rom	I must be gone and live, or stay and die.
Jul	Yond light is not daylight, I know it, I.
	Therefore stay yet, thou need'st not to be gone.
Rom	Let me be ta'en, let me be put to death,
	I am content, so thou wilt have it so.
	Come death and welcome, Juliet wills it so.
	How is't, my soul? Let's talk, it is not day.
Jul	It is, it is, hie hence, be gone, away.
	O now be gone, more light and light it grows.
	Enter Nurse.
Nur	Madam!
Jul	Nurse?
Nur	Your lady mother is coming to your chamber.
	The day is broke, be wary, look about. *[She exits.]*
Jul	Then window let day in, and let life out.
Rom	Farewell, farewell. One kiss and I'll descend.
	He climbs down.
Jul	Art thou gone so?
Rom	Farewell.

Therefore stay yet, thou need'st not to be gone.

Romeo   Let me be ta'en, let me be put to death,
I am content, so thou wilt have it so.
I'll say yon grey is not the morning's eye,
'Tis but the pale reflex of Cynthia's brow.   20
Nor that is not the lark whose notes do beat
The vaulty heaven so high above our heads.
I have more care to stay than will to go.
Come death and welcome, Juliet wills it so.
How is't, my soul? Let's talk, it is not day.   25

Juliet   It is, it is, hie hence, be gone, away.
It is the lark that sings so out of tune,
Straining harsh discords and unpleasing sharps.
Some say the lark makes sweet division.
This doth not so, for she divideth us.   30
Some say the lark and loathèd toad change eyes,
O now I would they had changed voices too,
Since arm from arm that voice doth us affray,
Hunting thee hence with hunt's-up to the day.
O now be gone, more light and light it grows.   35

Romeo   More light and light, more dark and dark our woes!

Enter Nurse.

Nurse   Madam!

Juliet   Nurse?

Nurse   Your lady mother is coming to your chamber.
The day is broke, be wary, look about.   *[She exits.]*   40

Juliet   Then window let day in, and let life out.

Romeo   Farewell, farewell. One kiss and I'll descend.

He climbs down.

Juliet   Art thou gone so? Love, lord, ay husband, friend,
I must hear from thee every day in the hour,
For in a minute there are many days.   45
O by this count I shall be much in years
Ere I again behold my Romeo!

Romeo   Farewell.
I will omit no opportunity
That may convey my greetings, love, to thee.   50

Juliet   O think'st thou we shall ever meet again?

Romeo   I doubt it not, and all these woes shall serve
For sweet discourses in our time to come.

Juliet   O God! I have an ill-divining soul.
Methinks I see thee now, thou art so low,   55
As one dead in the bottom of a tomb.
Either my eyesight fails, or thou look'st pale.

Romeo   And trust me love, in my eye so do you.
Dry sorrow drinks our blood. Adieu, adieu.   *Exit.*

17 **ta'en:** taken, arrested
18 **so thou wilt have it so:** if that is what you want
20 **reflex of Cynthia's brow:** the reflection of the moon goddess's face (Cynthia was another name for Diana, moon goddess)
21 **Nor that is not:** and that is not
22 **vaulty:** dome-like
23 **care:** desire

26 **hie hence:** hurry away from here

28 **sharps:** sharp musical notes
29 **sweet division:** a quick run of musical notes
30 **This doth not so:** I don't think so
31 **change:** exchange (from a folk tale told to explain why toads have more beautiful eyes than larks)
33 **arm from arm ... affray:** the lark's voice sends us from each other's arms in fear
34 **hunt's-up:** a song to wake hunters

40 **wary:** cautious

46 **count:** way of adding up
46 **much in years:** very old

50 **convey:** bring
52–3 **all these woes ... time to come:** we'll talk about these sorrows in the future
54 **I have an ill-divining soul:** I feel in my soul that bad things are going to happen

55 **so low:** so far down (the ladder)

59 **Dry:** thirsty

JULIET AND LADY CAPULET

- In pairs, read the *Working Cut*. One person reads Lady Capulet, and the other Juliet.

- As you read each line, repeat the last word before continuing.

1 By repeating the last word of every line, what do you notice about Juliet's responses?

- Read the extract again, but this time when Juliet refers directly to her mother – point at her.

- When Juliet speaks about Romeo or any outside force – point away from Lady Capulet.

- If Juliet speaks directly to the audience – point to the same spot each time as if the audience is present.

- Make sure that you really do point at a definite person or place.

2 Where is Juliet pointing to the most?

3 How often is Juliet deceiving her mother, saying something she means in one way, but which her mother understands differently? Quote and explain examples.

4 Explain the techniques used by Shakespeare to encourage the audience to sympathise with Juliet.

SHAKESPEARE'S WORLD
◇◇◇◇◇◇◇◇◇◇◇◇

Asides

Asides are common in Shakespeare's plays. When a character speaks, and some or all of the characters on stage can't hear, it is an aside. In this scene, when Juliet is talking to herself and her mother cannot hear, it is an aside. She is sharing her thoughts with the audience. This is an important part of Shakespeare's craft as a playwright. When a character speaks alone onstage, we call it a soliloquy. Shakespeare uses asides and soliloquies to tell us what a character is really thinking. When Romeo sees Juliet on the balcony, he asks the audience if he should speak to her. Here Juliet tells us how much she loves Romeo, even while Lady Capulet is plotting to kill him. In the original playhouse, as in today's Globe, nobody in the audience was very far from the stage. This means that asides and soliloquies are intimate moments, shared between the character and the audience.

Working Cut – text for experiment

Lady C	Why how now, Juliet?
Jul	Madam, I am not well.
Lady C	Evermore weeping for your cousin's death?
Jul	Yet let me weep, for such a feeling loss.
Lady C	So shall you feel the loss, but not the friend Which you weep for.
Jul	Feeling so the loss, Cannot choose but ever weep the friend.
Lady C	Well, girl, thou weep'st not so much for his death, As that the villain lives which slaughtered him.
Jul	What villain, madam?
Lady C	That same villain, Romeo.
Jul	*[Aside.]* Villain and he be many miles asunder. – God pardon him! I do, with all my heart, And yet no man like he doth grieve my heart.
Lady C	That is because the traitor murderer lives.
Jul	Ay, madam, from the reach of these my hands.
Lady C	We will have vengeance for it, fear thou not. Then weep no more, I'll send to one in Mantua, Shall give him such an unaccustomed dram, That he shall soon keep Tybalt company. And then I hope thou wilt be satisfied.
Jul	*[Aside.]* Indeed I never shall be satisfied With Romeo till I behold him, dead Is my poor heart so, for a kinsman vex'd? Madam, if you could find out but a man To bear a poison, I would temper it, That Romeo should, upon receipt thereof, Soon sleep in quiet. O, how my heart abhors To hear him named, and cannot come to him. To wreak the love I bore my cousin Upon his body that slaughtered him.
Lady C	Find thou the means, and I'll find such a man. But now I'll tell thee joyful tidings, girl.
Jul	What are they, I beseech your ladyship?
Lady C	Marry my child, early next Thursday morn, The gallant, young and noble gentleman, The County Paris, at Saint Peter's Church, Shall happily make thee there a joyful bride.
Jul	He shall not make me there a joyful bride.

Juliet	O Fortune, Fortune, all men call thee fickle.	60
	If thou art fickle, what dost thou with him	
	That is renowned for faith? Be fickle, Fortune,	
	For then I hope thou wilt not keep him long,	
	But send him back. *Enter Lady Capulet.*	
Lady Capulet	Ho daughter, are you up?	
Juliet	Who is't that calls? It is my lady mother.	65
	Is she not down so late, or up so early?	
	What unaccustomed cause procures her hither?	
Lady Capulet	Why how now, Juliet?	
Juliet	Madam, I am not well.	
Lady Capulet	Evermore weeping for your cousin's death?	
	What, wilt thou wash him from his grave with tears?	70
	An if thou couldst, thou couldst not make him live.	
	Therefore have done. Some grief shows much of love,	
	But much of grief, shows still some want of wit.	
Juliet	Yet let me weep, for such a feeling loss.	
Lady Capulet	So shall you feel the loss, but not the friend	75
	Which you weep for.	
Juliet	Feeling so the loss,	
	Cannot choose but ever weep the friend.	
Lady Capulet	Well, girl, thou weep'st not so much for his death,	
	As that the villain lives which slaughtered him.	
Juliet	What villain, madam?	
Lady Capulet	That same villain, Romeo.	80
Juliet	*[Aside.]* Villain and he be many miles asunder. —	
	God pardon him! I do, with all my heart,	
	And yet no man like he doth grieve my heart.	
Lady Capulet	That is because the traitor murderer lives.	
Juliet	Ay, madam, from the reach of these my hands.	85
	Would none but I might venge my cousin's death.	
Lady Capulet	We will have vengeance for it, fear thou not.	
	Then weep no more, I'll send to one in Mantua,	
	Where that same banished runagate doth live,	
	Shall give him such an unaccustomed dram,	90
	That he shall soon keep Tybalt company.	
	And then I hope thou wilt be satisfied.	
Juliet	*[Aside.]* Indeed I never shall be satisfied	
	With Romeo till I behold him, dead	
	Is my poor heart so, for a kinsman vex'd?	95
	Madam, if you could find out but a man	
	To bear a poison, I would temper it,	
	That Romeo should, upon receipt thereof,	
	Soon sleep in quiet. O, how my heart abhors	
	To hear him named, and cannot come to him.	100
	To wreak the love I bore my cousin	
	Upon his body that slaughtered him.	

60 **fickle:** changeable
61 **what dost thou:** what do you want from
62 **renowned for faith:** known to be faithful

66 **Is she not down … up so early:** I wonder if she's up early or hasn't been to bed
67 **procures her hither:** brings her here
68 **how now:** what's wrong

72 **have done:** stop weeping
73 **shows stills some want of wit:** is always foolish
74 **feeling:** deeply felt

77 **friend:** can also mean 'lover'; Juliet's mother talks of Tybalt, Juliet of Romeo. From this point, she is deliberately misleading her mother over her feelings for Romeo

81 **Villain and he … miles asunder:** Romeo is far from being a villain
83 **no man like he doth grieve my heart:** no man can cause me the distress he has

86 **Would:** I wish
86 **venge:** take revenge for

89 **runagate:** runaway
90 **unaccustomed dram:** unusual drink (of poison)

95 **vex'd:** made angry

97 **temper:** mix something into
98 **upon receipt thereof:** when he has it
99 **abhors:** hates
101 **wreak:** 'work' double meaning: have her revenge; show her love

Working Cut – text for experiment

Cap	Have you delivered to her our decree?
Lady C	Ay, sir, but she will none, she gives you thanks.
Cap	How, will she none? Doth she not give us thanks?
	Is she not proud? Doth she not count her blest,
	So worthy a gentleman to be her bridegroom?
Jul	Not proud you have, but thankful, that you have.
Cap	How, how, how, how? Chopped-logic? What is this?
	"Proud", and "I thank you", and "I thank you not".
	And yet "not proud", mistress minion you?
	Thank me no thankings, nor, proud me no prouds,
	But fettle your fine joints 'gainst Thursday next,
	To go with Paris to Saint Peter's Church,
	Or I will drag thee on a hurdle thither.
	Out you green-sickness carrion, out you baggage,
	You tallow-face!
Lady C	Fie, fie, what, are you mad?
Jul	Good father, I beseech you on my knees,
	Hear me with patience but to speak a word.
Cap	Hang thee young baggage, disobedient wretch!
	I tell thee what, get thee to church o' Thursday,
	Or never after look me in the face.
Nur	You are to blame, my lord, to rate her so.
Cap	Peace, you mumbling fool!
Lady C	You are too hot.
Cap	Thursday is near, lay hand on heart, advise.
	An you be mine, I'll give you to my friend.
	And you be not: hang, beg, starve, die in the streets,
	For, by my soul, I'll ne'er acknowledge thee,
	Nor what is mine shall never do thee good. *Exit.*

FROM THE REHEARSAL ROOM...

JULIET AND CAPULET

In groups of four or five, one person reads each part and one is a scribe (the scribe can also be the Nurse).

- Read through the *Working Cut*.
- Now, read it again. This time, before you say your own lines, repeat the most important word or phrase that the character before has said. The scribe writes these down.
- Discuss the choices – do you all agree?
- Read it again, and start saying your lines two or three words before the previous speaker has finished, so that your lines overlap.

1 How does the overlapping affect Juliet's relationship with her father?

- Read through the scene again. This time pause and count three seconds in your head before you start saying your speech.

2 How does this change the scene?

3 Whose point of view is the strongest in each of the different versions?

Juliet and Capulet, spring 2009.

Which of these two photos was taken first? Quote to support your answer.

Lorraine Burroughs, Vincent Brimble

A

B

Lady Capulet	Find thou the means, and I'll find such a man. But now I'll tell thee joyful tidings, girl.
Juliet	And joy comes well in such a needy time, What are they, I beseech your ladyship?
Lady Capulet	Well, well, thou hast a careful father, child! One who to put thee from thy heaviness Hath sorted out a sudden day of joy, That thou expect'st not, nor I looked not for.
Juliet	Madam, in happy time, what day is that?
Lady Capulet	Marry my child, early next Thursday morn, The gallant, young and noble gentleman, The County Paris, at Saint Peter's Church, Shall happily make thee there a joyful bride.
Juliet	Now, by Saint Peter's Church, and Peter too, He shall not make me there a joyful bride. I wonder at this haste, that I must wed Ere he that should be husband comes to woo. I pray you, tell my lord and father, madam, I will not marry yet, and when I do, I swear It shall be Romeo, whom you know I hate, Rather than Paris. These are news indeed!
Lady Capulet	Here comes your father, tell him so yourself, And see how he will take it at your hands.

Enter Capulet and Nurse.

Capulet	When the sun sets, the air doth drizzle dew, But for the sunset of my brother's son It rains downright. — How now? A conduit, girl? What, still in tears? Evermore show'ring? In one little body Thou counterfeits a bark, a sea, a wind. For still thy eyes, which I may call the sea, Do ebb and flow with tears. The bark thy body is, Sailing in this salt flood, the winds thy sighs, Who, raging with thy tears and they with them, Without a sudden calm will overset Thy tempest-tossed body. How now, wife? Have you delivered to her our decree?
Lady Capulet	Ay, sir, but she will none, she gives you thanks. I would the fool were married to her grave.
Capulet	Soft, take me with you, take me with you, wife. How, will she none? Doth she not give us thanks? Is she not proud? Doth she not count her blest, Unworthy as she is, that we have wrought So worthy a gentleman to be her bridegroom?
Juliet	Not proud you have, but thankful, that you have. Proud can I never be of what I hate, But thankful even for hate, that is meant love.
Capulet	How, how, how, how? Chopped-logic? What is this? "Proud", and "I thank you", and "I thank you not".

105 **in such a needy time:** at a time when we need it most

107 **careful:** caring
108 **heaviness:** sadness
109 **sorted out:** arranged
110 **nor I looked not for:** and I wasn't expecting
111 **in happy time:** how lucky

112 **Marry:** a mild oath – by Mary (Christ's mother)

115

118 **I wonder at:** I'm astonished at
119 **Ere he that ... comes to woo:** before the man who wants to be my husband has even begun to court me
120
123 **These are news indeed!:** what a thing to tell me

125 **at your hands:** from you

127 **the sunset of my brother's son:** Tybalt's death
129 **conduit:** water pipe
130
131 **Thou counterfeits:** you imitate
131 **bark:** ship
132 **still:** always

135

136 **Without:** unless there is

138 **our decree:** my decision

139 **she will none:** she won't do it
140

141 **Soft, take me with you:** hold on, explain
143 **count her:** consider herself
144 **wrought:** persuaded
146 **Not proud you have, but thankful:** I'm not pleased, but I am grateful
145
148 **thankful even for hate, that is meant love:** I'm grateful for what you have done out of love, but I hate the thing itself
149 **Chopped-logic:** over-clever arguments
150

95

Lady Capulet, Juliet (kneeling), Capulet, summer 2009.

1 What is the earliest point in the scene this photo might have been taken? Quote from the text to support your answer.

2 How has the director chosen to make Juliet look at this point in the scene? Explain your answer.

l–r Miranda Foster, Ellie Kendrick, Ian Redford

And yet "not proud", mistress minion you?
Thank me no thankings, nor, proud me no prouds,
But fettle your fine joints 'gainst Thursday next,
To go with Paris to Saint Peter's Church,
Or I will drag thee on a hurdle thither.
Out you green-sickness carrion, out you baggage,
You tallow-face!

Lady Capulet   Fie, fie, what, are you mad?

Juliet Good father, I beseech you on my knees,
Hear me with patience but to speak a word.

Capulet Hang thee young baggage, disobedient wretch!
I tell thee what, get thee to church o' Thursday,
Or never after look me in the face.
Speak not, reply not, do not answer me.
My fingers itch. Wife, we scarce thought us blest
That God had lent us but this only child,
But now I see this one is one too much,
And that we have a curse in having her.
Out on her, hilding!

Nurse   God in heav'n bless her!
You are to blame, my lord, to rate her so.

Capulet And why, my lady wisdom? hold your tongue,
Good prudence, smatter with your gossips, go.

Nurse I speak no treason.

Capulet   O, God gi' good-e'en.

Nurse May not one speak?

Capulet   Peace, you mumbling fool!
Utter your gravity o'er a gossip's bowl,
For here we need it not.

Lady Capulet   You are too hot.

Capulet God's bread, it makes me mad!
Day, night, hour, tide, time, work, play,
Alone, in company, still my care hath been
To have her matched. And having now provided
A gentleman of noble parentage,
Of fair demesnes, youthful, and nobly allied,
Stuffed, as they say, with honourable parts,
Proportioned as one's thought would wish a man —
And then to have a wretched puling fool,
A whining mammet, in her fortune's tender,
To answer, "I'll not wed, I cannot love.
I am too young, I pray you, pardon me."
But, and you will not wed, I'll pardon you!
Graze where you will you shall not house with me.
Look to't, think on't, I do not use to jest.
Thursday is near, lay hand on heart, advise.
An you be mine, I'll give you to my friend.
And you be not: hang, beg, starve, die in the streets,
For, by my soul, I'll ne'er acknowledge thee,

151 **mistress minion:** spoilt little madam
153 **fettle your fine joints:** get your fussy self ready
155 155 **hurdle:** rough wooden frame used to drag traitors to execution
156 **Out:** used to show disgust
156 **green-sickness carrion:** bloodless corpse
156 **baggage:** a good-for nothing woman
157 **tallow-face:** face as white as candle wax
160 157 **fie:** used to reproach someone for unsuitable behaviour

164 **My fingers itch:** I long to slap you
165 **but this only:** just one

168 **hilding:** a good-for nothing horse or woman
169 **rate her so:** scold her so violently
170

171 **smatter with your gossips:** babble away with your women friends
172 **God gi' good-e'en:** said to show he's exasperated

174 **Utter your gravity o'er a gossip's bowl:** say your piece when drinking with your friends
175

178–9 **still my care hath been To have her matched:** I've been constantly thinking about finding her a good husband
180
181 **fair demesnes:** with plenty of land and income
181 **nobly allied:** with important connections
184 **puling:** whining
185 185 **mammet:** doll
185 **in her fortune's tender:** when offered this good fortune
188 **and:** if
189 **Graze where you will ... with me:** you can fend for yourself, I won't have you in the house
190
190 **I do not use to jest:** I'm not joking
191 **advise:** think it over carefully
194 **acknowledge thee:** accept you as mine

EXPECTATIONS THEN AND NOW

- Read the *Working Cut*, and pick out all the places where modern family life is different.

- Discuss the differences between present day family life and family life in Shakespeare's time.

1 In society today what role could the Nurse have with the Capulet family?

2 What status would Juliet have in an Elizabethan family? How does it compare with a modern family?

- Work as a group to create two versions of this section of the scene, one Elizabethan, one modern. Show in each version how the conventions of family life at the time affect what happens.

- Compare both versions and discuss the similarities and differences in the interpretations with the rest of the class.

3 Which version had the most impact?

4 What words had the most effect in both versions of the scene?

Working Cut – text for experiment

Jul	O sweet my mother, cast me not away.
	Delay this marriage for a month, a week.
Lady C	Talk not to me, for I'll not speak a word.
	Do as thou wilt, for I have done with thee. *Exit.*
Jul	O God! O Nurse, how shall this be prevented?
	Some comfort Nurse.
Nur	I think it best you married with the County.
	O he's a lovely gentleman!
	Romeo's a dishclout to him.
	I think you are happy in this second match.
Jul	Speakest thou from thy heart?
Nur	And from my soul too, or else beshrew them both.
Jul	Amen.
Nur	What?
Jul	Well, thou hast comforted me marvellous much.
	Go in, and tell my lady I am gone,
	To make confession and to be absolved.
Nur	Marry, I will, and this is wisely done. *Exit.*
Jul	Ancient damnation! O most wicked fiend!
	I'll to the Friar to know his remedy,
	If all else fail, myself have power to die. *[Exit.]*

SHAKESPEARE'S WORLD

Family life

In this scene, Capulet is angry because Juliet disobeys him by saying she will not marry Paris. Shakespeare's audience lived in a world where the father or husband was the head of the household, and in charge of the family. The Church taught that children should obey their parents, and wives should submit to their husbands. This reflected a male-dominated society – only men could vote, go to university, or be a doctor or lawyer. Both Lady Capulet and Juliet were expected to obey Capulet in everything. Since Juliet is a girl, her boldness is even more troubling to her father – she is breaking two obligations, to obey as a child, and as a female. Many parents were strict with their children to teach them discipline and respect. People thought spoiling children was wrong, because the children would become rude and selfish. While this might seem harsh today, parents usually acted in their child's best interest. In the play, Capulet wants Juliet to marry Paris since he will be able to provide for her later in life. In Shakespeare's day, children's actions also showed others their social class. Juliet's disrespectfulness towards her father would be an insult to the training he had provided for her as a child. Parents expected their children to be obedient and show their high social status to their neighbours.

Director's view

Dominic Dromgoole
Director, summer 2009

Her father is horrendous, her mother lets her down, the Nurse eventually lets her down as well, and she was a small bird, Ellie [Kendrick, who played Juliet], with a wonderful innocence and a wonderful fragility. That is what I really wanted to do. Just see how much authority someone delicate and small could have.

Director's Note, 3.5

✔ After spending the night together, Romeo and Juliet part. He goes off to exile in Mantua.

✔ Juliet's mother arrives. She tells Juliet of the plan to marry her to Paris in three days.

✔ Juliet refuses – when her father arrives, she refuses again. He loses his temper, telling Juliet she must marry Paris or he will throw her out of his house.

✔ Her parents leave. Juliet asks the Nurse for her advice, which is that Juliet should marry Paris.

✔ Juliet says nothing, but privately rejects the Nurse and goes to ask for Friar Lawrence's help.

✔ How do Juliet's emotions change during this scene?

	Nor what is mine shall never do thee good.	195
	Trust to't, bethink you, I'll not be forsworn.	*Exit.*
Juliet	Is there no pity sitting in the clouds,	
	That sees into the bottom of my grief?	
	O sweet my mother, cast me not away.	
	Delay this marriage for a month, a week,	200
	Or, if you do not, make the bridal bed	
	In that dim monument where Tybalt lies.	
Lady Capulet	Talk not to me, for I'll not speak a word.	
	Do as thou wilt, for I have done with thee.	*Exit.*
Juliet	O God! O Nurse, how shall this be prevented?	205
	My husband is on earth, my faith in heaven,	
	How shall that faith return again to earth	
	Unless that husband send it me from heaven	
	By leaving earth? Comfort me, counsel me.	
	Alack, alack, that heaven should practise stratagems	210
	Upon so soft a subject as myself.	
	What say'st thou? Hast thou not a word of joy?	
	Some comfort Nurse.	
Nurse	Faith, here it is.	
	Romeo is banished, and all the world to nothing,	215
	That he dares ne'er come back to challenge you.	
	Or, if he do, it needs must be by stealth.	
	Then, since the case so stands as now it doth,	
	I think it best you married with the County.	
	O he's a lovely gentleman!	220
	Romeo's a dishclout to him. An eagle, madam,	
	Hath not so green, so quick, so fair an eye	
	As Paris hath. Beshrew my very heart,	
	I think you are happy in this second match,	
	For it excels your first. Or if it did not,	225
	Your first is dead, or 'twere as good he were,	
	As living here and you no use of him.	
Juliet	Speakest thou from thy heart?	
Nurse	And from my soul too, or else beshrew them both.	
Juliet	Amen.	230
Nurse	What?	
Juliet	Well, thou hast comforted me marvellous much.	
	Go in, and tell my lady I am gone,	
	Having displeased my father, to Lawrence' cell,	
	To make confession and to be absolved.	235
Nurse	Marry, I will, and this is wisely done.	*Exit.*
Juliet	Ancient damnation! O most wicked fiend!	
	Is it more sin to wish me thus forsworn,	
	Or to dispraise my lord with that same tongue	
	Which she hath praised him with above compare	240
	So many thousand times? Go, counsellor,	
	Thou and my bosom henceforth shall be twain.	
	I'll to the Friar to know his remedy,	
	If all else fail, myself have power to die.	*[Exit]*

195 **Nor what is mine ... thee good:** you'll get no inheritance from me
196 **be forsworn:** break my word

202 **that dim monument where Tybalt lies:** Tybalt's tomb

206 **My husband is ... in heaven:** I'm married, I made my vows before God

209 **By leaving earth:** by dying
210 **practise stratagems:** play tricks
211 **soft:** easy

215 **all the world to nothing:** I bet you anything
216 **challenge you:** claim you as his wife
217 **it needs must be by stealth:** it would have to be in secret
219 **the County:** Paris
221 **dishclout:** dishcloth
223 **Beshrew my very heart:** honestly (literal meaning 'curse my heart')
224 **happy:** lucky

226 **'twere as good he were:** he might as well be
227 **As living ... no use of him:** he's no use to you if you can't be together

233 **my lady:** my mother
237 **Ancient damnation!:** damn you, old woman
238 **more sin:** more sinful
238 **thus forsworn:** to break my marriage vows
239 **dispraise:** be critical of
239 **my lord:** my husband
240 **above compare:** as better than anyone
242 **Thou and my bosom ... be twain:** I won't share my thoughts with you again
243 **I'll to:** I'll go to
243 **his remedy:** his solution to the problem
244 **myself have power to die:** I'll find a way to kill myself

99

EXAMINER'S NOTES, 3.5

These questions help you to explore many aspects of *Romeo and Juliet*. At GCSE, your teacher will tell you which aspects are relevant to how your Shakespeare response will be assessed.

EXAMINER'S TIP

A good response

A good response may refer to effects on the character on stage and then to effects on people in the audience.

For example, the effect of this scene on Juliet is that she feels alone and desperate because she can't expect any help from her father, her mother or the Nurse.

The effect on the audience is that we hope the Friar may have a solution, that Romeo may come back to take her away, or that the Nurse may change her mind and help her.

1 Character and plot development

The beginning of this scene (lines 1–59) presents the two lovers in the most intimate and affectionate way, with some gentle humour and an undercurrent of danger. The audience is aware from Act 3 Scene 4 that Capulet has made his arrangements for Juliet's marriage to Paris, so the happiness of this scene is balanced by the knowledge that there is going to be major trouble soon.

1 Is the opening part of this scene tender and romantic or does it have some reminders of the dangers involved in their relationship?

2 How are Juliet's feelings for Romeo shown to be a mixture of wanting to be with him and wanting him to be safe?

2 Characterisation and voice: dramatic language

This scene moves swiftly from the two young lovers happy after their first night together, to Juliet's mother telling her she is to marry Paris, to her father, in a rage, insisting on her marrying Paris or he will disown her.

3 How does Romeo's imagery (lines 6–10) create a vivid sense of the early dawn?

4 How is Juliet's urgency conveyed in her lines 26–35?

5 How do Juliet's lines 93–102 show her attempt to express and conceal her emotions in discussion with her mother?

6 How is Capulet's attitude to his daughter conveyed by his way of speaking in lines 149–157?

7 How does the Nurse attempt to show her care for Juliet and do what her employers expect?

3 Themes and ideas

This is a scene of great contrasts: between Juliet as a young woman just married and as a daughter treated like a child by her father; between the happiness and harmony at the beginning of the scene, and the anger discord at the end; and between Juliet's closeness with Romeo at the start of the scene, and her isolation at the end, as she realises that even the Nurse is taking Juliet's parents' side. Throughout, Shakespeare makes the audience feel moved by ideas of love, duty, and fear that things are turning out tragically.

8 How do Lady Capulet's remarks about Romeo (lines 80–92) keep the theme of family feud and revenge in the audience's mind?

9 Do you think that Lady Capulet, as Juliet's mother, shows any understanding or sympathy with her daughter in this scene?

10 Which lines of Juliet's do you think an audience would find effective in saying what she means but in a way that her mother doesn't understand?

11 At which point in the scene do you think Juliet realises she is completely isolated with no-one she can turn to for help?

EXAMINER'S NOTES, 3.5

4 Performance

Performing this scene on screen gives plenty of scope for close-up shots of the lovers' faces and reactions to each other, but performing it on stage needs other ways of showing feelings.

12 If you were the director, how would you stage lines 1–36? Start by explaining whether you would use the upper stage or the main stage; then describe what you would have the actors do, and why you made these choices.

13 What props would you choose for Lady Capulet to use when announcing the wedding plan – a picture of Paris? A wedding dress? A portrait of her own marriage? Something else? Or nothing? Explain the reasons for your choice.

14 What advice would you give the actor playing Capulet about speaking his lines 126–138 and 149–157?

15 How would you advise the actor playing the Nurse about her attitude and feelings at these three points in the scene:
- lines 168–169
- line 173
- her speech 214–227?

5 Contexts and responses

Most readers and audiences will feel some sympathy for Juliet in this scene, but it is possible to see her as an immature girl who has behaved irresponsibly in a way that could cause her family great damage. There may be different responses to the scene according to the age, gender or culture of the individual people in the audience.

16 Parents and daughters – in what ways can a modern audience feel sympathy with Lady Capulet and with Juliet?

17 Actions and consequences – what could be the effect on Juliet's family if she told her parents the whole truth at this point in the play?

6 Reflecting on the scene

18 'Alack, alack, that heaven should practise stratagems
Upon so soft a subject as myself.'
How does this scene show that it is not just Fate's 'stratagems' that have created Juliet's desperate situation?

19 How does Shakespeare present the attitudes and feelings of Capulet in this scene?

20 How does Shakespeare present the changing relationship between Juliet and the nurse in this scene?

EXAMINER'S TIP

Writing about drama

Sometimes the success of a performance comes from what the audience sees, not just what it hears. Writing about visual business such as Romeo climbing down a rope ladder from the upper stage shows you are aware of technical aspects of performance.

USING THE VIDEO

Exploring interpretation and performance

If you have looked at the video extracts in Dynamic Learning, try this question.

The 2004 clip shows Romeo coming down the ladder, causing the audience to laugh. Do you think the scene is improved or not by introducing this humorous touch?

EXAMINER'S TIP

Reflecting on the scene

Writing about Capulet's range of voices, or Juliet as sadly isolated, or dramatic techniques, can be helped by referring to the way your understanding has developed by seeing a performance on stage or screen, or performing an aspect of the scene yourself or as part of a group.

A

Juliet and Paris, touring production, 2008.

1 What impression does this production give of Paris?

2 How well does this fit with the text in this scene? Quote to support your answer.

Dominique Bull, Perri Snowdon

SHAKESPEARE'S WORLD

Touring players

In Shakespeare's time, London was not the only place people could see professional actors. Groups of actors toured the country, playing in towns and the houses of the rich. When there was plague in London, the theatres were shut down to help stop the plague spreading. At these times even Shakespeare's company, the Lord Chamberlain's Men, would take some of their plays on tour.

The modern Globe also sends plays on tour round the country. The production of *Romeo and Juliet* shown in the photos on this page toured parts of the UK and Europe in 2008.

B

Enter Friar Lawrence and Paris.

Friar Lawrence On Thursday sir? The time is very short.

Paris My father Capulet will have it so,
And I am nothing slow to slack his haste.

Friar Lawrence You say you do not know the lady's mind?
Uneven is the course, I like it not. 5

Paris Immoderately she weeps for Tybalt's death,
And therefore have I little talked of love,
For Venus smiles not in a house of tears.
Now, sir, her father counts it dangerous
That she doth give her sorrow so much sway, 10
And in his wisdom hastes our marriage
To stop the inundation of her tears,
Which, too much minded by herself alone,
May be put from her by society.
Now do you know the reason of this haste. 15

Friar Lawrence *[Aside.]*   I would I knew not why it should be slowed. —
Look sir, here comes the lady towards my cell.

Enter Juliet.

Paris Happily met, my lady and my wife.

Juliet That may be, sir, when I may be a wife.

Paris That "may be" must be, love, on Thursday next. 20

Juliet What "must be" shall be.

Friar Lawrence   That's a certain text.

Paris Come you to make confession to this father?

Juliet To answer that, I should confess to you.

Paris Do not deny to him that you love me.

Juliet I will confess to you that I love him. 25

Paris So will ye, I am sure, that you love me.

Juliet If I do so, it will be of more price,
Being spoke behind your back, than to your face.

Paris Poor soul, thy face is much abused with tears.

Juliet The tears have got small victory by that, 30
For it was bad enough before their spite.

Paris Thou wrong'st it more than tears with that report.

Juliet That is no slander, sir, which is a truth,
And what I spake, I spake it to my face.

Paris Thy face is mine, and thou hast slandered it. 35

Juliet It may be so, for it is not mine own.
Are you at leisure, holy father, now,
Or shall I come to you at evening mass?

3 **I am nothing ... his haste:** I have no reason to want to slow him down
4 **the lady's mind:** what Juliet thinks of it
5 **Uneven is the course:** this is not the normal way to do this
8 **Venus smiles not:** the goddess of love is not happy
9 **counts it:** thinks it is
10 **doth give her sorrow so much sway:** lets her grief overwhelm her
12 **inundation:** flood
13 **too much minded by herself alone:** thought about too much when she's on her own
14 **put from her by society:** pushed aside by company
16 **I would I knew not ... be slowed:** if only I didn't know why it should be delayed
18 **Happily:** fortunately
21 **a certain text:** a saying – that's right
27 **more price:** greater value
29 **much abused with tears:** disfigured by crying
30 **small victory:** hardly any gain
31 **For it was ... their spite:** I wasn't a beauty before they set to work
32 **Thou wrong'st ... with that report:** you do it more harm than the tears, saying that
33 **slander:** untruthful criticism

Colin Hurley
Friar Lawrence, spring 2009

I have to [have a plan] because there's another sobbing teenager on the floor in front of me. She pulls out a knife. She plays the suicide card. So, that puts me in a position where the only card I can play is, 'Well, how about something that is a bit like that – but not.'

So, her emotional state just forced the issue. So I don't think this is something I would do lightly, but it's our only hope. So, there it is, and I'm confident because I've got the big man on my side – because I am a Friar! I'm confident that if she does the right things I can get a letter to lover boy; and okay, it's Plan B but at least they'll be together. The distance will help the emotions to calm down hopefully. There's a saying isn't there, that to really value something, you have to look at it as if for the first time, or as if for the last time. And I think the absence of their daughter will make them appreciate her more.

I didn't want the Friar to be Machiavellian and 'Aha! I'm glad you said that because I have this vial.' So, I did a terrible thing when I – I wasn't sure which vial. I'd got the potion in, 'and take thou...this one, I think it is.' Hoping it was the right one. They need to be improvising.

Ellie Kendrick
Juliet, summer 2009, on meeting Paris

In this scene Juliet is continuing that double-ness that she has started with the Nurse and her parents, when she has to completely mask her true feelings. And yet she uses words which are semi-true, and she shows an immense power of language and logic, and real quick thinking in this scene, which is just astounding.

So she falls into this rhyme with Paris, this very awkward witty repartee that they have together, when we were playing it, we played it so that Paris thought it was an enjoyable game, and was really getting into it and thought it was funny and witty and a good laugh, whereas Juliet is only just holding onto it, because she has just had the most terrible news, but yet she shows an immense fortitude of character by being able to mask all that. It is interesting the way they fall into this rhyme in this awkward way, because it is almost like a parody of the original interaction between Romeo and Juliet – that beautiful rhyming sonnet that they have together, and here that is deconstructed in a awkward, almost embarrassing, but slightly humorous interchange between Paris and Juliet.

The kiss that they have together, we played that as Paris very confidently believing that he owns Juliet now as his wife-to-be, and just lunges in and goes for it, while she is absolutely terrified and rigid. Almost crying, but trying to mask it, because obviously it is a terrible thing to happen, to be kissed by the man who is potentially going to take you away from the one you are in love with.

FROM THE REHEARSAL ROOM...

WHAT I SAY AND WHAT I THINK

- In groups of three, read lines 18–43. One person reads Paris, one person Friar Lawrence, and the third reads Juliet.
- Read through a second time. This time, after you have read the lines, say in your own words what you think your character is really thinking. Is it the same as what you just said?

1 What does this activity tell you about Paris and Juliet's relationship at this point in the play?

2 Which words in the extract reveal each character's real emotions?

- Paris' attempt to kiss Juliet may be
  - formal (kiss her hand)
  - friendly (a kiss on the cheek)
  - a passing kiss on the lips
  - sexual.
- Juliet may:
  - avoid or refuse the kiss
  - passively accept the kiss
  - join in.
- Discuss which best fits what is happening in this scene.

3 If you were directing the play, how would you stage the kiss? Explain your reasons.

4 What is the Friar's role in this part of the scene?

Ellie Kendrick
Juliet, summer 2009, on suicide

I think that Juliet is completely serious when she suggests that she will commit suicide if she has to marry Paris, simply because Romeo has become her life. Especially as she has abandoned all of her family, she has abandoned everything for him, because he is the sole purpose now of her life and so if she has to leave him, there is no point in going on living for her. I think she is totally serious. I don't think it is just an idle teenage instance of hyperbole, I think it is really serious, and quite terrifying for the Friar, which is why he proposes this mad solution to it – because he really believes her.

Friar Lawrence	My leisure serves me, pensive daughter, now.	
	My lord, we must entreat the time alone.	40
Paris	God shield I should disturb devotion.	
	Juliet, on Thursday early will I rouse ye,	
	Till then, adieu, and keep this holy kiss.	

Exit Paris.

Juliet	O shut the door, and when thou hast done so	
	Come weep with me, past hope, past care, past help.	45
Friar Lawrence	O Juliet, I already know thy grief,	
	It strains me past the compass of my wits.	
	I hear thou must, and nothing may prorogue it,	
	On Thursday next be married to this County.	
Juliet	Tell me not, Friar, that thou hear'st of this,	50
	Unless thou tell me how I may prevent it.	
	If in thy wisdom thou canst give no help,	
	Do thou but call my resolution wise,	
	And with this knife, I'll help it presently.	
	God joined my heart and Romeo's, thou our hands.	55
	And ere this hand, by thee to Romeo sealed,	
	Shall be the label to another deed,	
	Or my true heart with treacherous revolt	
	Turn to another, this shall slay them both.	
	Therefore, out of thy long-experienced time,	
	Give me some present counsel, or behold	60
	'Twixt my extremes and me this bloody knife	
	Shall play the umpire, arbitrating that	
	Which the commission of thy years and art	
	Could to no issue of true honour bring.	65
	Be not so long to speak, I long to die,	
	If what thou speak'st speak not of remedy.	
Friar Lawrence	Hold daughter, I do spy a kind of hope,	
	Which craves as desperate an execution	
	As that is desperate which we would prevent.	70
	If, rather than to marry County Paris,	
	Thou hast the strength of will to slay thyself,	
	Then is it likely thou wilt undertake	
	A thing like death, to chide away this shame,	
	That cop'st with death himself to 'scape from it.	75
	And if thou darest, I'll give thee remedy.	
Juliet	O bid me leap, rather than marry Paris,	
	From off the battlements of any tower,	
	Or walk in thievish ways, or bid me lurk	
	Where serpents are. Chain me with roaring bears,	80
	Or hide me nightly in a charnel-house,	
	O'er-covered quite with dead men's rattling bones,	
	With reeky shanks and yellow chapless skulls.	
	Or bid me go into a new-made grave	
	And hide me with a dead man in his shroud,	85
	(Things that to hear them told have made me tremble),	

39 **My leisure serves me:** I'm free

39 **pensive:** double meaning: thoughtful; sad

39 **daughter:** he is her spiritual father

40 **entreat the time alone:** need to be alone

41 **shield:** forbid

42 **rouse:** wake

45 **care:** spiritual help

47 **It strains me past the compass of my wits:** I can't think of an answer

48 **prorogue:** postpone

53 **Do thou but call my resolution wise:** just say I'm making the right decision

54 **I'll help it presently:** I'll carry it out now

56 **ere:** before

57 **Shall be the label to another deed:** will be given to another man in marriage

58 **true:** faithful

59 **this:** the knife

59 **them both:** her hand and heart

60 **time:** life

61 **present counsel:** advice, now

62 **'Twixt:** between

62 **my extremes:** my appalling situation

63–5 **arbitrating that ... honour bring:** providing the answer that you, for all your experience, cannot give

67 **speak not of remedy:** doesn't give an answer

68 **Hold:** wait

69–70 **Which craves ... we would prevent:** which will take as much courage as killing yourself

74 **A thing like death:** something similar to death

74 **chide away:** drive away

74 **this shame:** marrying Paris

75 **That cop'st with ... 'scape from it:** if you can face the idea of death to escape it

79 **thievish ways:** dangerous places full of thieves

81 **charnel-house:** a place where bones were stored when graves were re-used for more recent burials

83 **reeky shanks:** smelly shinbones

83 **chapless:** missing the lower jaw

Friar Lawrence, 2004.

Which line or lines do you think Friar Lawrence was speaking when this photo was taken? Quote the line or lines and explain your reasons.

John McEnery

Director's Note, 4.1

✔ Paris tells Friar Lawrence he is to marry Juliet in three days (Thursday).

✔ Juliet arrives, and is uncomfortable as Paris treats her as his love.

✔ Paris leaves so Juliet can confess to the Friar.

✔ Juliet is desperate, and threatens suicide; Friar Lawrence comes up with a plan:

● Juliet goes home and agrees to marry Paris

● but on Wednesday night she makes sure the Nurse does not sleep in her room, and she takes a drug Friar Lawrence gives her, which will make her seem dead

● she will be in a coma for 42 hours, long enough to be buried in the Capulet vault

● Friar Lawrence and Romeo will be there when she wakes, and she and Romeo can go off in exile together.

✔ Who benefits from the Friar's plan?

	And I will do it without fear or doubt, To live an unstained wife to my sweet love.		88 **unstained:** faithful
Friar Lawrence	Hold then. Go home, be merry, give consent To marry Paris. Wednesday is tomorrow,	90	

And I will do it without fear or doubt,
To live an unstained wife to my sweet love.

88 unstained: faithful

Friar Lawrence Hold then. Go home, be merry, give consent
To marry Paris. Wednesday is tomorrow,
Tomorrow night look that thou lie alone,
Let not thy nurse lie with thee in thy chamber.
Take thou this vial, being then in bed,
And this distilling liquor drink thou off,
When presently through all thy veins shall run
A cold and drowsy humour. For no pulse
Shall keep his native progress, but surcease.
No warmth, no breath, shall testify thou livest,
The roses in thy lips and cheeks shall fade
To many ashes, thy eyes' windows fall
Like death when he shuts up the day of life.
Each part, deprived of supple government,
Shall stiff and stark and cold appear like death,
And in this borrowed likeness of shrunk death
Thou shalt continue two and forty hours,
And then awake as from a pleasant sleep.
Now when the bridegroom in the morning comes
To rouse thee from thy bed, there art thou dead.
Then, as the manner of our country is,
In thy best robes uncovered on the bier,
Thou shalt be borne to that same ancient vault
Where all the kindred of the Capulets lie.
In the mean time, against thou shalt awake,
Shall Romeo by my letters know our drift,
And hither shall he come, and he and I
Will watch thy waking, and that very night
Shall Romeo bear thee hence to Mantua.
And this shall free thee from this present shame,
If no inconstant toy nor womanish fear,
Abate thy valour in the acting it.

90

91 **look that thou lie:** make sure you sleep
93 **vial:** very small bottle
94 **distilling liquor:** strong liquid
94 **drink thou off:** drink up completely
95 **When presently:** at once
96 **A cold and drowsy humour:** a feeling of cold and sleepiness
96-7 **For no pulse ... but surcease:** your pulse will seem to stop
100 **many:** pale

102 **supple government:** the power to move

104 **borrowed likeness:** imitation

109 **as the manner of our country is:** in the way we do things here
110 **bier:** the moveable stand a body is carried to the grave on
111 **vault:** tomb
113 **against thou shalt wake:** in preparation for when you wake
114 **our drift:** what we have planned

117 **bear thee hence:** take you away

119 **inconstant toy:** childish change of mind
120 **Abate thy valour:** weaken your courage

95

100

105

110

115

120

Juliet Give me, give me! O, tell not me of fear!

122 **prosperous:** lucky

Friar Lawrence Hold, get you gone, be strong and prosperous
In this resolve. I'll send a friar with speed
To Mantua with my letters to thy lord.

Juliet Love give me strength and strength shall help afford.
Farewell, dear father.   *They exit.*

125 **shall help afford:** will provide my help

125

ACT 4 SCENE 2

Enter Capulet, Lady Capulet, Nurse, and Servants.

Capulet So many guests invite as here are writ.   *[Exit a Servant.]*
Sirrah, go hire me twenty cunning cooks.

Servant You shall have none ill, sir, for I'll try if they can lick
their fingers.

Capulet How canst thou try them so?

5

Servant Marry sir, 'tis an ill cook that cannot lick his own

1 **So many guests ... here are writ:** here's a list of the guests to be invited
2 **cunning:** skilful
3 **none ill:** no bad ones
3-4 **try if they can lick their fingers:** test them to see if they lick their fingers (good cooks were supposed to do so)

Juliet, summer 2009.

1 What line or lines is Juliet speaking? Explain why the lines or lines you have chosen fit the image.

2 The photo doesn't show us who Juliet is looking at. Who is it? Give reasons for your answer.

Ellie Kendrick

Director's Note, 4.2

✔ Capulet is organising the wedding feast.

✔ Juliet returns, apologises, and says she will marry Paris.

✔ Overjoyed, Capulet moves the wedding forward to Wednesday.

✔ How close to the truth is Juliet's speech about Paris?

fingers. Therefore he that cannot lick his fingers goes
not with me.

Capulet	Go, be gone. *[Exit Servants.]*	
	We shall be much unfurnished for this time. —	10
	What, is my daughter gone to Friar Lawrence?	
Nurse	Ay forsooth.	
Capulet	Well, he may chance to do some good on her.	
	A peevish self-willed harlotry it is. *Enter Juliet.*	
Nurse	See where she comes from shrift with merry look.	15
Capulet	How now, my headstrong, where have you been gadding?	
Juliet	Where I have learnt me to repent the sin	
	Of disobedient opposition	
	To you and your behests, and am enjoined	
	By holy Lawrence to fall prostrate here,	20
	And beg your pardon. Pardon, I beseech you,	
	Henceforward I am ever ruled by you.	
Capulet	Send for the County, go tell him of this.	
	I'll have this knot knit up tomorrow morning.	
Juliet	I met the youthful lord at Lawrence' cell,	25
	And gave him what becomèd love I might,	
	Not stepping o'er the bounds of modesty.	
Capulet	Why, I am glad on't. This is well. Stand up.	
	This is as't should be. Let me see the County.	
	Ay, marry, go I say, and fetch him hither.	30
	Now, afore God, this reverend holy friar,	
	Our whole city is much bound to him.	
Juliet	Nurse, will you go with me into my closet,	
	To help me sort such needful ornaments	
	As you think fit to furnish me tomorrow?	35
Lady Capulet	No, not till Thursday; there is time enough.	
Capulet	Go, Nurse, go with her. We'll to church tomorrow.	
	Exit Juliet and Nurse.	
Lady Capulet	We shall be short in our provision,	
	'Tis now near night.	
Capulet	Tush, I will stir about,	
	And all things shall be well, I warrant thee, wife:	40
	Go thou to Juliet, help to deck up her;	
	I'll not to bed tonight; let me alone;	
	I'll play the housewife for this once. What, ho!	
	They are all forth. Well, I will walk myself	
	To County Paris, to prepare up him	45
	Against tomorrow. My heart is wondrous light,	
	Since this same wayward girl is so reclaimed. *Exit all.*	

10 We shall be ... for this time: we won't be ready in time
12 Ay forsooth: yes, indeed
14 A peevish self-willed harlotry it is: she's a moody, stubborn little madam
15 shrift: confession
16 my headstrong: my stubborn child
16 gadding: wandering off to
19 behests: commands
19 enjoined: instructed
20 fall prostrate: throw myself at your feet
22 Henceforward: from now on
22 I am ever ruled: I will always obey
24 this knot: the marriage
25 the youthful lord: Paris
26 gave him what becomèd love I might: showed him as much love as was suitable
32 is much bound to him: owes him a great deal
33 closet: private room
34 sort: choose
34 needful: necessary
35 fit to furnish me: suitable to wear
38 shall be short in our provision: won't have enough food and drink
39 Tush: don't be foolish
39 stir about: get it done
40 warrant: promise
41 deck up her: choose what she'll wear
42 let me alone: let me deal with it
44 forth: out of the house
45–6 prepare up him Against tomorrow: tell him the wedding's now tomorrow
47 reclaimed: obedient, my favourite again

SHAKESPEARE'S WORLD

Beds

The Chamberlain's Men would not have used as many props as a modern theatre company. Many of the major props which they did have are used in *Romeo and Juliet*. There are the swords (for the fight scenes) and the torches (to help the audience imagine the dark). In this scene the company's biggest prop was used: the bed.

Sometimes the bed was used behind doors or curtains at the back of the stage, which were opened to show it. We call this a 'discovery'. On other occasions, the bed was pushed onto the stage itself. In this scene, a 'discovery' allows Juliet to be found by the Nurse, but the dramatic impact would be greater if the bed is on stage.

Shakespeare used the bed in a number of other plays, including *Othello*, and *Henry IV Part 2*.

FROM THE REHEARSAL ROOM...

POWER WORDS

This activity looks at the *Working Cut* of Juliet's soliloquy (lines 14–57). Each member of the group is given one or more lines.

- Choose three words that seem most important in your line. These can be any words you like. For example, from the first line you could choose *faint, fear* and *veins*.

- The group reads the *Working Cut* out loud, each person just saying the 'power' words, not the whole line.

- Now read the *Working Cut* again. This time each person reads their whole line, giving special emphasis to the 'power' words.

1 What kind of words have people chosen?

2 What themes do the words highlight in the soliloquy?

3 What type of sounds and atmosphere do the words create?

4 What might the 'power' words tell you about Juliet's thoughts and feelings at the beginning, middle and end of her soliloquy?

Working Cut – text for experiment

Jul I have a faint cold fear thrills through my veins.
I'll call them back again to comfort me.
Nurse! — What should she do here?
My dismal scene I needs must act alone.
Come vial. What if this mixture do not work at all?
Shall I be married then to-morrow morning?
[Taking out a dagger.]
No, no, this shall forbid it. Lie thou there.
What if it be a poison, which the Friar
Subtly hath ministered to have me dead.
I fear it is, and yet methinks it should not,
For he hath still been tried a holy man.
How, if when I am laid into the tomb,
I wake before the time that Romeo
Come to redeem me? There's a fearful point.
Shall I not, then, be stifled in the vault,
And there die strangled ere my Romeo comes?
Or if I live, is it not very like
The horrible conceit of death and night,
Together with the terror of the place,—
Where bloody Tybalt, yet but green in earth,
Lies festering in his shroud, where, as they say,
At some hours in the night spirits resort —
Alack, alack, is it not like that I,
So early waking, what with loathsome smells,
Run mad — O if I wake, shall I not be distraught?
And madly play with my forefather's joints,
And pluck the mangled Tybalt from his shroud,
And in this rage, with some great kinsman's bone,
As with a club, dash out my desp'rate brains?
Romeo, Romeo, Romeo, here's drink. I drink to thee!

ACT 4 SCENE 3

Enter Juliet and Nurse, a bed with curtains on stage.

Juliet

Ay, those attires are best. But gentle nurse
I pray thee leave me to myself tonight.
For I have need of many orisons
To move the heavens to smile upon my state,
Which, well thou know'st, is cross and full of sin.

Enter Lady Capulet.

Lady Capulet

What, are you busy, ho? Need you my help?

Juliet

No madam, we have cull'd such necessaries
As are behoveful for our state tomorrow.
So please you, let me now be left alone,
And let the Nurse this night sit up with you,
For I am sure you have your hands full all
In this so sudden business.

Lady Capulet

         Good night.
Get thee to bed and rest for thou hast need.

Exit Lady Capulet and Nurse.

Juliet

Farewell. God knows when we shall meet again.
I have a faint cold fear thrills through my veins
That almost freezes up the heat of life.
I'll call them back again to comfort me.
Nurse! — What should she do here?
My dismal scene I needs must act alone.
Come vial. What if this mixture do not work at all?
Shall I be married then tomorrow morning?

[Taking out a dagger.]

No, no, this shall forbid it. Lie thou there.
What if it be a poison, which the Friar
Subtly hath ministered to have me dead,
Lest in this marriage he should be dishonoured,
Because he married me before to Romeo?
I fear it is, and yet methinks it should not,
For he hath still been tried a holy man.
How, if when I am laid into the tomb,
I wake before the time that Romeo
Come to redeem me? There's a fearful point.
Shall I not, then, be stifled in the vault,
To whose foul mouth no healthsome air breathes in,
And there die strangled ere my Romeo comes?
Or if I live, is it not very like
The horrible conceit of death and night,
Together with the terror of the place,
As in a vault, an ancient receptacle,
Where for this many hundred years the bones
Of all my buried ancestors are packed,
Where bloody Tybalt, yet but green in earth,
Lies festering in his shroud, where, as they say,
At some hours in the night spirits resort —

---

1 **attires:** clothes

3 **orisons:** prayers
4 **state:** circumstances
5 **cross:** unfavourable, not what I want
5 **full of sin:** because she's married already

7 **cull'd:** picked out
8 **behoveful:** needed
8 **state:** ceremony

15 **faint cold fear:** a fear that makes me feel cold and close to fainting

18 **What should she do here?:** what use could she be?
19 **dismal:** disastrous, fatal
20 **vial:** very small bottle

24 **Subtly hath ministered:** has cunningly given me
25 **Lest in ... be dishonoured:** in case he's found out and disgraced at the wedding
28 **still been tried:** always been shown to be
29 **How, if:** what if

31 **redeem:** save, rescue
32 **stifled:** suffocated
33 **healthsome:** fresh, healthy
34 **strangled:** choked, dead from lack of air
34 **ere:** before
36 **The horrible conceit of death and night:** the awful thoughts of death and darkness

41 **yet but green in earth:** only recently buried

43 **resort:** meet in

Alack, alack, is it not like that I,
So early waking, what with loathsome smells,
And shrieks like mandrakes torn out of the earth,
That living mortals, hearing them, run mad –
O if I wake, shall I not be distraught,
Environéd with all these hideous fears.
And madly play with my forefather's joints,
And pluck the mangled Tybalt from his shroud,
And in this rage, with some great kinsman's bone,
As with a club, dash out my desp'rate brains?
O look, methinks I see my cousin's ghost
Seeking out Romeo that did spit his body
Upon a rapier's point. Stay, Tybalt, stay!
Romeo, Romeo, Romeo, here's drink. I drink to thee!

She drinks, and falls on the bed, within the curtains.

44 **is it not like:** isn't it likely
46 **mandrakes:** plants said to scream when pulled up, causing those who heard the screams to go mad and die
49 **Environéd with:** surrounded by
52 **rage:** madness
55 **spit:** skewer
56 **stay!:** stop!

Director's Note, 4.3

- ✔ Lady Capulet and the Nurse leave Juliet alone for the night.
- ✔ Juliet is scared. She worries what might happen – if the drug does not work, if Friar Lawrence has actually given her poison, if she wakes too early ...
- ✔ She takes the drug.

ACT 4 SCENE 4

Enter Lady Capulet and Nurse.

Lady Capulet Hold, take these keys and fetch more spices, Nurse.

Nurse They call for dates and quinces in the pastry.

Enter Capulet.

Capulet Come, stir, stir, stir! The second cock hath crowed,
The curfew-bell hath rung, 'tis three o'clock.
Look to the baked meats, good Angelica,
Spare not for the cost.

Nurse Go you cot-quean, go,
Get you to bed. Faith, you'll be sick tomorrow
For this night's watching.

Capulet No, not a whit. What? I have watched ere now
All night for less cause, and ne'er been sick.

Lady Capulet Ay, you have been a mouse-hunt in your time;
But I will watch you from such watching now.

Exit Lady Capulet and Nurse.

Capulet A jealous hood, a jealous hood!

Enter three or four servants with cooking-spits, logs and baskets.

Now, fellow, what's there?

First Servant Things for the cook, sir, but I know not what.

Capulet Make haste, make haste. *[Exit First Servant.]*
Sirrah, fetch drier logs.
Call Peter, he will show thee where they are.

Second Servant I have a head, sir, that will find out logs,
And never trouble Peter for the matter. *He exits.*

Capulet Mass and well said, a merry whoreson, ha!
Thou shalt be logger-head. Good faith, 'tis day. *Music offstage.*

2 **pastry:** room where pastry was made
4 **curfew-bell:** bell rung in the early morning when the watchmen went off duty and the gates were unlocked
5 **Angelica:** the name of a female servant in the room, or the Nurse
6 **Spare not for:** don't hold back because of
6 **cot-quean:** man who interferes in women's business of running the house
8 **watching:** staying awake
9 **not a whit:** not in the slightest
11 **mouse-hunt:** woman-chaser
12 **watch you from such watching:** keep an eye on you to stop that
13 **hood:** woman

20 **Mass:** short for 'by the Mass'; an oath
20 **merry whoreson:** cheerful bastard
21 **logger-head:** double meaning: chief log fetcher; a blockhead/fool

The County will be here with music straight,
For so he said he would, I hear him near.
Nurse! Wife! What ho? What, Nurse, I say!
Enter Nurse.   Go waken Juliet, go and trim her up.
I'll go and chat with Paris. Hie, make haste,
Make haste, the bridegroom he is come already.
Make haste I say.   *Exit Capulet.*

22 **straight:** any minute

25 25 **trim her up:** get her dressed

SHAKESPEARE'S WORLD

Curfews

The curfew was originally a bell rung at the time at night when people had to put their fires and candles out. Over the years, 'curfew' came to mean more than just putting out fires and candles. The bell was rung when the gates of a city or town were shut at night. People were expected to stay indoors after the bell had rung. Sometimes, usually in times of political unrest, there were laws passed enforcing this.

Elizabeth I issued a curfew in 1595, which was around the time that Shakespeare was writing *Romeo and Juliet*. This particular curfew was an attempt to control crime, which was on the increase, especially in cities. The curfew bell was rung in London at nine o'clock at night, and anyone found outside could be arrested and put in prison. The 'Watch' – volunteers like modern Special Constables – patrolled the streets, to make sure the law was obeyed. The curfew was lifted at dawn, and the bell was rung again to tell the people that a new day had begun. It is this second bell that Capulet refers to here, and so the phrase has connotations of the freedom and activity that sunrise brought.

Director's Note, 4.4

✔ The Capulets are up all night preparing for the feast.
✔ When he hears Paris' musicians coming, Capulet sends the Nurse to wake Juliet.

Capulet and Lady Capulet, watched by the Nurse, summer 2009.

1 What does the photo suggest about the mood in the Capulet household in this scene?

2 Pick a line or lines that you think were being spoken when the photo was taken. Quote from the text to support your answer.

l–r Ian Redford, Miranda Foster, Penny Layden

A

FROM THE REHEARSAL ROOM...

STAGING

The Nurse does not raise the alarm until line 14.

- In pairs, read lines 1–16.
- Each time you get to a question mark, exclamation mark or full stop, change reader.
- Read the extract again: what could the Nurse be doing before she discovers Juliet's body?

1 What is the Nurse concentrating on at the start of this scene?

2 Why does it take her so long to decide Juliet is dead?

SHAKESPEARE'S WORLD

◇◇◇◇◇◇◇◇◇◇◇◇

An Elizabethan wedding day

The day began with friends taking the bride and groom from the brides' house to the church, accompanied by musicians, dancers and guests. Afterwards, the couple gave money to the poor who waited outside the church to congratulate them. There was then a feast, usually at the bride's parents' house. The feast usually included roast or boiled meats, breads, pastries, cake, spiced wine, beer and mince pies. In the play, the Capulets prepare by inviting guests, hiring cooks and fetching pastries and spices. Capulet says 'spare not for the cost'.

B

A: Nurse and Juliet, 2004; B: 'Enter Friar Lawrence and County Paris with Musicians', 2004. Paris with the black cloak, Lady Capulet and Juliet by the bed, Capulet seated.

1 At what point, during the first 16 lines, do you think Photo A was taken? Give reasons for your answer.

2 How will the entry of Paris and friends (dancing) and the musicians have affected the mood of the scene?

3 In Photo B, what is Lady Capulet doing? Why do you think the director decided to include this?

A: Bette Bourne, Kananu Kirimi

[The Nurse goes to bed.]

Nurse   Mistress, what mistress? Juliet? Fast, I warrant her, she.   1 **Fast:** fast asleep
— Why lamb, why lady? Fie, you slugabed!
Why love I say? Madam? Sweetheart? Why bride?
What, not a word? You take your pennyworths now.   4 **take your pennyworths now:** sleep while you can
Sleep for a week, for the next night, I warrant,   5
The County Paris hath set up his rest   6 **set up his rest:** decided
That you shall rest but little, God forgive me.
— Marry, and amen, how sound is she asleep?
I needs must wake her. Madam, madam, madam!
Ay, let the County take you in your bed,   10   10 **take you:** double meaning: arrive and find you; have sex with you
He'll fright you up, i' faith. Will it not be?   11 **fright you up:** startle you awake
[She opens the bed curtains.]   12 **dressed, and in ... down again:** dressed, and then gone back to sleep in your clothes
What, dressed, and in your clothes, and down again?
I must needs wake you. Lady, lady, lady?   13 **I must needs:** I really have to
Alas, alas! Help, help! My lady's dead!
O wereaday, that ever I was born!   15   15 **wereaday:** alas
Some *aqua vitae*, ho! My lord! My lady!   16 *aqua vitae:* brandy

Enter Lady Capulet.

Lady Capulet   What noise is here?

Nurse   O lamentable day!

Lady Capulet   What is the matter?

Nurse   Look, look. O heavy day!   18 **heavy:** unhappy

Lady Capulet   O me, O me, my child, my only life.   19 **my only life:** the only child I have
Revive, look up, or I will die with thee!   20
Help, help! Call help!   *Enter Capulet.*

Capulet   For shame, bring Juliet forth, her lord is come.

Nurse   She's dead. Deceased. She's dead. Alack the day!

Lady Capulet   Alack the day, she's dead, she's dead, she's dead!

Capulet   Ha! Let me see her. Out, alas, she's cold: 25
Her blood is settled and her joints are stiff.   26 **is settled:** isn't moving round her body
Life and these lips have long been separated.
Death lies on her like an untimely frost   28 **untimely:** coming at the wrong time, out of season
Upon the sweetest flower of all the field.

Nurse   O lamentable day!

Lady Capulet   O woeful time!   30

Capulet   Death, that hath ta'en her hence to make me wail,   31 **ta'en her hence:** taken her away
Ties up my tongue, and will not let me speak.

Enter Friar Lawrence and County Paris with Musicians.

Friar Lawrence   Come, is the bride ready to go to church?

Capulet   Ready to go, but never to return.
O son, the night before thy wedding day   35
Hath Death lain with thy wife. There she lies,   36 **lain with:** slept with

Lady Capulet, Capulet, Juliet (on the bed), Friar Lawrence, and Paris, summer 2009.

1 Who are the men standing behind the stairs?

2 Who is speaking when the photo was taken, and which lines might they be saying? Quote to support your answer.

l–r Miranda Foster, Ian Redford, Ellie Kendrick, Rawiri Paratene, Tom Stuart

SHAKESPEARE'S WORLD

Funeral customs

Church bells were rung to tell people somebody had died. Until the funeral, Elizabethans usually watched the corpse day and night. This was both a mark of respect and kept the corpse safe. In England the body was usually buried within two or three days of death, but in the world of the play Juliet's funeral must be the same day or the next day. In simple funerals a few family members carried the body to be buried. More elaborate funerals had a horse-drawn carriage and many more mourners. As with weddings, local people watched funerals. The corpses of wealthy and important people were dressed in expensive clothes and ornaments. The wealthy also wore special funeral clothes in black, and draped black cloth around the carriage which carried the coffin. At the grave, people threw pieces of rosemary, the herb of remembrance, onto the body. After the burial, there was a funeral feast. People ate mutton, beef, cheese and bread. They drank wine and beer. As in the play, wealthy families often had their own large family tomb in the churchyard.

Flower as she was, deflowered by him.
Death is my son-in-law, Death is my heir,
My daughter he hath wedded. I will die,
And leave him all. Life, living, all is Death's. 40

Paris
Have I thought long to see this morning's face,
And doth it give me such a sight as this?

Lady Capulet
Accursed, unhappy, wretched, hateful day!
Most miserable hour that e'er time saw
In lasting labour of his pilgrimage. 45
But one, poor one, one poor and loving child,
But one thing to rejoice and solace in,
And cruel Death hath catched it from my sight!

Nurse
O woe! O woeful, woeful, woeful day!
Most lamentable day, most woeful day, 50
That ever, ever, I did yet behold!
O day, O day, O day, O hateful day,
Never was seen so black a day as this.
O woeful day, O woeful day!

Paris
Beguiled, divorcèd, wrongèd, spited, slain! 55
Most detestable Death, by thee beguiled,
By cruel, cruel thee quite overthrown.
O love, O life! Not life, but love in death!

Capulet
Despised, distressèd, hated, martyred, killed!
Uncomfortable time, why cam'st thou now 60
To murder, murder our solemnity?
O child, O child! My soul and not my child,
Dead art thou! Alack my child is dead,
And with my child, my joys are burièd.

Friar Lawrence
Peace, ho, for shame! Confusion's cure lives not 65
In these confusions. Heaven and yourself
Had part in this fair maid, now heaven hath all,
And all the better is it for the maid.
Your part in her you could not keep from death,
But heaven keeps his part in eternal life. 70
The most you sought was her promotion,
For 'twas your heaven she should be advanced,
And weep ye now, seeing she is advanced
Above the clouds, as high as heaven itself?
O in this love, you love your child so ill 75
That you run mad, seeing that she is well.
She's not well married, that lives married long,
But she's best married, that dies married young.
Dry up your tears, and stick your rosemary
On this fair corse, and, as the custom is, 80
And in her best array, bear her to church.
For though fond nature bids us all lament,
Yet nature's tears are reason's merriment.

Capulet
All things that we ordainèd festival,
Turn from their office to black funeral. 85
Our instruments to melancholy bells,

37 **deflowered by him:** her virginity taken by Death

41 **Have I thought long ... morning's face:** I've waited so impatiently for this morning

45 **In lasting labour of his pilgrimage:** on the long hard journey of all those years
47 **solace in:** take comfort from
48 **hath catched it:** has snatched this child

55 **Beguiled:** cheated
60 **Uncomfortable:** without comfort
61 **murder our solemnity:** kill her and so kill our celebration
65-6 **Confusion's cure ... these confusions:** we can't sort things out until we all calm down
67 **Had part in:** shared
69 **Your part:** the mortal part (her body)
70 **his part:** her soul
71 **her promotion:** social advancement (through marriage)
72 **'twas your heaven she should be advanced:** the best you could imagine for her was to marry well
75-6 **O in this love ... that she is well:** you love your child so little that you go mad with grief despite the fact she's in the best possible place
77-8 **She's not well married ... dies married young:** she's better off dying young and going to heaven than marrying well here
79 **rosemary:** herb of remembrance, used at funerals
80 **corse:** corpse
81 **array:** clothes and ornaments
82 **fond nature:** foolish natural feeling
83 **nature's tears are reason's merriment:** our natural sorrow should really, if we think about it, be joy
84 **things we ordainèd festival:** wedding preparations
85 **office:** intended use
85 **to black funeral:** to serve her funeral

	Our wedding cheer to a sad burial feast,	
	Our solemn hymns to sullen dirges change,	88 **sullen dirges:** gloomy funeral hymns
	Our bridal flowers serve for a buried corse,	
	And all things change them to the contrary. 90	90 **contrary:** opposite
Friar Lawrence	Sir, go you in, and madam, go with him,	
	And go Sir Paris, every one prepare	
	To follow this fair corse unto her grave.	
	The heavens do lour upon you for some ill,	94 **lour:** frown
	Move them no more by crossing their high will. 95	

Exit Capulet, Lady Capulet, Paris, and Friar Lawrence,
each putting rosemary on the body, and shutting the bed
curtains.

First Musician	Faith, we may put up our pipes and be gone.	96 **may put up our pipes and be gone:** might as well pack up our instruments and go
Nurse	Honest goodfellows, ah, put up, put up,	
	For well you know, this is a pitiful case.	98 **pitiful case:** very sad situation
First Musician	Ay, by my troth, the case may be amended.	99 **the case may be amended:** double meaning: the situation could be improved; his music case needs mending

Exit Nurse, the Musicians start to follow.
Enter Peter.

Peter	Musicians, O musicians, "Heart's ease, Heart's ease": O, 100 and you will have me live, play "Heart's ease".	
First Musician	Why "Heart's ease"?	
Peter	O, musicians, because my heart itself plays "My heart is full of woe": O play me some merry dump to comfort me. 105	104 **merry dump:** cheerful, sad song (which would be impossible)
First Musician	Not a dump we, 'tis no time to play now.	
Peter	You will not then?	
First Musician	No.	
Peter	I will then give it you soundly.	
First Musician	What will you give us? 110	
Peter	No money, on my faith, but the gleek. I will give you the minstrel.	111 **the gleek:** I'll mock you 111–2 **I will give you the minstrel:** I'll call you minstrels (wandering beggars that usually played music badly)
First Musician	Then I will give you the serving-creature.	
Peter	Then will I lay the serving-creature's dagger on your pate. I will carry no crotchets, I'll *re* you, I'll *fa* you. Do 115 you note me?	113 **the serving-creature:** suggesting Peter is a bad servant 115 **pate:** head 115 **I will carry no crotchets:** double meaning: I won't put up with your nonsense; I won't put up with your music. Start of a run of musical puns
First Musician	An you *re* us, and *fa* us, you note us.	
Second Musician	Pray you put up your dagger and put out your wit. Then have at you with my wit.	118 **put up:** put away 118 **put out your wit:** show some sense

Peter	I will dry-beat you with an iron wit, and put up my iron 120 dagger. Answer me like men:
	   When griping grief the heart doth wound,
	   And doleful dumps the mind oppress,
	   Then music with her silver sound
	Why "silver sound"? Why "music with her silver sound"? 125
	What say you, Simon Catling?
		120 **dry-beat you with an iron wit:** I'll use my sharp wit to beat you without drawing blood
		126 **Catling:** named after a string for a musical instrument made from catgut

Many productions cut the end of this scene. In the Globe's summer 2009 production, it was played.

1 Why might directors choose to cut this part of the scene?

2 Which actor is playing Peter? Give reasons for your answer.

a)   b)   c)

First Musician   Marry, sir, because silver hath a sweet sound.

Peter   Prates. What say you, Hugh Rebeck?

Second Musician   I say "silver sound", because musicians sound for silver.

Peter   Prates too. What say you, James Soundpost?   130

Third Musician   Faith, I know not what to say.

Peter   O I cry you mercy, you are the singer, I will say for you. It is "music with her silver sound", because musicians have no gold for sounding.

    Then music with her silver sound,   135
    With speedy help doth lend redress.   *Exit Peter.*

First Musician   What a pestilent knave is this same!

Second Musician   Hang him, Jack! Come, we'll in here, tarry for the mourners, and stay dinner.   *They exit.*

ACT 5 SCENE 1

Enter Romeo.

Romeo   If I may trust the flattering truth of sleep,
My dreams presage some joyful news at hand.
My bosom's lord sits lightly in his throne.
And all this day an unaccustomed spirit
Lifts me above the ground with cheerful thoughts.   5
I dreamt my lady came and found me dead
(Strange dream that gives a dead man leave to think.)
And breathed such life with kisses in my lips,
That I revived and was an emperor.
Ah me, how sweet is love itself possessed,   10
When but love's shadows are so rich in joy!
    Enter Balthasar, Romeo's servant, in riding boots.
News from Verona. How now Balthasar?
Dost thou not bring me letters from the Friar?
How doth my lady? Is my father well?
How doth my lady Juliet? That I ask again,   15
For nothing can be ill, if she be well.

Balthasar   Then she is well, and nothing can be ill.

127 **silver hath a sweet sound:** when given in payment
128 **Prates:** nonsense
128 **Rebeck:** a type of violin
129 **sound for silver:** play music for money
130 **Soundpost:** part of a violin
132 **you are the singer:** you sing, you don't 'say' (talk)
136 ***doth lend redress:*** puts things right
137 **What a pestilent knave is this same:** he's a pain in the neck
138 **tarry:** hang around
139 **stay:** wait for

Director's Note, 4.5

✔ The Nurse finds Juliet, and believes she is dead.

✔ She calls the Capulets, who are grief-stricken.

✔ Paris arrives with his musicians; he too becomes distraught.

✔ Friar Lawrence tells them to rejoice because she has gone to heaven, and starts to arrange the funeral.

✔ Afterwards, Peter jokes with the musicians.

1 **the flattering truth of sleep:** what my dreams tell me
2 **presage:** predict
3 **bosom's lord:** heart
4 **unaccustomed spirit:** unusual cheerfulness
7 **leave:** permission
10 **itself possessed:** experienced in reality
11 **but love's shadows:** just dreams of love

Romeo and the Apothecary, summer 2009.

This photo (A), and the one at the top of page 122 (B), both come from between the entrance of the Apothecary (line 57) and the end of the scene (on page 123).

1 Which photo was taken earlier in this section of the scene? Quote from the text to support your answer.

2 Romeo describes the Apothecary as desperately poor.

a) What did they do in the summer 2009 production to show this? (Photo A)

b) What did they do in the spring 2009 production, which was in modern dress, to show this? (Photo B)

c) Which do you think was most successful? Give reasons for your answer.

Adetomiwa Edun, Graham Vick

SHAKESPEARE'S WORLD

What was an apothecary?

An apothecary was someone who made and prescribed medicine, similar to a chemist today. Apothecaries also sold spices, plants, oils, chemicals, and the ingredients for cosmetics and perfumes.

Doctors were expensive in Shakespeare's time, so people often went to apothecaries for treatment. Many apothecaries had some medical training, but they were not seen as professional people. Doctors were. So apothecaries charged a fee, but could not charge as much as doctors. Sometimes priests or monks treated poor people for free, using similar medicines. In *Romeo and Juliet* Friar Lawrence clearly makes herbal medicines. Apothecaries often first prescribed vinegar to patients to prevent infection. Other medicines included arsenic, sage, dried toad, lavender, rose, bay leaf, wormwood, liquorice and mint. It was against the law to sell poison, as the apothecary in this scene tells Romeo. However, apothecaries had access to various poisonous substances and people were prepared to pay a lot for poison.

A

Her body sleeps in Capel's monument,
And her immortal part with angels lives.
I saw her laid low in her kindred's vault, 20
And presently took post to tell it you.
O pardon me for bringing these ill news,
Since you did leave it for my office, sir.

Romeo
Is it even so? Then I deny you, stars. —
Thou know'st my lodging, get me ink and paper, 25
And hire post-horses, I will hence tonight.

Balthasar
I do beseech you, sir, have patience.
Your looks are pale and wild, and do import
Some misadventure.

Romeo
                    Tush, thou art deceived.
Leave me, and do the thing I bid thee do. 30
Hast thou no letters to me from the Friar?

Balthasar
No, my good lord.

Romeo
                 No matter. Get thee gone,
And hire those horses, I'll be with thee straight.
Well, Juliet, I will lie with thee tonight.   *Exit Balthasar.*
Let's see for means. O mischief, thou art swift 35
To enter in the thoughts of desperate men.
I do remember an apothecary,
And hereabouts 'a dwells, which late I noted
In tattered weeds, with overwhelming brows,
Culling of simples. Meagre were his looks, 40
Sharp misery had worn him to the bones.
And in his needy shop a tortoise hung,
An alligator stuffed, and other skins
Of ill-shaped fishes. And about his shelves
A beggarly account of empty boxes, 45
Green earthen pots, bladders, and musty seeds,
Remnants of packthread, and old cakes of roses
Were thinly scattered, to make up a show.
Noting this penury, to myself I said,
"An if a man did need a poison now, 50
Whose sale is present death in Mantua,
Here lives a caitiff wretch would sell it him."
O this same thought did but forerun my need,
And this same needy man must sell it me.
As I remember, this should be the house. 55
Being holiday, the beggar's shop is shut.
What ho! Apothecary!   *Enter Apothecary.*

Apothecary
              Who calls so loud?

Romeo
Come hither man. I see that thou art poor,
Hold, there is forty ducats, let me have
A dram of poison, such soon-speeding gear 60
As will disperse itself through all the veins,
That the life-weary taker may fall dead
And that the trunk may be discharged of breath
As violently as hasty powder fired
Doth hurry from the fatal cannon's womb. 65

---

18 **Capel's monument:** the Capulet tomb
19 **immortal part:** soul
21 **presently took post:** set off as fast as possible on a relay of hired horses
23 **Since you did leave it for my office:** but when you left you told me to bring news
24 **Is it even so?:** so that's what's happened
24 **I deny you, stars:** I won't accept the influence of the stars on events
26 **post-horses:** horses hired from inns, used to travel long distances quickly, by changing tired horses at other post inns
28–9 **do import Some misadventure:** nothing good can come of acting now
29 **Tush:** don't be foolish
35 **Let's see for means:** how can I do it
35 **mischief:** evil
37 **apothecary:** someone who prepared and sold medicines
38 **hereabouts 'a dwells:** he lives around here
38 **which late I noted:** I saw him recently
39 **tattered weeds:** ragged clothes
39 **overwhelming brows:** overgrown, uncared for eyebrows
40 **Culling of simples:** picking herbs for medicines
40 **Meagre were his looks:** he looked thin
42 **needy:** run-down
45 **A beggarly account of:** a few tattered
46 **bladders:** used to hold liquids
47 **packthread:** string
47 **cakes of roses:** pressed rose petal bars
49 **penury:** obvious lack of money
51 **present death:** punishable by immediate execution
52 **a caitiff wretch:** a poor man desperate enough
53 **forerun:** run ahead of
56 **holiday:** a saint's day; no one worked

59 **ducats:** gold coins
60 **dram:** a small quantity
60 **soon-speeding gear:** stuff that works fast
63 **the trunk:** the body
63 **discharged of breath:** stop breathing
64 **hasty powder:** gunpowder
65 **cannon's womb:** inside of the cannon

Director's view

Bill Buckhurst
Director, spring 2009

What we've discovered is that when Romeo leaves his fate with the stars, he's constantly going 'you be my guide', he believes in a larger power than himself which is guiding him on life's journey. And then when he's told the news of Juliet's death he says, 'I defy you stars', another pivotal point in the play. He suddenly comes of age and takes responsibility for his own actions, and what does he do? He goes and kills himself.

Director's Note, 5.1

✔ In Mantua, Romeo gets a message from a servant, telling him that Juliet is dead.
✔ Romeo decides to go to Juliet's tomb, and kill himself there, to be with her.
✔ He buys poison from an Apothecary.
✔ The audience know to expect a message to Romeo from Friar Lawrence. How might that affect the audience as this scene develops?

Romeo and the Apothecary, spring 2009.

James Alexandrou, Shane Zaza

Friar John and Friar Lawrence, summer 2009.

This photo was taken while Lawrence said: 'and the neglecting it May do much danger.' (lines 19–20)

1 What has Friar John done to provoke Friar Lawrence's anger?

2 Could the director and actors have chosen to play this scene in another way, without anger? Explain your answer.

James Lailey, Rawiri Paratene

Apothecary	Such mortal drugs I have, but Mantua's law Is death to any he that utters them.
Romeo	Art thou so bare and full of wretchedness, And fear'st to die? Famine is in thy cheeks, Need and oppression starveth in thy eyes, Contempt and beggary hangs upon thy back. The world is not thy friend, nor the world's law. The world affords no law to make thee rich. Then be not poor, but break it, and take this.
Apothecary	My poverty, but not my will, consents.
Romeo	I pay thy poverty, and not thy will.
Apothecary	Put this in any liquid thing you will And drink it off, and if you had the strength Of twenty men, it would dispatch you straight.
Romeo	There is thy gold, worse poison to men's souls, Doing more murder in this loathsome world Than these poor compounds that thou mayst not sell. I sell thee poison, thou hast sold me none. Farewell, buy food, and get thyself in flesh. — Come, cordial and not poison, go with me To Juliet's grave, for there must I use thee. *They exit.*

Glossary (right column):

66 **mortal:** deadly
67 **he that utters:** man that sells
68 **bare:** poor
69 **And fear'st:** yet still fear
71 **Contempt and beggary hangs upon thy back:** how the world despises you is clear from the pitiful state of your clothes
73 **affords:** gives you
75 **My poverty, but not my will, consents:** poverty forces me to take it, but I don't want to
79 **dispatch you straight:** kill you instantly
82 **poor compounds:** wretched mixtures
84 **get thyself in flesh:** put some flesh on your bones
85 **cordial:** medicine to make you well

ACT 5 SCENE 2

Enter Friar John and Friar Lawrence by different doors.

Friar John	Holy Franciscan friar, brother, ho!
Friar Lawrence	This same should be the voice of Friar John. Welcome from Mantua, what says Romeo? Or, if his mind be writ, give me his letter.
Friar John	Going to find a barefoot brother out, One of our order, to associate me, Here in this city visiting the sick, And finding him, the searchers of the town Suspecting that we both were in a house Where the infectious pestilence did reign, Sealed up the doors, and would not let us forth, So that my speed to Mantua there was stayed.
Friar Lawrence	Who bare my letter then to Romeo?
Friar John	I could not send it — here it is again — Nor get a messenger to bring it thee, So fearful were they of infection.
Friar Lawrence	Unhappy fortune! By my brotherhood, The letter was not nice but full of charge, Of dear import, and the neglecting it May do much danger. Friar John, go hence, Get me an iron crow and bring it straight Unto my cell.
Friar John	Brother, I'll go and bring it thee. *He exits.*

Glossary (right column):

4 **if his mind be writ:** if he's written to me
5 **barefoot brother:** Franciscan friar
6 **associate me:** travel with me (friars were supposed to travel in pairs)
8 **searchers:** official who viewed dead bodies to find the cause of death
10 **pestilence:** plague
11 **forth:** out
12 **my speed to Mantua there was stayed:** I couldn't go to Mantua
13 **bare:** took
15 **Nor get:** nor could I get
18 **nice:** trivial
18 **charge:** serious information
19 **Of dear import:** vitally important
21 **an iron crow:** a crow-bar
21 **straight:** at once

Friar Lawrence	Now must I to the monument alone,
	Within this three hours will fair Juliet wake, 25
	She will beshrew me much that Romeo
	Hath had no notice of these accidents.
	But I will write again to Mantua,
	And keep her at my cell till Romeo come.
	Poor living corse, closed in a dead man's tomb! 30

ACT 5 SCENE 3

Enter Paris and his Page, who carries flowers and a torch.

Paris	Give me thy torch, boy. Hence, and stand aloof,
	Yet put it out, for I would not be seen.
	Under yond yew trees lay thee all along,
	Holding thy ear close to the hollow ground,
	So shall no foot upon the churchyard tread, 5
	Being loose, unfirm with digging up of graves,
	But thou shalt hear it. Whistle then to me,
	As signal that thou hearest some thing approach.
	Give me those flowers. Do as I bid thee, go.
Page	[Aside.] I am almost afraid to stand alone 10
	Here in the churchyard, yet I will adventure.

The page moves away. Paris strews the grave with flowers.

Paris	Sweet flower, with flowers thy bridal bed I strew.
	O woe, thy canopy is dust and stones,
	Which with sweet water nightly I will dew,
	Or wanting that, with tears distilled by moans. 15
	The obsequies that I for thee will keep,
	Nightly shall be to strew thy grave and weep.

The Page whistles.

	The boy gives warning, something doth approach,
	What cursèd foot wanders this way tonight,
	To cross my obsequies and true love's rite? 20
	What, with a torch? Muffle me, night, awhile.

Paris moves away. Enter Romeo and Balthasar, with a torch, mattock, and an iron crow-bar.

Romeo	Give me that mattock and the wrenching iron.
	Hold, take this letter. Early in the morning
	See thou deliver it to my lord and father.
	Give me the light. Upon thy life, I charge thee, 25
	Whate'er thou hear'st or seest, stand all aloof,
	And do not interrupt me in my course.
	Why I descend into this bed of death
	Is partly to behold my lady's face,
	But chiefly to take thence from her dead finger 30
	A precious ring, a ring that I must use
	In dear employment. Therefore hence, be gone.
	But if thou, jealous, dost return to pry
	In what I further shall intend to do,
	By heaven I will tear thee joint by joint, 35
	And strew this hungry churchyard with thy limbs.
	The time and my intents are savage-wild,
	More fierce and more inexorable far
	Than empty tigers, or the roaring sea.

124

ACT 5 SCENE 3

24 **the monument:** the Capulet tomb
26 **beshrew me much:** abuse me
27 **these accidents:** what's happened
30 **corse:** corpse

Director's Note, 5.2

✔ Friar John tells Friar Lawrence he was not able to deliver the message to Romeo.
✔ Friar Lawrence rushes to Juliet's tomb, so she does not wake alone.

1 **stand aloof:** wait over there
2 **Yet put it out:** put the torch out
3 **Under yond yew trees ... along:** lie on the ground under those yew trees
6 **Being:** because it is
10 **stand:** stay
11 **adventure:** risk it
12 **Sweet flower:** Juliet
12 **strew:** scatter
13 **canopy:** bed covering
14 **sweet water:** perfumed water
14 **dew:** sprinkle
15 **wanting:** lacking
15 **distilled:** made from
16 **obsequies:** memorial rites

20 **cross:** interrupt
21 **Muffle me:** hide me

22 **mattock:** digging tool
22 **wrenching iron:** crow-bar
23 **Hold:** wait
25 **charge:** command
26 **all aloof:** well away
27 **my course:** what I'm doing

31-2 **I must use In dear employment:** I need for an important purpose
33 **jealous:** suspicious

38 **inexorable:** unstoppable
39 **empty tigers:** hungry tigers

Balthasar	I will be gone, sir, and not trouble you.	40
Romeo	So shalt thou show me friendship. Take thou that,	
	[He gives Balthasar money.]	
	Live and be prosperous, and farewell, good fellow.	
Balthasar	*[Aside.]* For all this same, I'll hide me hereabout,	
	His looks I fear, and his intents I doubt. *[Moves away.]*	

Romeo starts to open the tomb.

Romeo	Thou detestable maw, thou womb of death,	45
	Gorged with the dearest morsel of the earth.	
	Thus I enforce thy rotten jaws to open,	
	And in despite I'll cram thee with more food.	
Paris	This is that banished haughty Montague,	
	That murdered my love's cousin, with which grief	50
	It is supposèd, the fair creature died,	
	And here is come to do some villainous shame	
	To the dead bodies. I will apprehend him.	
	[Steps out.]	
	Stop thy unhallowed toil, vile Montague,	
	Can vengeance be pursued further than death?	55
	Condemnèd villain, I do apprehend thee.	
	Obey and go with me, for thou must die.	
Romeo	I must indeed, and therefore came I hither.	
	Good gentle youth, tempt not a desperate man.	
	Fly hence and leave me. Think upon these gone,	60
	Let them affright thee. I beseech thee, youth,	
	Put not another sin upon my head	
	By urging me to fury. O be gone!	
	By heaven, I love thee better than myself,	
	For I come hither armed against myself.	65
	Stay not, be gone, live, and hereafter say,	
	A madman's mercy bid thee run away.	
Paris	I do defy thy conjurations,	
	And apprehend thee for a felon here.	
Romeo	Wilt thou provoke me? Then have at thee, boy!	70

They fight.

Page	*[Aside.]* O Lord they fight! I will go call the watch. *[Exit.]*	
Paris	O I am slain! If thou be merciful,	
	Open the tomb, lay me with Juliet. *[He dies.]*	
Romeo	In faith I will, Let me peruse this face.	
	Mercutio's kinsman, noble County Paris!	75
	What said my man, when my betossèd soul	
	Did not attend him as we rode? I think	
	He told me Paris should have married Juliet.	
	Said he not so? Or did I dream it so?	
	Or am I mad, hearing him talk of Juliet,	80
	To think it was so? O give me thy hand,	
	One writ with me in sour misfortune's book.	
	I'll bury thee in a triumphant grave. *[Opens the grave.]*	
	A grave? O no, a lantern, slaughtered youth.	

44 **His looks I fear, and his intents I doubt:** I don't like the look of him, I fear he might do something desperate

45 **maw:** stomach

46 **Gorged with the dearest morsel of the earth:** full, having taken the most precious thing on earth (Juliet)

48 **in despite:** despite the fact you're full

48 **more food:** another dead body (himself)

51 **the fair creature:** Juliet

53 **apprehend:** arrest

54 **unhallowed toil:** unholy work (breaking into the tomb)

58 **therefore came I hither:** that's why I came here

59 **tempt not:** don't provoke

60 **these gone:** the dead in the tomb

65 **armed against myself:** to kill myself

68 **I do defy thy conjurations:** I won't listen to your appeals

69 **felon:** criminal

74 **peruse:** look at

76 **betossèd:** disturbed, whirling

77 **attend him:** listen to him

78 **should have:** was going to

82 **One writ with me in sour misfortune's book:** we've both been brought tragedy by fate

84 **a lantern:** a small tower on top of a building with glass on all sides to let in a lot of light

125

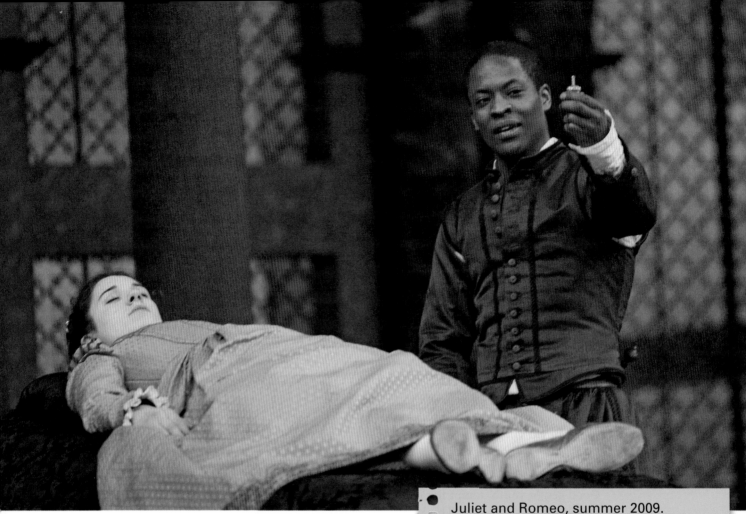

Juliet and Romeo, summer 2009.

Which of Romeo's lines between 88 and 120 best fits with this photo? Quote to support your answer.

Ellie Kendrick, Adetomiwa Edun

MONOLOGUE AS DUOLOGUE

- In pairs, read Romeo's monologue as a duologue (lines 74–120).
- Each time you get to a question mark, exclamation mark or full stop, change reader until the next punctuation mark. Continue this pattern to the end of the soliloquy.

1 What do you notice immediately about Romeo's soliloquy?

2 Why does Romeo ask so many questions?

3 What effect do Romeo's questions have on the audience?

- Read the extract again. This time look for the significant changes in Romeo's speech – the places where his thoughts change.
- Divide the monologue into clearly defined sections.
- Each block should represent either a change in Romeo's thoughts, a realisation, a decision and/ or action.

- Once you have broken the speech into significant sections, **add a title** to each chunk of text, to 'sum up' each section.

4 Looking at each section, how does Romeo begin to make sense of the sequence of events that have happened since his banishment?

5 What does Romeo see when he looks closely at Juliet?

6 What type of language and imagery does Romeo use to describe Juliet in death?

7 What options does Romeo believe that he has at this point in the play?

8 How does Romeo see death at this stage in the play? How does it differ from earlier in the play? Why has his opinion of death changed in this scene?

For here lies Juliet, and her beauty makes   85
This vault a feasting presence full of light.
Death, lie thou there, by a dead man interred.
                    [Laying Paris in the tomb.]
How oft when men are at the point of death
Have they been merry? Which their keepers call
A light'ning before death? O how may I   90
Call this a light'ning? O my love, my wife,
Death that hath sucked the honey of thy breath,
Hath had no power yet upon thy beauty.
Thou art not conquered. Beauty's ensign yet
Is crimson in thy lips and in thy cheeks,   95
And Death's pale flag is not advancèd there.
Tybalt, liest thou there in thy bloody sheet?
O what more favour can I do to thee
Than with that hand that cut thy youth in twain
To sunder his that was thine enemy?   100
Forgive me, cousin. Ah, dear Juliet,
Why art thou yet so fair? Shall I believe
That unsubstantial death is amorous,
And that the lean abhorrèd monster keeps
Thee here in dark to be his paramour?   105
For fear of that, I still will stay with thee,
And never from this palace of dim night
Depart again. Here, here will I remain
With worms that are thy chamber-maids. O here
Will I set up my everlasting rest   110
And shake the yoke of inauspicious stars
From this world-wearied flesh. Eyes, look your last.
Arms, take your last embrace. And lips, O you
The doors of breath, seal with a righteous kiss
A dateless bargain to engrossing Death.   *[Kisses her.]* 115
Come bitter conduct, come unsavoury guide,
Thou desperate pilot, now at once run on
The dashing rocks thy sea-sick weary bark.
Here's to my love! *[He drinks.]* O true apothecary,
Thy drugs are quick. Thus with a kiss I die.   *[He dies.]* 120

Enter Friar Lawrence, with a lantern, crowbar, and spade.

Friar Lawrence   Saint Francis be my speed! How oft tonight
Have my old feet stumbled at graves? Who's there?

Balthasar   Here's one, a friend, and one that knows you well.

Friar Lawrence   Bliss be upon you. Tell me, good my friend,
What torch is yond that vainly lends his light   125
To grubs and eyeless skulls? As I discern,
It burneth in the Capel's monument.

Balthasar   It doth so, holy sir, and there's my master,
One that you love.

Friar Lawrence   Who is it?

Balthasar   Romeo.

Friar Lawrence   How long hath he been there?

Balthasar   Full half an hour.   130

---

86 **feasting presence:** room where guests are welcomed before a feast
88 **at the point of death:** waiting for execution
89 **keepers:** jailers
90 **light'ning:** easing of sorrow

94 **ensign:** flag

96 **is not advancèd:** has not taken over

99 **cut thy youth in twain:** killed you while you were so young
100 **sunder his that was thine enemy:** end your enemy's (Romeo's) life
101 **cousin:** Tybalt
103–5 **unsubstantial death is amorous ... his paramour:** skeleton-like Death loves you and keeps you here to be his lover
106 **still:** always

111 **shake the yoke of inauspicious stars:** throw off my unlucky fate

115 **A dateless bargain to engrossing Death:** an everlasting contract with Death who gets everything
116 **conduct:** guide
117 **pilot:** navigator that guides a ship into harbour
118 **sea-sick weary bark:** ship, sick of sailing (Romeo's body)
119 **true:** honest, truthful
121 **be my speed:** help me

124 **Bliss be upon you:** bless you
125 **is yond:** is that over there
126 **As I discern:** it seems to me

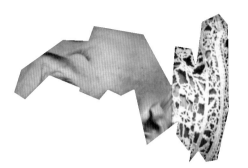

SHAKESPEARE AND THE DIRECTOR

This activity asks you to decide how to stage lines 140–167.

- In groups of three, one reads Juliet, one reads the Friar and one is the director, supervising the scene.
- Read the text aloud several times.
- As well as the printed stage directions, identify the exact words that are prompts for sound effects, props, and actions for the actors.
- List all the props you will need to play the scene, where the props are positioned on the stage and/or who the props are with.
- Working with your director, decide how to stage and block this section of the scene, following all the new stage directions that you have identified from the text.

1 List the new stage directions you chose, and exactly where in the text each one comes.

2 How did your group know these stage directions would be sensible?

3 How does Shakespeare build up the tension in the scene?

4 How does Shakespeare ensure that the scene flows smoothly?

Juliet and Romeo, 2004.

The stage direction for this kiss is in square brackets [ ]. This shows it is not in the printed text from Shakespeare's time. We have added it to help readers, by telling them what people in the theatre would see on stage.

1 Why did we put it at this exact point? Quote from the text to support your answer.

2 Are there any other places in this speech (lines 161–167) where a director could choose to have Juliet kiss Romeo? Again, quote to support your answer.

Kananu Kirimi, Tom Burke

Actor's view

Ellie Kendrick
Juliet, summer 2009

At first I played Juliet as being very confused and dazed, and then gradually, this horrible realisation dawns upon her, when she sees that everything is not quite right.

The Friar very hurriedly tells her that something terrible has happened, but then just runs away. And she gradually discovers the poison in his hand, and I think it is, obviously, a really heartbreaking moment. The lines speak for themselves here. I think the lines are much more affecting if they are spoken with real honesty. They are really heartbreaking. So we played it with Juliet almost subdued in grief here, and then she very quickly makes the decision to die herself.

I don't think Juliet would ever consider the Friar's suggestion of being hidden with the nuns. Romeo is the meaning of her life. She threatens to commit suicide earlier, and is deadly serious in that, and here she doesn't consider it for a moment, she says, 'Go, get thee hence, for I will not away.' In our production Juliet was very definite about that. Obviously very sad, but there is no doubt in her mind, that if Romeo is there, she needs to be there as well.

Friar Lawrence	Go with me to the vault.
Balthasar	I dare not, sir.
	My master knows not but I am gone hence,
	And fearfully did menace me with death
	If I did stay to look on his intents.
Friar Lawrence	Stay then, I'll go alone. Fear comes upon me.
	O much I fear some ill unthrifty thing.
Balthasar	As I did sleep under this yew tree here,
	I dreamt my master and another fought,
	And that my master slew him.
Friar Lawrence	Romeo!

He goes to the tomb, and sees blood and weapons on the ground.

Alack, alack, what blood is this, which stains
The stony entrance of this sepulchre?
What mean these masterless and gory swords
To lie discoloured by this place of peace?

[He enters the tomb.]

Romeo! O, pale! Who else? What, Paris too?
And steeped in blood? Ah, what an unkind hour
Is guilty of this lamentable chance?   *Juliet wakes.*
The lady stirs.

Juliet	O comfortable Friar, where is my lord?
	I do remember well where I should be,
	And there I am. Where is my Romeo?
Friar Lawrence	I hear some noise lady. Come from that nest
	Of death, contagion, and unnatural sleep.
	A greater power than we can contradict
	Hath thwarted our intents. Come, come away.
	Thy husband in thy bosom there lies dead,
	And Paris too. Come, I'll dispose of thee
	Among a sisterhood of holy nuns.
	Stay not to question, for the watch is coming.
	Come, go, good Juliet, I dare no longer stay.
Juliet	Go, get thee hence, for I will not away.

Exit Friar Lawrence.

What's here? A cup closed in my true love's hand?
Poison, I see, hath been his timeless end.
O churl, drunk all? And left no friendly drop
To help me after? I will kiss thy lips,
Haply some poison yet doth hang on them,
To make me die with a restorative.   *[Kisses him.]*
Thy lips are warm.

Enter Page and the Watch.

First Watchman	Lead boy, which way?
Juliet	Yea, noise? Then I'll be brief. O happy dagger!

[Taking Romeo's dagger.]

This is thy sheath, there rust, and let me die.

She stabs herself and falls.

---

132 **knows not but I am gone from hence:** thinks I've gone away
133 **fearfully did menace:** threatened me in a very frightening way
136 **some ill unthrifty thing:** something dreadfully wasteful and evil
141 **sepulchre:** tomb
142 **masterless:** abandoned
142 **gory:** bloodstained
143 **by this place of peace:** near this tomb, where bodies lie at peace
145 **unkind:** cruel circumstance
146 **this lamentable chance:** tragic accidental meeting
148 **comfortable:** reassuring
152 **contagion:** infectious disease
154 **thwarted our intents:** ruined our plans
156-7 **dispose of thee Among ... of holy nuns:** hide you in a nunnery
158 **Stay not to question:** don't ask questions now
162 **hath been his timeless end:** has killed him
163 **churl:** bad-mannered person
164 **To help me after:** for me to take to follow you (into death)
165 **Haply:** perhaps
166 **restorative:** double meaning: brings back to life; takes her to be with him
169 **brief:** quick
169 **happy:** found at just the right moment

First Watchman (left of left-hand pillar), Capulet and Lady Capulet (left of grave), Romeo and Juliet, the Prince, and other Watchmen in the background, spring 2009.

1 Which are the earliest and latest lines at which this photo could have been taken? Explain your answer.

2 What are the two Watchmen at the back holding, and why?

3 Look back to page 3. Where was the photographer when he took this shot?

l–r Ben Aldridge, Vincent Brimble, Golda Rosheuvel, James Alexandrou, Lorraine Burroughs, Nick Khan

Page	This is the place, there where the torch doth burn.	170 **This:** her body
First Watchman	The ground is bloody, search about the churchyard. Go, some of you, whoe'er you find attach. *[Some exit.]* Pitiful sight! Here lies the County slain, And Juliet bleeding, warm, and newly dead 175 Who here hath lain these two days burièd. Go tell the Prince, run to the Capulets, Raise up the Montagues. Some others search. *[More exit.]* We see the ground whereon these woes do lie, But the true ground of all these piteous woes 180 We cannot without circumstance descry.	173 **whoe'er you find attach:** arrest anyone you find 179 **these woes:** Paris, Romeo and Juliet 180 **the true ground:** the reasons for 181 **without circumstance descry:** understand without more information

Enter some of the Watch, with Balthasar.

Second Watchman	Here's Romeo's man. We found him in the churchyard.	
First Watchman	Hold him in safety, till the Prince come hither.	183 **in safety:** so he can't get away

Enter another Watchman and Friar Lawrence.

Third Watchman	Here is a friar, that trembles, sighs, and weeps. We took this mattock and this spade from him, 185 As he was coming from this churchyard side.	
First Watchman	A great suspicion, stay the friar too.	187 **A great suspicion, stay the friar too:** that looks very suspicious, don't let him go away

Enter the Prince, with attendants.

Prince	What misadventure is so early up, That calls our person from our morning's rest?	188 **What misadventure is so early up:** what awful thing has happened this early

Enter Capulet and Lady Capulet.

Capulet	What should it be, that they so shriek abroad?	190 190 **What should it be, that they so shriek abroad?:** what is everyone yelling about?
Lady Capulet	O the people in the street cry "Romeo", Some "Juliet", and some "Paris", and all run With open outcry toward our monument.	
Prince	What fear is this which startles in your ears?	194 **What fear is this which startles in your ears?:** what are you frightened of?
First Watchman	Sovereign, here lies the County Paris slain, 195 And Romeo dead, and Juliet, dead before, Warm and new killed.	
Prince	Search, seek, and know how this foul murder comes.	
First Watchman	Here is a friar, and slaughtered Romeo's man, With instruments upon them, fit to open 200 These dead men's tombs.	200 **instruments:** tools
Capulet	O heavens! O wife, look how our daughter bleeds! This dagger hath mista'en, for, lo, his house Is empty on the back of Montague, And it mis-sheathed in my daughter's bosom! 205	203 **hath mista'en:** has lost its way 203 **his house:** the dagger's sheath 204 **Montague:** Romeo 205 **it:** the dagger
Lady Capulet	O me, this sight of death, is as a bell That warns my old age to a sepulchre. *Enter Montague.*	207 **warns my old age to a sepulchre:** calls me to my grave
Prince	Come Montague, for thou art early up To see thy son and heir now early down.	209 **early down:** dead before you were up 210 **is dead tonight:** died in the night
Montague	Alas, my liege, my wife is dead tonight, 210	

Capulet, Watchman (with torch), Prince, Lady Capulet, Juliet and Romeo (on the tomb), Paris (foot of the tomb), Friar Lawrence, Friar John, two Watchmen (with torches), Montague, 2004.

1 Friar Lawrence is speaking (between line 230 and 260).

   a) How has the director staged the scene?

   b) Why do you think he chose to stage it like this? Explain your answer.

2 Which line or lines do you think Lawrence was speaking when the photo was taken? Quote from the text to support your answer.

l–r Bill Stewart, John Paul Connolly, Joel Trill, Melanie Jessop, Kananu Kirimi, Tom Burke, Callum Coates, John McEnery, Rhys Meredith, Terry McGinity

Grief of my son's exile hath stopped her breath.
What further woe conspires against mine age?

Prince Look, and thou shalt see.

Montague O thou untaught! What manners is in this,
To press before thy father to a grave?

Prince Seal up the mouth of outrage for a while,
Till we can clear these ambiguities,
And know their spring, their head, their true descent.
And then will I be general of your woes,
And lead you even to death. Meantime forbear,
And let mischance be slave to patience.
Bring forth the parties of suspicion.

Friar Lawrence I am the greatest, able to do least,
Yet most suspected, as the time and place
Doth make against me, of this direful murder.
And here I stand, both to impeach and purge,
Myself condemnèd, and myself excused.

Prince Then say at once what thou dost know in this.

Friar Lawrence I will be brief, for my short date of breath
Is not so long as is a tedious tale.
Romeo, there dead, was husband to that Juliet,
And she, there dead, that's Romeo's faithful wife.
I married them, and their stol'n marriage-day
Was Tybalt's doomsday, whose untimely death
Banished the new-made bridegroom from this city,
For whom (and not for Tybalt) Juliet pined.
You, to remove that siege of grief from her,
Betrothed, and would have married her perforce
To County Paris. Then comes she to me,
And with wild looks bid me devise some means
To rid her from this second marriage,
Or in my cell there would she kill herself.
Then gave I her (so tutored by my art)
A sleeping potion, which so took effect
As I intended, for it wrought on her
The form of death. Meantime, I writ to Romeo,
That he should hither come as this dire night,
To help to take her from her borrowed grave,
Being the time the potion's force should cease.
But he which bore my letter, Friar John,
Was stayed by accident, and yesternight
Returned my letter back. Then all alone,
At the prefixèd hour of her waking,
Came I to take her from her kindred's vault,
Meaning to keep her closely at my cell
Till I conveniently could send to Romeo.
But when I came some minute ere the time
Of her awaking, here untimely lay
The noble Paris and true Romeo dead.
She wakes, and I entreated her come forth,
And bear this work of heaven with patience

211 Grief of: grief over
214 thou untaught: rude boy
215 To press before: to push in front of
216 Seal up the mouth of outrage: quieten your grief
217 clear these ambiguities: find out what happened
218 their spring, their head, their true descent: what caused these events
219 be general of your woes: lead you in mourning and punish those responsible
220 even to death: executing the guilty if necessary
220 forbear: keep your feelings under control
221 let mischance be slave to patience: let patience rule your misery
222 parties of suspicion: suspects
223 the greatest: the most suspected
225 Doth make against me: throw suspicion on me
226 impeach: accuse
226 purge: clear (of blame)
229 my short date of breath: the short time I have left to live
233 stol'n: secret
234 Tybalt's doomsday: the day Tybalt died
237 that siege of grief from her: the grief that shut her up
238 perforce: by force
240 devise some means: work out a way
243 so tutored by my art: as I have learned from my studies
245-6 wrought on her The form of death: made her seem dead
247 as: on
253 prefixèd: prearranged
255 closely: hidden
257 ere: before
259 true: faithful
260 entreated: begged
261 this work of heaven: what has happened

133

PUNISHED AND PARDONED

At the end of the play, the Prince has to decide who to punish and who to pardon.

- In groups of three, read the *Working Cut* and consider who you think should be punished for their actions and who should be pardoned.

1 How do Capulet and Montague react to the loss of their children in the final scene?

- Using the evidence from the whole play, build a balanced argument, to present to the Prince, that will justify your group's decisions on who to punish and who to pardon.

- Remember, you need to find evidence in the text to support your recommendations to the Prince.

- Once you have built your argument, decide on how you will present your case to the Prince. Each group should present their argument and the Prince (teacher) can decide what action to take.

2 Explain who you think deserves to be pardoned. Quote to support your answer.

3 Explain who you think deserves to be punished. Quote to support your answer.

Working Cut – text for experiment

Prin	This letter doth make good the Friar's words, Their course of love, the tidings of her death. And here he writes that he did buy a poison Of a poor 'pothecary, and therewithal Came to this vault to die, and lie with Juliet. Where be these enemies? Capulet, Montague? See what a scourge is laid upon your hate That heaven finds means to kill your joys with love. And I, for winking at your discords too, Have lost a brace of kinsmen. All are punished.
Cap	O brother Montague, give me thy hand, This is my daughter's jointure, for no more Can I demand.
Mont	But I can give thee more. For I will raise her statue in pure gold.
Cap	As rich shall Romeo's by his lady's lie.
Prin	Go hence, to have more talk of these sad things, Some shall be pardoned, and some punishèd. For never was a story of more woe Than this of Juliet, and her Romeo.

Two Watchmen (with lanterns), Balthasar, Montague, Prince, Capulet (over Juliet and Romeo's corpses), Friar Lawrence, Watchman (with torch), Paris (dead), summer 2009.

1 Which line or lines were being spoken when the photo was taken? Quote from the text to support your answer.

2 Compare the photos on pages 130, 132, and this page – they show the last scene in the three productions we have been following.

a) What are the similarities?

b) What are the differences?

c) If you were the director, how would you stage the end of this scene?

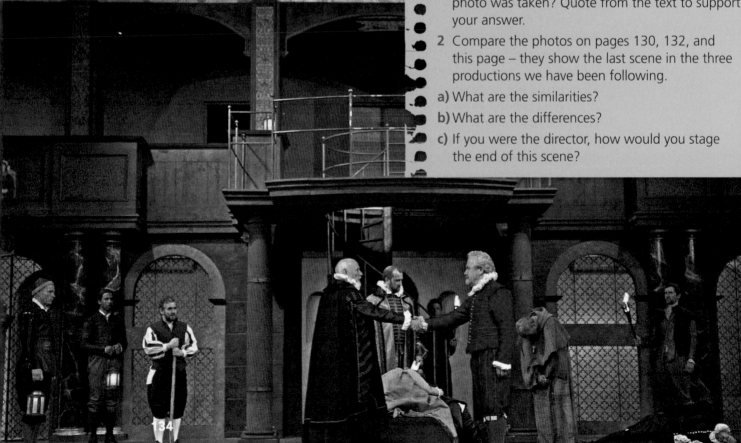

But then a noise did scare me from the tomb,
And she, too desperate, would not go with me,
But, as it seems, did violence on herself.
All this I know, and to the marriage
Her nurse is privy. And if aught in this
Miscarried by my fault, let my old life
Be sacrificed, some hour before his time,
Unto the rigour of severest law.

Prince   We still have known thee for a holy man.
Where's Romeo's man? What can he say to this?

Balthasar   I brought my master news of Juliet's death,
And then in post he came from Mantua
To this same place, to this same monument.
This letter he early bid me give his father,
And threatened me with death, going in the vault,
If I departed not, and left him there.

Prince   Give me the letter, I will look on it.
Where is the County's page, that raised the watch?
Sirrah, what made your master in this place?

Page   He came with flowers to strew his lady's grave,
And bid me stand aloof, and so I did.
Anon comes one with light to ope the tomb,
And by and by my master drew on him,
And then I ran away to call the watch.

Prince   This letter doth make good the Friar's words,
Their course of love, the tidings of her death.
And here he writes that he did buy a poison
Of a poor 'pothecary, and therewithal
Came to this vault to die, and lie with Juliet.
Where be these enemies? Capulet, Montague?
See what a scourge is laid upon your hate
That heaven finds means to kill your joys with love.
And I, for winking at your discords too,
Have lost a brace of kinsmen. All are punished.

Capulet   O brother Montague, give me thy hand,
This is my daughter's jointure, for no more
Can I demand.

Montague   But I can give thee more.
For I will raise her statue in pure gold,
That while Verona by that name is known,
There shall no figure at such rate be set
As that of true and faithful Juliet.

Capulet   As rich shall Romeo's by his lady's lie,
Poor sacrifices of our enmity.

Prince   A glooming peace this morning with it brings,
The sun, for sorrow, will not show his head.
Go hence, to have more talk of these sad things,
Some shall be pardoned, and some punishèd.
For never was a story of more woe
Than this of Juliet, and her Romeo.   *They all exit.* 310

265
270
275
280
285
290
295
300
305

to the marriage her nurse is privy: her nurse knew about the marriage
266 **aught in this miscarried:** anything went wrong
267 **some hour before his time:** before my natural time to die
268 **Unto the rigour of severest law:** as the harshest possible punishment
270 **still have known thee:** have always thought you were
272 **in post:** as fast as possible
274 **early:** early the next morning
275 **going in:** as he went into
279 **made your master:** was your master doing
282 **Anon comes one:** just then someone arrived
283 **by and by:** soon after
285 **make good:** confirm
288 **therewithal:** with it (the poison)
291 **scourge:** punishment
292 **your joys:** your children
293 **winking at your discords:** letting you quarrel so
294 **a brace:** a pair, two
291 **jointure:** payment made to the bridegroom's family by the bride's family on marriage
300 **There shall no figure at such rate be set:** no one will be seen as more important
301 **Romeo's:** a statue to Romeo
302 **Poor sacrifices to our emnity:** both victims of our hatred
304 **glooming:** dark, clouded

Director's Note, 5.3

✔ Paris and Romeo fight outside Juliet's tomb. Romeo kills Paris.
✔ Romeo enters the tomb, and drinks poison, kissing Juliet as he dies.
✔ Friar Lawrence arrives; Juliet wakes and sees Romeo's body.
✔ They hear a noise. The Friar flees. Juliet stabs herself.
✔ The Watchmen arrive followed by the Prince, the Capulets and Montague.
✔ Friar Lawrence tells what happened. Montague and Capulet end the feud.
✔ The Prince says, 'Some shall be pardoned, and some punished.' Who should be punished?

EXAMINER'S NOTES, 5.3

These questions help you to explore many aspects of *Romeo and Juliet*. At GCSE, your teacher will tell you which aspects are relevant to how your Shakespeare response will be assessed.

EXAMINER'S TIP

A good response

A good response may make links between details in a scene and one before or after. This can show either that Shakespeare is sustaining an aspect of plot or character (i.e. doing something to reinforce it) or developing an aspect of plot or character (i.e. making it more varied or complex).

For example, Paris, whose wish to marry Juliet made her take her desperate choice of action, appears in the last scene to have strong feelings for her, and becomes a victim himself. Shakespeare could have left him out of the play after his previous appearance, but added something to his character and the plot by writing him into this scene as a character the audience may sympathise with.

USING THE VIDEO

Reflecting on the scene

If you have looked at the video extracts in Dynamic Learning try these questions.

When Juliet wakes she recognises Friar Lawrence and talks to him, without noticing Romeo. She notices him only when Friar Lawrence says 'Thy husband in thy bosom there lies dead.'

What are the advantages and disadvantages of staging it like this?

❶ Character and plot development

The scene begins with Paris, who has come to grieve at Juliet's tomb. This results in another fight, and another death – before Romeo's death and Juliet's that follows. The scene ends with the families agreeing to end the feud that has caused so much conflict and grief.

1. Paris says he will come to grieve at Juliet's tomb every night in 'true love's rite'. Do you think Shakespeare intends him to be a man sincerely in love with Juliet?
2. Quote from the text to show how Shakespeare uses Romeo's instructions to Balthasar (lines 22–24) to show that he has been rational and organised in what he has decided to do.
3. How does Shakespeare show that this latest fight and death is not something caused by Romeo's impetuous nature?
4. Romeo thinks he has heard that Paris was due to marry Juliet, but his attitude is not one of jealousy or anger. He sees him as a fellow-sufferer of Fate, and lays his body next to Juliet's. What does this suggest about Romeo's character at the end of the play?

❷ Characterisation and voice: dramatic language

In this last scene, several characters are developed beyond their previous appearances – Paris, Friar Lawrence, The Prince and Capulet. Each of these speaks in a way that we have not heard them speak before, as a result of the events that have occurred. Other voices, too, are added to create a scene of conclusion – Balthasar, the Watchmen and the Page.

5. What aspects of his speech make Romeo seem in control of his feelings and his actions in his speech to Paris (lines 58–68)?
6. How does Shakespeare make Juliet's final speeches similar to Romeo's final speech (Juliet: lines 160–170; Romeo: lines 118–120)?
7. What is there to suggest that Friar Lawrence feels responsible for the tragic outcome of his plan?
8. How is Capulet's attitude here different from his attitudes before?

❸ Themes and ideas

Although the deaths of Romeo and Juliet are tragic, they each want to die rather than carrying on living without the other. This makes the theme of togetherness in death a major part of the final scene.

The scene also ends with some good brought about by their deaths, as the rival families agree to stop their feud that has caused so much harm. This introduces the theme that tragic events can have positive outcomes. Capulet, Montague and The Prince draw a line under all that has happened, bringing in the idea of reconciliation.

9. Which of the lovers' references to death suggest that they do not fear it, but see it as a welcome solution?
10. In what ways does Shakespeare's ending of the play suggest that the adults have learned something from the tragic events?

EXAMINER'S NOTES, 5.3

11 Friar Lawrence explains his part in the events leading up to the lovers' deaths, and adds that the Nurse knew all about the secret marriage. What do you think Capulet would say to her when he next sees her?

4 Performance

This is a very crowded scene, with at least 15 actors on stage – Paris, Paris' Page, Romeo, Balthasar, Friar Lawrence, Juliet, at least three Watchman, The Prince, his attendants, Capulet, Lady Capulet and Montague. Apart from the deaths of Paris, Romeo and Juliet, we learn that Romeo's mother has also died, of grief.

12 What advice would you give the actor playing Friar Lawrence about his leaving the tomb after line 160?

13 What advice would you give him about telling the truth and excusing himself in his speech (lines 229–271)?

14 Although Montague and Capulet have closing speeches, Lady Capulet has nothing to say after line 207. Do you think that Shakespeare has made a mistake, or do you think he had a reason for this?

15 What would you advise the actor playing Lady Capulet to do from her last line to the end of the play?

5 Contexts and responses

The play was written a long time ago, and set in a far-away place, but modern audiences will see some of the play's events and situations as familiar. Family conflict, forbidden love and plans that go wrong are familiar to most people, but we may have a different take on any of them, according to our values, preferences and experiences.

16 'Star-crossed', 'unlucky' or 'they brought it all on themselves': what do you think is the main cause of all that went wrong?

17 Who do you think has most to learn today from what happens in this play: parents or teenagers?

18 What would you have done if you had been in the position of either the Nurse or Friar Lawrence?

6 Reflecting on the play

19 Do you think that Shakespeare wanted the audience to think that such tragic events were a matter of Fate?

20 Friar Lawrence's role could be a simple one as part of plot design, but Shakespeare has made him more complex and interesting than that. What do you think makes him more complex and interesting as a character?

21 In a play which ends tragically and includes tragic episodes, there are also scenes of comic humour. What effect on the audience do you think Shakespeare intended these scenes to have?

EXAMINER'S TIP

Writing about drama

Dramatic writing has to keep an audience engaged. If every Act and Scene creates the same mood, it is hard to keep interest for three hours in the theatre. Shakespeare builds in variety and contrast in moods, adding rude jokes and comic behaviour (with the servants, Act 1 Scene 1 and the Nurse, Act 2 Scene 4) in a tragedy like *Romeo and Juliet*, to vary the mood.

EXAMINER'S TIP

Reflecting on the play

When you have finished reading and watching *Romeo and Juliet*, you should have some overview of what Shakespeare has written. These questions will be useful in coming to a personal view of the play as a whole.

1 Is it a play which gives us some insight into life in Shakespeare's time?

2 Is it a play which gives us some insight into life in our own time?

3 Is it a play which can be admired because it has lots to please and interest a paying audience, or a serious study of human behaviour?

4 Is it a play which some people can enjoy reading, rather than watching?

5 Is it a play which you will remember for anything other than answering your GCSE questions?

1	The Prologue introduces the play with its themes of fate, love, and death.
1.1	Montagues and Capulets fight in the street. The Prince orders them to stop and threatens that any further fighting will be punishable by death. Romeo admits to Benvolio that he is in love with Rosaline.
1.2	Capulet tells Paris to woo Juliet, but that she is too young to marry. Benvolio persuades Romeo to go the Capulet's feast, in disguise, where he will find Rosaline and other women who are as beautiful.
1.3	Lady Capulet tells Juliet and the Nurse that Paris wants to marry Juliet.
1.4	Mercutio mocks Romeo for being in love. Benvolio urges them to go to the Capulet ball.
1.5	Romeo and his friends arrive disguised at the Capulet ball. Tybalt recognises and would attack the enemy Romeo, but is stopped by Capulet. Tybalt plans revenge. Romeo and Juliet meet and fall in love. They then learn that they are the children of the feuding families.
2	The Chorus confirms that Romeo and Juliet are in love and are determined to be together at any cost.
2.1	Benvolio and Mercutio look for Romeo who has hidden from them.
2.2	Romeo overhears Juliet speak of her love for him. He tells her that he loves her. They agree to marry.
2.3	Romeo tells Friar Lawrence that he is no longer in love with Rosaline but is in love with Juliet. Lawrence eventually agrees to marry them.
2.4	Mercutio, Benvolio and Romeo meet. Romeo gives the Nurse a message for Juliet with the news that Lawrence will marry them that afternoon at his cell.
2.5	The Nurse gives Juliet the message.
2.6	Juliet meets Romeo at Friar Lawrence's cell. They leave with Lawrence to be married.
3.1	Tybalt tries to provoke a fight with Romeo; Mercutio fights Tybalt instead and is fatally wounded. Romeo, ashamed, challenges Tybalt and kills him. Romeo flees. The Prince orders Romeo's banishment.
3.2	Juliet longs for Romeo. The Nurse tells her of Tybalt's death, and of Romeo's banishment. Juliet despairs but the Nurse tells her she will bring Romeo to her, secretly, that night.
3.3	Friar Lawrence tells Romeo that he has been banished. Distraught, Romeo attempts suicide. Friar Lawrence sends Romeo to Juliet but tells him he must leave for Mantua before daybreak.
3.4	Capulet tells Paris that he can marry Juliet in 3 days' time.
3.5	After spending the night with Juliet, Romeo leaves for Mantua. Lady Capulet tells Juliet she must marry Paris; Juliet refuses; Capulet threatens to disown her. The Nurse advises Juliet to marry Paris.
4.1	Juliet meets Paris at Friar Lawrence's cell. Paris leaves. Friar Lawrence comes up with a plan: she should agree to marry Paris but take a drug that will make everyone think she has died. Friar Lawrence will tell Romeo and they will wait for her in the tomb until she awakes and then take her away.
4.2	Juliet returns home and tells her parents that she will marry Paris. Capulet moves the wedding forward to Wednesday.
4.3	Juliet sends her mother and the Nurse away and goes to bed. She takes the drug.
4.4	Capulet, his wife, and the Nurse prepare for the wedding.
4.5	The Nurse finds Juliet, all believe she is dead. Friar Lawrence starts to arrange the funeral.
5.1	In Mantua Romeo receives a message that Juliet is dead and has been put in the family tomb. He buys poison intending to kill himself by her side.
5.2	Friar Lawrence discovers that Romeo has not received his message and hurries to Juliet's tomb.
5.3	Paris fights Romeo in Juliet's tomb. Paris is killed. Romeo takes the poison. Friar Lawrence arrives; Juliet wakes and finds Romeo dead. They hear a noise. Friar Lawrence flees and Juliet stabs herself. The Watch arrive and Friar Lawrence and Balthasar are arrested. The Prince, the Capulets and Montague arrive. Friar Lawrence reveals what has happened. The families agree to end their feud.

How to write a good response to *Romeo and Juliet* for GCSE English Literature

Whatever Controlled Assessment task or examination questions you take will be based on some of the Assessment Objectives below. Your teacher will tell you which ones are relevant to how your Shakespeare response will be assessed.

If you are taking GCSE English or GCSE English Language, some of the examples for the GCSE English Literature Assessment Objectives may be of use when preparing for your response to *Romeo and Juliet*. Your teacher will tell you which ones are relevant to how your Shakespeare response will be assessed.

GCSE English Literature Assessment Objectives

AO	Assessment Objective	Key word used for each AO, below
1	Respond to texts critically and imaginatively; select and evaluate relevant textual detail to illustrate and support interpretations.	**Response**
2	Explain how language, structure and form contribute to writers' presentation of ideas, themes and settings.	**Language**
3	Make comparisons and explain links between texts, evaluating writers' different ways of expressing meaning and achieving effects.	**Comparison/Links**
4	Relate texts to their social, cultural and historical contexts; explain how texts have been influential and significant to self and other readers in different contexts.	**Contexts**

❶ Response

If you are assessed on Response (AO1), you need to:
- understand what you have read and can prove that you understand
- show some judgement based on informed knowledge about plays, language and Shakespeare but also based on your own feelings, attitudes and preferences
- always support what you write with relevant reference or quotation.

How do you show you can do this?

Write a comment on what Romeo says, showing not just that you understand what he means, but how you can justify your comment by further comment on a detail of quotation. Look at the two examples below, about Act 1 Scene 5:

Rather than: *Although he used to think Rosaline was more beautiful than anyone else, now he thinks the same about Juliet.*

Write something such as: *Although he used to think Roasaline was more beautiful than anyone else, when he said 'The all-seeing sun/Ne'er saw her match since first the world begun' he now thinks the same about Juliet, saying 'So shows a snowy dove trooping with crows,/As yonder lady oe'r her fellows shows.'*

Now try it yourself with the question:
What are Tybalt's feelings in Act 1 Scene 5 lines 54–61?

Rather than: *Tybalt is really angry because he thinks Romeo has come to the party to make fun of the Capulets and he thinks this is an insult to his family,* using one or two quotations, write a short paragraph in response showing that he jumps to conclusions about Romeo and takes his family reputation seriously.

EXAMINER'S TIP

Response
- Respond thoughtfully and sensitively to the text.
- Pick out short, relevant phrases or quotations from the play to back up your ideas.
- Explain and analyse the quotations.

2 Language

If you are assessed on Language (AO2), you need to have a good understanding of the writer's craft, including Shakespeare's technical skill in:

- choice of language
- composition of a text in scenes
- making people and situations believable
- making themes and ideas interesting.

How do you show you can do this?

Write a comment which shows that Shakespeare has used particular words and images in a speech so as to have an impact on the audience. Look at the two examples below, about Act 3 Scene 1:

Rather than: *Shakespeare shows Romeo trying to avoid a fight between Tybalt and himself and Mercutio by using calming language.*

Write something such as: *Shakespeare shows Romeo trying to avoid a fight between Tybalt, himself and Mercutio by using calming language to both of them: 'And so, good Capulet, which name I tender/As dearly as my own', and 'Gentle Mercutio, put thy rapier up.'*

Now try it yourself with the question:
How does Shakespeare suggest a change in Romeo's feelings in Act 3 Scene 5 lines 105–111?

Rather than: *Romeo's feelings change completely because Mercutio has been killed*, using one or two quotations, write a short paragraph in response showing that he feels responsible for Mercutio's death and that falling in love with Juliet has spoiled his reputation by making him weak.

3 Comparison/Links

If you are assessed on Comparison/Links (AO3), you need to:

- see what is similar in texts (e.g. themes. settings, situations) and what is different in texts (e.g. authors' attitudes, values, style and appeal to readers)
- give your opinion of how well the writers have used their craft to create effects on readers/audiences.

How do you show you can do this?

Your comparison or links with *Romeo and Juliet* will depend on the linked text you are studying. The example below uses the word 'Text' to reflect this. It shows a comparison/link with a text where a setting can be directly described and *Romeo and Juliet* where Shakespeare has to use characters to set the scene, through their dialogue.

If commenting on Shakespeare's skill in creating a sense of time and place (Act 3 Scene 5, for example), rather than: *In this Text the scene can be set by the author building a description directly into the narrative and setting but in Romeo and Juliet Shakespeare has to let the characters set the scene through what they say.*

EXAMINER'S TIP

Language

- Write about why Shakespeare has chosen particular words or phrases to get his meaning across.
- Write about the theme(s) of the play.
- Write about the setting of the play/particular scene.

Write something such as: *In this Text the writer can build a description of a scene into the narrative and setting by telling the reader, for example: 'The first faint hints of light'. In Romeo and Juliet, Shakespeare has to create a sense of place and mood by what the characters say, as in: 'what envious streak/Do lace the severing clouds in yonder east./Night's candles are burnt out, and jocund day/Stands tiptoe on the misty mountain tops.' This is where dialogue fills in the details of what's happening or what's happened off stage.*

Now try it yourself with the question:
How does Shakespeare show changing attitudes and feelings in two of the plays you have studied?

Rather than: *Shakespeare shows changing moods by writing lines which need to be spoken with a different tone of voice,* using one or two quotations, write a short paragraph in response, showing how Shakespeare puts together lines addressed to different people, expressing different attitudes and feelings in different tones of voice. Compare it with an example of how a sense of mood is created in your linked Text.

④ Contexts

If you are assessed on Contexts (AO4), you need to:

- understand something about the culture that is reflected in the text because of the time or place it was written, or how it reflects some aspect of the author's experience
- think about and explain what it is in your own life and culture that makes you interested (or not interested) in the text you have studied
- consider a personal response, but always remember to put your personal feelings in a context of attitudes, values and beliefs that make up your personal culture. The most important thing about social, cultural, or historical contexts is 'What's changed?' and 'What's stayed the same?'.

How do you show you can do this?
Rather than: *Capulet thought that Juliet should obey her parents and be grateful that he had found her a suitable husband.*

Write something such as: *In Shakespeare's day, the audience may have thought that Capulet was doing his best to find Juliet a suitable husband, and that marriage was too important to be left to youngsters' emotions. But a modern audience would have more of a view of youngsters' rights, and think that getting married is a personal choice, and not something to do for business, or without loving someone.*

Now try it yourself with the question:
'Star-cross'd lovers, victims of circumstances or reckless youngsters?' How many different audiences think any of these matched Shakespeare's view of the characters presented in the play?

Rather than: *In Shakespeare's day, people were more superstitious so they would have thought that what happens in the play was caused by Fate, and that the lovers were star-cross'd, like Shakespeare says in the Prologue at the start,* using one or two quotations, write a short paragraph in response, showing that a modern audience may see social influences and personality having more influence on people's behaviour.

EXAMINER'S TIP

Comparison/Links
Think about what is similar and what is different about the texts and the way they are written.

EXAMINER'S TIP

Contexts
- Show you understand the times in which the play is **set**.
- Show you understand the times in which the play was **written**.
- Show you understand how the events of Shakespeare's day may have had an influence on his work.

Although you need to have an understanding of these issues, remember that the play itself is your main focus. Only mention details about the playwright or period if it is relevant to what you are discussing about the play.

EXAMINER'S TIP

Assessment based on exams
- Focus on the question clearly throughout your whole answer.
- Know the text in detail.
- Select key details from the text to support your points and ideas.
- Show understanding and appreciation of the language used by Shakespeare and explain the effect of the words he has chosen.
- Include a strong personal response at the end – don't simply repeat what you have written in your introduction.

Key terms

These key terms provide a starting place for exploring key aspects of *Romeo and Juliet*. At GCSE, your teacher will tell you which examples are most relevant to how your Shakespeare response will be assessed.

THEMES AND IDEAS

Conflict

The long running feud between the Capulets and Montagues Prologue 1–5 Despite the Veronan law, both sides continue 1.1.35–45 The feud directly causes the deaths of Mercutio 3.1.87, Tybalt 3.1.129, Paris 5.3.54–73, and, indirectly, the deaths of Romeo: 5.3.120 and Juliet: 5.3.169–70 Some characters work for peace; e.g. the Prince 1.1.74–90, Benvolio 1.1.58–9, Lady Montague 1.1.72–3; others revel in the conflict; e.g. Sampson and Gregory 1.1.36–45, Tybalt 1.1 63–5 Characters experience internal conflict, e.g. over loyalties – Juliet when Romeo is Tybalt's murderer 3.2.73–9, Romeo over fighting Tybalt 3.1.59–69 until Mercutio is slain 3.1.120–30

Love

Courtly love

Romeo's idealistic, unrequited love for Rosaline 1.1.203–232 makes him avoid friends 1.1.116–124, moody 1.1.126–134 secretive 1.1.141–6, sad 1.1.183–9, powerless and unfulfilled 1.1.203–19 and suffer 1.3.55–8 It amuses Romeo's friends 2.1.8–22; 2.4.13–5 Romeo believes it blinds him to other womens' charms 1.1.227–231 and 1.2.88–93

Arranged marriages

Common in Shakespeare's time, Capulet's choice for Juliet, Paris, strengthens family ties and transfers wealth. Capulet believes arranged marriages should not be entered into too early 1.2.12–3 and tells acceptable suitor, Paris, to win Juliet's 'heart' 1.2.16–9 Lady Capulet asks Juliet if she can choose to love Paris who offers status and wealth 1.3.75–91 Juliet agrees to try to obey her parent's wishes 1.3.93–5 After Juliet falls in love with Romeo she is unable to choose to be in love with Paris instead. When Juliet refuses Paris, Capulet tries to force Juliet to obey by threatening to banish her 3.5.192–4

Passionate love

Natural, and more powerful than either hatred, death 2.2.66–84 or family ties 3.2.96–126 It overcomes boundaries of family feuds 2.2.51 and 2.2.69, reconciles individuals 2.2.144; 2.3.49–54 and, potentially, their families when Romeo turns from foe to friend 3.1.59–61 It makes lovers happy 2.4.49–79, strengthens characters 4.2.125, is worth risking death for 2.2.76–8, 82–4 and is fulfilled by marriage; but if it is too strong, it is dangerous 2.6.9–16: thwarted, it leads to the deaths of Romeo 5.3.120 and Juliet 5.3.169–70

Lust

Source of comedy in bawdy jokes 46–53; act of hate 1.1.14–6; a response of the eyes and so easily changes its focus 1.2.47–51; 1.2.96–9; contrasts with the fidelity and purity of Romeo and Juliet's passionate love 2.2.35–9

Hatred

Drives the feud 1.1.11–69, contrasts with love and peace 1.1.63–5, results in bloodshed, and must be constrained by the law 1.1.76–90; it drives Lady Capulet to seek Romeo's execution 3.1.175–180, Tybalt to duel with Romeo, and, later, Paris. It is punished with loss 5.3.293–5

Fate and fortune

The Prologue describes Romeo and Juliet as 'star–crossed lovers' coming from 'fatal loins' whose 'death–marked' future is frequently foreshadowed in characters' speeches 1.4.107–114; 3.5.200–3 and in images 2.2.184 The characters express a sense of fate; e.g. Romeo 1.4.107–14; 2.6.6–8, Juliet 2.1.134–5; 3.2.21–2; 3.5.54–7 Juliet calls on fate to help 3.5.60–4 Friar Lawrence's speech foreshadows events 2.3.19–22. Romeo dreams Juliet finds him dead 5.1.6–8

Light and dark

Romeo brings light; e.g. to the dark masquerade ball 1.4.35–9; light is an image of time and life passing 1.4.43–5 Juliet is symbolised as light 2.2.2–4 True love is revealed in the darkness 2.2 and night is the time for passion 3.2.1–31 Dawn heralds Romeo's departure 3.5.9–15 and misery 3.5.36 The final, tragic suicides and deaths all take place in the darkness of the vault

Secrecy/concealment

Lovesick Romeo conceals himself from Benvolio 1.1.117–124, and 2.1 and the reason for his unhappiness 1.1.138 Romeo hides his identity to attend the Capulet's masked ball 1.5; he hides below Juliet's balcony 2.2 and overhears her declaration of love 2.2.33–49 There are secret meetings 2.4.160–3, a secret marriage 2.5 and secret plans 2.5.72 Juliet conceals her love for Romeo 3.5.81–3, marriage 3.5, 4.1.19, grief at Romeo's banishment 3.5.76–7, and plans to avoid marrying Paris 3.5.241–2 Father Lawrence's secret plan 4.2.89–120 will conceal the lovers. Drugged Juliet is concealed in the tomb to wait for Romeo

Time

The play's events are compressed into four days. Images of time passing include death 1.2.14 –15, loss of light 1.4.43–5, birds; i.e. nightingale symbolises night, lark day 3.5.1–6 The time for stars is the time for love 1.2.25 Events are often foreshadowed 1.2.86–8 Characters set appointments 2.2.169 which are thwarted 2.5.1–3; yearning makes time seem long 2.2.170 Capulet forces Juliet to marry Paris quickly 3.5 188–94 leads to Father Lawrence's poison plot 4.1.68 and the

lovers' deaths. Events overlap creating irony; e.g. as Capulet fixes Thursday as the date of Juliet's marriage to Paris, upstairs Romeo and Juliet consummate their marriage 3.4 and 3.5 News of Juliet's 'death' reaches Romeo before the letter from Friar Lawrence 5.1.17–21

Gender

Men fight 1.1.55, feud 1.1.87–90, hold power as fathers 1.2.17–9 and political leaders 1.1.89–90, use women to cement relationships, transfer wealth and secure family bonds and status through arranged marriages 1.2.12–3 Romeo fears his love for Juliet makes him 'effeminate' 3.1.112–13 but he goes on to avenge Mercutio's death by slaying Tybalt. Women are objects of desire 1.5.42–51, meant to obey fathers 3.4.13, 159–62, 4.2.22 and husbands 4.2.41 Female rule, shown by Queen Mab, only causes dreams of wish fulfilment and madness 1.4.55–95

Religion and myths

Images of pagan classical Greek and Roman deities are associated with courtly love 2.1.11–15; e.g. Cupid, giving lovers 'wings' and skill at dancing 1.4.17–18, then causes unrequited lover's suffering 1.4.19–22; Dian the virgin huntress 1.1.204 Queen Mab is associated with dreams, wish fulfilment and madness 1.4. 55–95 Courtly love is a religion 1.2.88–93, replaced by Romeo and Juliet's pure, passionate love which is associated with Christian imagery: pilgrims, saints, shrines 1.5.92–105, sin and purification 1.5.106

Appearance and reality

Rosaline appears the ideal woman 1.2.88–93, 2.1.18–20, until Romeo sees Juliet 1.5.42–51 Juliet only appears ready to obey and marry Paris 3.5.233–5; she will only appear dead 4.1.93–108 Romeo believes drugged Juliet really is dead 5.3.91–105 The Prince asks for reality to be explained by Benvolio 3.1.150–174 and Friar Lawrence 5.3.231–264

Youth versus age

Age is associated with withering 1.2.11, canker, the roots of the feud 1.1.88, no longer dancing 1.5.29 In Friar Lawrence age brings wisdom love, faith 2.3.1–44, 4.5.65–76 Youth is associated with fighting 1.1.55–65, 3.1.86, 5.3.71, strong emotions, true love 2.2.90–135, 2.4.49–79, passion 3.2.1–28, despair 3.3.29–47, courage 4.3.20–57 and death 1.1.55–65, 3.1.86, 5.3.71, 5.3.120, 5.3.169–70

Order versus chaos

Order, such as the implementing of law 1.1.89–90, 3.1.184–195, 3.1.184–196, arranged marriages, or traditions of courtly love maintain peace and stability. If order is disrupted it leads to disorder/chaos; e.g. giving illiterate Peter a reading task 1.2.39–41; leads to Romeo gatecrashing the ball; Juliet marrying outside her father's choice leads to the tragedy

Death

Men duel and kill each other: 1.1.55–65, 3.1.86, 5.3.71 Death is the punishment for murder 1.1.89–90 but avenging murder leads to Romeo's banishment 3.1.185–196 Romeo and Juliet's love is death-marked Prologue Romeo foretells his death 1.4.108–14 Juliet foreshadows her suicide 2.1.134–7 and Romeo his 3.3.43–6 Juliet fears Romeo's death 3.5.54–7 and her own 4.3.31–4 Both Romeo and Juliet threaten to kill themselves, Romeo: 3.3.107–9; 5.1.34–35; Juliet: 3.5.244 and 4.1.54, 4.1.76–85 and do so, Romeo: 5.3.120, Juliet: 5.3.169–70

CHARACTERISATION AND VOICE

Characterisation

The skill of making an actor playing a part do it so well that the audience believes he is a real person, with a distinct personality, attitude, feelings and behaviour. Characterisation can be reported such as Romeo's 1.1.125–136, or revealed; e.g. the Nurse's rambling prose.1.3.18–44

Voice see Examiner's Tips p 34

LANGUAGE

Alliteration

Words begin with same sounds: 'Now old desire doth in his death-bed lie' 2.1.1 'all my fortunes at thy foot I'll lay/And follow thee…' 2.2.147–81

Allusions

Indirect references to other texts especially the classics and mythology see religion and myths; e.g. the use of a Chorus echoes classical Greek dramas

Antithesis

The use of opposites such as light and dark; e.g. 'More light and light, more dark and dark our woes!' 3.5.36 Pairing of opposites in an expression is an oxymoron

Epithets

Sum up character's natures: The fiery Tybalt 1.1.102

Hyperbole

Exaggeration used to emphasize a point; e.g. Romeo's first descriptions of Juliet: 'The brightness of her cheek would shame those stars' 2.2.19

Iambic pentameter

A pattern of 5 pairs of unstressed then stressed syllables in a line; e.g. the Prologue and 'But soft! What light through yonder window breaks?'

Shared lines

Where different characters complete an iambic pentameter, increases the pace e.g. 2.2.25

Imagery

Language which creates impressions by association and suggestion. Romeo and Juliet's true love described using images

from the Christian religion; e.g. pilgrims, saints, shrines 1.5.92–105, 2.2.55, baptism, angels 2.2.26–32 Whereas courtly love is described through pagan and classical religion, ancient myths etc: 2.1.11–15; Juliet's beauty is associated with brilliant light 1.5.42 and 2.2.14–21. Unhappy love is associated with avoiding natural light 1.1.128–133 and darkness 1.1.133–5 Suffering love is associated with smoke, sea 3.5.130–7, an extended metaphor and madness 1.1.185–8, clouds 1.1.127, being weighed down unable to dance 1.4.14–6 Fiery images describe strong emotions; e.g. falling in love 1.5.42, rage 1.1.77 or characters driven by hate; e.g. fiery Tybalt 1.1.102 Animal imagery used as insults 1.1.7 and 10, feuding, hate driven men are beasts 1.1.76 Birds to compare women's beauty 1.2.87, 1.5.46, or time passing 3.5.1–6 Romeo wishes he were Juliet's bird 2.2.183 Poison 4.3.57, 5.3.119–20, 5.3.160–5

Irony

Because the Prologue and chorus reveal the plot, speeches foreshadowing future events can create irony; e.g. 'compare her [Rosaline's] face with some that I shall show, And I will make thee think thy swan a crow' 1.2.86–7 Swans are faithful, only having one mate, crows are birds of death. Romeo states he'll suffer if he stops loving Rosaline 1.2.88–93 Romeo's marriage will kill Juliet 2.1.134–5 Mercutio's death will lead to others 3.1.117–8 Juliet dreads waking too early 4.3.31–2 but wakes too late. After marrying Romeo, Juliet hides her true feelings creating dramatic irony 3.5. 96–102 Situational irony; e.g. events overlapping: while Capulet fixes Thursday for Juliet to marry Paris, upstairs, Romeo and Juliet consummate their marriage 3.4 and 3.5

Onomatopoeia

Where sounds of words echo their sense; e.g. 'Who, nothing hurt withal hiss'd him in scorn' 1.1.105

Oxymorons

Phrases made up of opposites such as 'Beautiful tyrant, fiend angelical', 'Ravenous dove-feathered raven! Wolvish–ravening lamb' 3.2.75–6

Personification

Words used to put human or animal characteristics onto non-human or animal things, e.g. 'limping winter treads' 1.2.28, death as Juliet's husband e.g. 'And death, not Romeo, take my maidenhead' 3.2.137

Rhyming couplets

Used to round off scenes Prologue, 1.3.100–1, 2.2. 189–90, create memorable exits 1.5.90–1, express heightened emotions; e.g. Romeo's speech at first seeing Juliet 1.5.42–3, Juliet's discovery she's in love with a Montague 1.5.1.137–40

Sonnets

14-line poems, in iambic pentameter following a rhyme scheme – often

ababcdcdefefgg. There are three in the play: The First Chorus (Prologue); Romeo and Juliet's first meeting, 1.5.92–105, the Second Chorus at the start of Act 2

Symbolism

Romeo carries the torch and so bears light, symbolic of bringing love and passion, into Juliet's house 1.4.12

Word play

E.g. 'sycamour' = sick amour 1.1.114 and 1.1.1–4 ; puns such as: **collier** (coal vendor) which sound like **choler** (anger) and **collar** (hangman's noose)

PERFORMANCE: STAGECRAFT AND THEATRICALITY

Stagecraft

Stage directions in text such as Benvolio commenting on putting on his mask 1.4.30–2 Clues in the text to guide actors; e.g. repetition of part suggests sword thrusts: 1.1.107; sound effects e.g. 'Hist' 2.2.159; the progression from Romeo kissing Juliet's hand, to their hands meeting and finally they kiss on the lips 1.5.92–106

Theatricality

Swordfights 1.1.and 3.1; dancing at masked ball 1.5.24; Romeo conceals himself below the balcony with Juliet appearing above 2.2

Soliloquy

Characters speaking alone to the audience reveal their inmost thoughts and feelings; e.g. 2.2.1–8, 3.2.1–31, 4.3.14–57

Suspense

Juxtaposition creates dramatic tension; e.g. at the ball, as Romeo speaks of falling in love with Juliet, his identity is discovered by his enemy, Tybalt 1.5.52

Symbolism

An idea is represented by an object; e.g. Romeo carries the torch and so bears light, symbolic of bringing love and passion, into Juliet's house 1.4.12

CONTEXTS

Contexts within the play that create a scene or mood.

Characters alone on stage seem more vulnerable and courageous; e.g. Juliet deciding to take the poison 4.3, and kill herself 5.3.161–70; grim atmosphere at the tomb where Tybalt, then Paris and finally Romeo and Juliet lie dead 5.3

Context around the play

For example, the way that ideas, customs and events of the period, are reflected in the play: see notes on duelling, courtly love, arranged marriages.

Context of performance

Where and how it is performed and how that affects the audience's understanding; e.g. characters in modern costume or Elizabethan dress

Globe Education Shakespeare

Series Editors: Fiona Banks, Paul Shuter, Patrick Spottiswoode

Steering Committee: Fiona Banks, Hayley Bartley, Paul Shuter, Patrick Spottiswoode, Shirley Wakley

Romeo and Juliet

Editors: Fiona Banks, Paul Shuter

Consultant: Shirley Wakley

Play text: Hayley Bartley, Ryan Nelson, Paul Shuter, Patrick Spottiswoode

Glossary: Jane Shuter

Assessment: Senior moderators and senior examiners including Peter Thomas, Paula Adair, Tony Farrell; key terms index: Clare Constant

From the rehearsal room: Fiona Banks, Adam Coleman, Sarah Nunn, Yolanda Vazquez

Shakespeare's World Farah Karim-Cooper, Gwilym Jones, Amy Kenny, Paul Shuter:

Dynamic Learning: Hayley Bartley

Progression: Georghia Ellinas, Michael Jones

Globe Education would like to thank our dedicated team of Globe Education Practitioners – who daily bring rehearsal room practices into the classroom for young people at Shakespeare's Globe and around the world. Their work is the inspiration for this series.

Playing Shakespeare with Deutsche Bank
The spring 2009 production of *Romeo and Juliet*, which features in this book, was the 2009 *Playing Shakespeare with Deutsche Bank* production. This is Globe Education's flagship project for London schools, with 16,000 free tickets given to students for a full-scale Shakespeare production created specifically for young people.

Photo credits
All photographs are from the Shakespeare's Globe photo library.
Andy Bradshaw, 2004 production: 10, 12 (left), 22, 38, 42, 60, 74, 82, 84, 88 (left), 106, 114, 128, 132; Manuel Harlan, spring 2009 production: 8 (lower), 12 (right), 26, 30, 36, 40, 44 (right), 46, 58 (top left), 66 (lower), 68 (upper), 78, 81, 88 (right), 94, 122 (upper), 130; John Haynes, summer 2009 production: 8 (upper), 14, 17, 20, 28, 44 (left), 48, 50, 58 (right and lower left), 64, 66 (upper), 68 (lower), 71, 76, 90, 96, 108, 113, 116, 119, 120, 122 (lower), 126, 134; James Erskine: 62, 102; Pete le May: 3 (lower); John Tramper: 3 (upper)

Orders: please contact Bookpoint Ltd, 130 Milton Park, Abingdon, Oxon OX14 4SB.
Telephone: (44) 01235 827720. Fax: (44) 01235 400454. Lines are open 9.00 – 5.00, Monday to Saturday, with a 24-hour message answering service. Visit our website at www.hoddereducation.co.uk

© The Shakespeare Globe Trust, 2011
First published in 2011 by
Hodder Education,
An Hachette UK Company
338 Euston Road
London NW1 3BH

Impression number   5 4 3 2 1
Year   2016 2015 2014   2013 2012 2011

All rights reserved. Apart from any use permitted under UK copyright law, no part of this publication may be reproduced or transmitted in any form or by any means, electronic or mechanical, including photocopying and recording, or held within any information storage and retrieval system, without permission in writing from the publisher or under licence from the Copyright Licensing Agency Limited. Further details of such licences (for reprographic reproduction) may be obtained from the Copyright Licensing Agency Limited, Saffron House, 6–10 Kirby Street, London EC1N 8TS.

Cover photo Ellie Kendrick and Adetomiwa Edun, summer 2009, photo by John Haynes
Typeset in Garth Graphic Regular 10pt by DC Graphic Design Limited, Swanley Village, Kent
Printed in Dubai

A catalogue record for this title is available from the British Library

ISBN: 978 1444 13664 7